CARBON
Copy

A NOVEL BY:

AZAREL

ESSENCE MAGAZINE BESTSELLING AUTHOR OF
BRUISED 2 & DADDY'S HOUSE

Life Changing Books in conjunction with Power Play Media
Published by Life Changing Books
P.O. Box 423 Brandywine, MD 20613

Library of Congress Cataloging-in-Publication Data;

www.lifechangingbooks.net

ISBN- (10) 1-934230677 (13) 978-1934230671
Copyright ® 2009

Acknowledgements

Clearly, I don't have a clue where to begin. I have so much to be thankful for and so many people to acknowledge. First off, it is with God's grace that I have my health and He's allowed me to write and operate as CEO of Life Changing Books. Thank You!

A special thanks must go out to my supportive family. My husband truly supports the endeavors of my company and all of my other over-the-top dreams. I am so blessed to have you. You make me realize dreams do come true when you have people in your life who truly love and support you. So, a special thanks to my beautiful daughters, who allow me to juggle motherhood and my business ventures. You're now becoming miniature CEO's in the making. Keep making top notch grades, shipping books on the side, and creating your own companies. To my sister, Tam (shout out to Hush Boutique), Gram, and my parents thank you for always being there when I need you. You are appreciated.

Of course I have to acknowledge my babysitters. What would I do without you? I'll say it again, what would I do without you?(smile). My mother Linda, my grandmother, Elizabeth, and my niece, Kinae, you help me in so many ways. I can't thank you enough. If you ever need anything, a hug, a shoulder to cry on, my right leg, whatever just ask!

I want to send a special shout out to all my test readers. These are the ladies who say-I hate it, I love it, change it, and all the other stuff that I can't say. So, Cheryl, Shannon, Aschundria, Virginia, and last but not least Tonya, I thank you for keeping it real. Shout outs to Lisa Williams, honorary LCB for life staff member, Kim Gloster aka Em, Danielle Adams, and all my other folks who got my back- too many to name. You know who you are! To my cousin, Jeremy Vick, thanks for all the times you held the kiosk down. To my other cousin, Jeremiah Allen, thanks for always willing to carry some books (smile).

    To my brother- in- law, Don. I'm not sure whether you know it or not, but the board meetings work. It gets the wheels churning and thinking about how to move into the future. We don't always see eye to eye, but you are truly appreciated. For years, you've been helping to create the LCB blueprint for success and discussing this VP salary. Hold tight! It's coming…let's talk about it on the next book (smile).

    People always ask me, "How do you do it all? You've got fourteen authors, and 36 titles to manage." The answer to that lies in three ladies. Leslie Allen, Nakea Murray, and Tasha Simpson are the ladies of LCB who make it happen for me. Ladies, I can't thank you enough…but I'll try. Thank you. Thank you. Thank you. Thank you. Thank you. Thank you. Thank you. Thank you.

    Thanks to the best graphics team. Dashawn Taylor, Kevin Carr, and Kellie. You all are top notch. To Hakim of Black and Nobel, Sidi of Harlem Book Center, Nati of African World Books, and Zahir of Empire Books. You all have hung in there with me for years, so I just want you all to know you're appreciated.

    To my authors on the grind with me, I thank you all for your endless support. I'll see you at the top. Remember, stay humble, stay on your grind, and keep writing bestsellers.

    Until next time, pick up a copy of my other titles, Bruised 1 and 2, Daddy's House, or take it way back with A Life to Remember. Hit me up on myspace.com/azarel the author or www.lifechangingbooks.net.

Peace,

Azarel

One . . .

Where all the deceit began. . .

Manipulation at its finest, I told myself opening his bedroom door slowly. I had always been super confident and capable of pulling anything off. Yet this move was on another level.

I slipped into his room unannounced wearing a sexy, red lace one piece. No panties underneath. It was half past one and his girlfriend wasn't expected back until after 2:00 a.m. My role as a guest in their home had gone from a simple overnight stay to a major violation.

His room, completely dark, blended in with the color of his skin. I crept cautiously near the side of the bed searching for the exact location of his entire body. Without a clear visual, there was that overwhelming sense of smell…his smell…the one I loved so well. It was combined with a strong stench of alcohol.

Who was I to turn my nose up? It was after all the alcohol that had given me the chance to get close. There he was on his back, deep beneath the black silk sheets. His arms and sexy braids lay exposed for me to feel. I pulled the sheets

1

back gradually, slipping my body up against his. The warmness my body felt rubbing against his skin had me going wild. Yet his long legs remained stiff, as if he were dead.

No doubt, he wouldn't know the difference between me and the love of his life. I'd only talked to him a brief moment just an hour before, when he stumbled in the house bragging about the entire bottle of Hennessy he'd drank by himself. I figured if he happened to awaken from his drunken stupor, he'd never know the difference.

Without hesitation, I reached over, caressing his manhood, getting an arousal instantly. Two moans later, he breathed heavily, turned flat on his back, and grabbed me by my shoulders lightly. It was clear he wanted me on top, yet lacked the strength to do anything, even open one eye.

Like a scavenger, I took charge thinking I may never have the same moment again. I found myself on top of him, grinding hard, and holding his left hand hostage, firmly on my ass. Even drunk, he got it up. The entrance was slow, but soothing. He moved a little, but nothing like his woman had bragged. I found myself working overtime, sweating like a Sumu wrestler trying to keep him hard, as the alcohol had his spirit incoherent. I fucked him hard, while he gave me a few weak pumps.

Suddenly, he released then instantly turned over, flipping me off of him like we weren't in the same bed. "Dammit," I screamed inside. "Two minutes! What the fuck?" I desperately needed to have an orgasm.

At that very moment everything changed. The sound of her clicking heels making their way toward their bedroom had my heart pounding. My mind flipped through different scenarios of how my situation could play out. I was known to be a bad bitch, had claimed to have no fear of anything. But the reality was, it wasn't the right time to claim my man.

I hopped up as the adrenalin swept through my veins.

2

My head darted around the room starting with the door, then toward the bathroom. The window was out of the question. Then the best hiding spot came to mind.

The sounds of her heels clicking had gotten louder, and my heart beat even faster. Quickly, I pulled the sheets back over him with poise; just glad that I'd been in touch with his sweet dick. Within seconds, I'd kissed him on the cheek, and jetted underneath the bed. The door flung open, and my half-naked body clung to the stiff floorboards. While she walked near the bed, I made sure to lay still, my face touching the cold hardwood floor. My assumption, she was checking on her man.

"Drunk again," I heard her say. "Umph."

For several minutes, she fumbled around in the dark making noisy sounds and walking to and from the master bathroom. I closed my eyes wondering how long I would remain on the floor. Maybe for a few minutes or a half an hour. Maybe all night. My escape would have to come when I knew she was sound asleep. Instead of complaining, I took the time to create my action plan and vowed to one day make him mine.

Two

Dominique

Not what I expected for my big day…I thought chills would infiltrate my body, making pimples appear all over my honey-colored arms. Even moisture seeping through my thong would've given me a sign. The thought of being one of those chicks who got married in May and ended up in Divorce Court by August made my skin crawl. I hoped like hell Derrick was really the one; the one who would change my life, and put me on the throne where I belonged.

He appeared to be what I always wanted; a strong black man with bottomless pockets. He was a drug-dealer turned real-estate mogul, which worked fine for me. I wasn't big on community anyway. I just wanted the lifestyle of the rich and famous with a fine brotha attached to my arm.

Derrick was a deep chocolate brotha, just the way I liked my men. He talked a good game always making it seem like he was rolling in success and basking in the good life; a life I badly wanted. He even stood six foot three with a slender build and walked as if he paid cash for his confidence. It seemed to be a miracle for me to land a guy who measured up to Rapheal, my sister's man. He was dark too, just sexier with

5

more loot. My sister Monique, always got major attention in life, and especially since she'd been dating Rapheal's fine-ass. Little did she know, I'd had a piece of him, too.

I stopped thinking for a moment hoping it would make the sweat building underneath my armpits come to a halt. Standing on the white aisle runner and hearing the song, *Here Comes the Bride*, made it clear my walk of commitment would start shortly. All eyes were on me as I waited for the coordinator to fix the train on my gown.

My wedding dress had cost my man a whopping $10,000. He resisted at first, but I explained to him that Vera Wang wasn't big on discounts, and that a pussy strike would take place if necessary. I had searched every state, every Vera Wang Bridal shop, and every online opportunity trying to find her perfect creation. I ended up with a tantalizing, strapless, form-fitting bodice gown. It flared at the bottom like a princess, had a four foot train, and was accompanied by a satin sash which made my waist appear to be even smaller. To top things off, it showed off my curvaceous shape.

It was important for me to shine because it was *my day*, all about *me*, I kept telling myself. And of course I had to out-shine Monique. She had out-shined me all our lives; always snagging the big fish, always winning, and always getting the notoriety. Well today, I made sure to put her ass in a plain, loose fuchsia bridesmaid's dress along with my other two bridesmaids. No need for a Maid of Honor, because no one was gonna be honored on my day but me. Monique may have been born my twin sister, but on my wedding day she was nothing more than a place holder at the altar.

The pianist hit a note which startled me just as my stepfather, Steve walked up beside me and grabbed my arm.

"It's show time," he uttered. "You nervous?"

I ignored him. Even turned my head.

As far as I was concerned, he was an accomplice to my

mother who never thought this day would come. They both thought I was incapable of landing a husband. I hit him with a half-ass smile like I really wanted him to give me away. Before I knew it, we'd started down the aisle and listened to the oohs and ahhs. Just the thought of me, Dominique, making people envious had me on cloud nine. I looked to my left noticing all of my mother's friends who had come to see her unfit daughter get married, the one they thought would be single forever. Some folks bit at their nails, some talked to their neighbors, while others looked on nonchalantly as if they attended by force. Fuck'em all I wanted to say.

As I made my way further up the aisle, I shot fake grins to all my aunts and uncles sitting in the pews looking on in amazement. One even shook her head. I wanted to yell out, "Bitch, leave!" But I didn't. Instead, I simply looked ahead at my future husband standing next to the pastor and his best man, Greg.

It was crazy how for a quick second, my eyes zoomed in on Greg. It was impossible not to admire him from head-to-toe. He was still stocky and thick, built like a wrestler. It was difficult trying to pretend as if his muscles weren't bulging through his tux. I stared like a groupie backstage after a show, but snapped out of it quick when Derrick shot me a strange look. It was one I'd never seen before and couldn't explain. It could've been an expression of love, but who was I to pretend to know what love really felt like. All I knew was that Derrick loved *me*, he'd given *me* a three carat rock, and now waited patiently at the altar for *me*, his princess. Meanwhile, I watched him like a germ under a microscope. All along I wondered if I should actually go through with it.

With each additional step, visions flashed through my mind of what life had in store for us; big house, big cars, loads of jewelry, and plenty of cash to spare. Everything troubled me. I was like a teen with Attention Deficit Disorder. It seemed impossible to settle my thoughts.

Less than three feet away from my future husband, I glared then smiled at him. Strangely, he didn't smile back. I figured he was nervous because I certainly was, so I cut him some slack. He kept fidgeting, and allowing his hands to play around with his jaws. I could tell he was in deep thought, and seemed to be getting worse. Greg leaned over and whispered something in his ear. Suddenly, Derrick's disposition changed and he was back. He shot me a reassuring look which made me grin slightly and turn to my mother on the front row.

I gave her a sign letting her know everything was okay. I surely didn't want to bring any attention her way. My mother already stood out as the only mixed person in the room. And her beautiful dark hair, and foreign features always caused people to stare anyway. I shot her a quick grin. She simply frowned a bit. I knew the look. She wanted to ask me, "What the heck was going on?"

Then matters got worse. Greg's girlfriend, Angel, sat on the second row on Derrick's side grinning wickedly. She had bright red hair and gave off a devilish smirk like Lucifer himself. She kept mouthing words to me which were difficult at first. Then I got it. "You got some explaining to do."

She was like a school-aged child teasing me. I thought, *What the hell does she mean*? I peeped over my shoulder wondering if one of my flames was in the building, or maybe an old boyfriend who wanted revenge. I figured her comment had nothing to do with Greg. She couldn't possibly have known about that, I convinced myself. I panicked big time. Maybe that was why Derrick behaved so strangely. I had to think fast. Something had to be done, so I grabbed his hand and massaged it softly letting him know whatever the problem was it would be okay. Then a breakthrough came. He looked me in the eye.

Everything was good, I told myself. My breaths eased

slightly. I would be married in less than twenty minutes and would make my mother proud. I was the first of her three children to jump the broom, beating Monique by just six months. Monique announced her wedding to Rapheal first, but I wasn't about to let that bitch marry before me. Besides, they'd postponed it twice. And as soon as I got to the hotel, I had planned on screwing Derrick's brain's out so I would be the first to have a baby. I prayed the child would look like me, but have Rapheal's personality.

I mean Derrick was fine, but didn't possess the pizzazz and swagger that Rapheal did. In reality, Derrick was sloppy seconds as far as I was concerned, and Raphael could have his spot any day.

Once again, I couldn't stay focused. My eyes darted around the church and focused in on all the Tiger Lily flower arrangements. Tiger Lilies were my favorite because they rep- resented me to the fullest…wide and exotic. My side was packed out while Derrick had about four rows of family and friends. My cousins Shawna, and Jennifer sat in the second row just behind my mother, waving like crazy. It made me feel good to see them in good spirits because they'd fought my nuptials hard. They were my road dogs and naturally never wanted me to marry Derrick. In their minds it would end our late nights out on the town, and our creeping with the fellas. In their eyes, it would all stop. But from where I sat, I was getting married, not dying. I would still hang out from time to time, and clubs would never be off limits. Derrick would have to deal with the real me. It's in my blood and lock down wouldn't be tolerated.

Before long, the pastor had his Bible open and the cer- emony moved along swiftly. It seemed like we were on the clock and had to be out of the church within the hour. The pastor was already at…, "Dominique, do you take this man to be your husband, to love and respect him, honor and cherish him, in sickness and in health, in prosperity and in adversity, so long as you both shall live?"

I almost fainted.

I was really giving up my freak card. No more male targets, no more scouting for the right man to show Monique up. It was over.

"I do," I finally said.

Then the torch passed to Derrick. He was read all the same vows and then the ultimate, "… so long as you both shall live?"

The pastor paused…waiting patiently for a response.

All of a sudden Derrick developed a weird expression like he'd been sucked into the twilight zone. He drifted off as if he were day dreaming, then started sweating and twitching again. He turned to his boy, Greg, who's eyeballs had damn near popped out of his head. Then he turned to his mother, then to my mother. He played a crazy game of peek-a-boo with his face.

I got crazy nervous wondering if he knew. How would he have found out? I counted to ten, then backwards again, and again praying that I wouldn't get embarrassed at the altar. The church had gotten noisy; of course a lot of chatter about Derrick's behavior. Then all of a sudden, it stopped.

"I do," Derrick told the pastor uneasily.

My rapid breaths slowed and I reduced the intensity of the frown on my face. Derrick would have to be dealt with later. Although he said yes, the embarrassment was too much to bear. I saw my crazy-ass sister off to my left cheesing, showing every tooth in her mouth. She liked that type of bull-shit; always did. Anything to make me less of a woman and to keep her in the Queen bitch seat. She needed to act her age. At twenty-seven, one would think she was beyond the jeal-ously bullshit. Apparently, she wasn't.

Well I was married now, and she *was not*. As soon as I

heard, "You may kiss the bride," I got wild, wrapped my arms around Derrick and slobbed him down. Greg studied our lip action like he wanted to join in. When Derrick turned to embrace his father, I stuck my tongue out seductively at Greg. I just wanted to tease him, letting him know I'd gotten my man successfully, unlike what he'd told me.

"Dominique Robinson," I repeated to myself as I grabbed Derrick's arm and headed down the aisle to exit the church. Contrary to what I'd initially thought, it was indeed, the happiest day of my life.

An hour later, we all stood outside under the white garden tent at the fabulous Piedmont Room hidden from the hot Atlanta sun. How an early day in May could be so hot shocked me. Our wedding party had already been introduced and so had Derrick and I…of course as husband and wife. Dinner, which consisted of grilled shrimp, lobster and steak were going to be served shortly, so I spent a little time walking around to each table mingling with my guests, and showing off my ring to everyone who would allow me the opportunity to gloat.

Although I never agreed with the wedding coordinator on much of anything, she had the place looking fabulous. Fuchsia and silver colors along with silk draped ceilings and crystal chandeliers adorned the tent. The towering nineteen inch floral center pieces were simply amazing as well as the Chavari chairs and specialty linen. She managed to make an outside event look like a five star wedding at a luxurious ballroom. I watched closely as each guest sat at their table admiring the personalized cookie favors and votive candles on each table.

All of a sudden Monique started tapping on a glass

with her fork. She loved to be the show stopper, so it didn't surprise me how elegantly she tapped.

"I'm ready to make my toast," she announced in her usual white-girl dialect. She spoke like a true northerner every day of her life, and I especially hated how she enunciated each syllable.

"Everyone grab a glass. The waiters are coming around now. And please….stand up. This will call for a standing ovation."

The sound of the chairs screeching across the stone flooring irritated me, but this was rare, a compliment coming from my twin. She'd shocked me, but pleasantly.

She raised her half-filled champagne glass and began.

"Dominique, I want to thank you. You make things exciting and entertaining for the rest of us, and now I'm sure your husband will enjoy all your shenanigans. I'm sure it will be a lot of fun and add excitement to both of your lives. He has no idea all the things you're capable of. You never cease to amaze me," she said sarcastically.

Of course laughter filled the room. Everyone became smitten by her.

"Well even today," she continued. "Just think; you bought a new car yesterday just like mine, just a different color, and never even told me, your older sister by six minutes." She grinned my way and everyone laughed again. "Well, at least it's a BMW."

They laughed again. I didn't think the shit was funny but crossed my arms and continued listening to the tramp.

"So good luck to you and your perfect man. I'm just happy that you found each other and that you're my sister." She got even more emotional and ended with, "So here's to Dominique and Derrick."

Everyone in the room gulped their champagne, including Derrick. He took two glasses to the head and waited for

12

the third as the waiters walked around refilling the glasses for the Best Man's toast.

Obviously Monique's speech was a hit. It brought tears to my mother's eyes. It was what she always wanted, for us to be close, the way she expected twins to feel about one another. She rushed over to Monique and squished her head in between her hands.

"You're such a great woman," she told her.

"You're too kind."

"No, seriously. You are."

I ignored the slap in my face from my mother and watched Greg spring into action. We all had a glass of bubbly in our hands ready for his toast. As Monique walked over to hand Greg the microphone, Derrick shocked us all by snatching it from Monique's hand.

"I have a testimony!" Derrick shouted.

Greg looked his way and spread his arms widely. "What the fuck, man?" he whispered and motioned with his mouth. "Give me the mic," he gritted through his teeth.

"I know you want the best for me," Derrick told him loudly with a superficial smirk, "but I need the microphone for a minute. I got a story to tell."

"Now?" Greg questioned nicely.

"Yes, now!" Derrick's response seemed cold as if he had some sort of problem.

"Honey, Greg is supposed to do the toast," I whispered in my husband's direction.

"Stay back, honey," he ordered in a deranged voice.

I thought… okay, this man has had way too much to drink. I contemplated grabbing the mic then decided against it. Everyone had their eyes pointed in our direction expecting to hear the toast, and now my husband had the floor talking about a fuckin' testimony.

"Let me tell you a short fairy tale that I hope each of

you never experience."

His words had me nervous as hell. I couldn't figure out where he was going and decided to move closer so I could help my man. He was clearly going through something and needed me to save him. Maybe he had huge financial problems in his business, or maybe there was something going on with his health that he never shared with me.

"Honey," I interrupted. "Now is not the time."

"Oh, it's the perfect time! Sweetheart!" he shouted, making sure his eyes crinkled as he said *sweet*.

His voice became more powerful, more emotional, yet he struggled to get the words out. He was damn near in tears. *Bitch-ass,* I said underneath my breath.

"You see, I thought I died and had gone to heaven when Dominique entered my life. It was like a gift from God…you know better than hitting the lottery. Look at her," he shouted. "My beautiful China doll."

People around the room smiled, a few laughed, and some let out sighs of joy. For me, I wasn't easily fooled. This shit was bad.

Derrick continued, "She won me over real quick," he added in a humorous tone. "Then she won my family over." He paused. "Then she won Greg over."

I stopped all movement and assumed the blood ceased to flow through my veins anymore. Had he said what I thought? Greg? Did he say Greg? Did he know?

"Yes, that's right, ladies and gentleman. My wife loves me so much she felt like she needed to get to know everyone in my life extremely well. Well today, I have a gift for Dominique, my beautiful wife and Greg, my best man."

His face showed defeat. He was hurt.

"If you all will take a moment to look under your seat, there's a special gift from them to you."

My eye lids opened wide and my heart skipped a beat.

What gift from me? I looked over at my mother who was already going underneath her seat just like all the other scavengers in the room. I knew it was bad by the way some covered their mouths and others gasped. Then Derrick spoke once again.

"Isn't that wonderful?" He laughed crazily after taking another sip from his drink. "See, my wife loved me so much she thought she needed to fuck my best man!"

I darted over to my sister who had a wide smirk spread across her face. I snatched her 4x6 photo from her hand and placed my eyes on the startling image of Greg on top of me. His bare ass covered the majority of the picture, with my head hanging off the bed and the remaining parts of my naked–ass pinned underneath. My facial expressions gave it all away. Everyone could tell I was enjoying it, so hollering rape wouldn't work.

Most people have a sister who would've helped them out of a bad situation, but mine just stood with a menacing look, shaking her head back and forth. My body began to shiver, and my temperature rose. So, I picked up a half-empty champagne glass off a nearby table and downed it. I managed to grin when I was done, hoping my situation would go away.

No one had to tell me my complexion had changed from honey to pale. It was obvious, and would probably have no pigment left in my skin at all if Derrick didn't end his humiliating tirade. I needed help in unscrambling what Derrick was trying to say. Was I still his wife, or was this all a joke? What was my next move? I wondered standing in the middle of the floor with all eyes on me.

Derrick's words caused quite a stir in the room and long gasps came about. There wasn't any loud outbursts from the crowd, no extra movements, only clear disappointment. In a desperate attempt to amend the situation, I pulled on the end of his tux, saying to him, "We need to talk."

"Never again!" he shouted in front of everyone. He even moved away from me quickly like I had a disease. "We're done!"

I had been taught by my brother, whenever you got caught doing wrong, you have the right to remain silent. *Damn, I wish he had been here to help me.*

I saw Derrick looking at me, giving me the evil eye. He didn't have to say another word- his eyes revealed everything. But I couldn't remain silent. My life fumbled right before me. Derrick pulled off his wedding band and dropped it into a nearby champagne glass and left the room. My monthly bills had to be paid, my car note especially, the BMW Derrick told me we couldn't afford.

I felt like I'd been hit with twenty high-powered bullets. My soul burned and the look of defeat spread across my face.

When my mother walked up to me, I closed my eyes as fast as possible. I couldn't face her short frame even though I was 5'7 and she only 4'11. With her height and squeaky voice she could never intimidate anyone but me. Yet, I only wanted to make her proud of me. Instantly, she started pointing and shaking her finger at me like a two-year-old child.

"You ought to be ashamed, Dominique! It's the ultimate betrayal."

Steve co-signed from behind. "Yeah."

"Look Ruby, I don't wanna discuss it. Shit, you don't know what happened and you're blaming me. And Steve you shut the hell up!"

Her mouth flew open and remained that way for several seconds before she could speak. I was positive she was into her feelings about me calling her Ruby. I did that often to make her feel less than a mother.

"What is there to figure out, child? You are naked, on

the bed with another man. And he happens to be your husband's best friend."

"Yeah, your ex-husband's best friend," Angel remarked, passing by my mother's backside.

I snapped. I knew somebody had helped Derrick to humiliate me. I started with Angel. With one leap, I was on her back, wedding dress and all. She screamed. She tried to take back her bright hair that I had tangled inside the palm of my hand. I called her every name in the book, hoping people would see her as the villain.

"Why the hell would you cut and paste me into those pictures with your man!" I shouted loudly. I hoped everyone who'd gathered around us was listening clearly. "I'ma beat your ass for trying to ruin my day!" I said between punches.

Several people had surrounded us, calling out my name, begging me to stop, including Greg. Somehow he had slipped away when all the attention was on me about the photo. Now he was back to defend his girl. With one blink I saw him from the corner of my eye. Then I saw the champagne bottle raised in the air, and coming my way. The sound was horrific. Glass splattered everywhere. He'd got me   hit me straight in the forehead. Damn, he was tryna kill me. Where was my help? Where was my sister? Where was my husband?

Three

Monique

The noise level in P'F Changs kept me from thinking clearly. It would be my first get together with my sister since her disastrous wedding. Although it had been two months, it seemed more like two years. It was weird, but I sorta missed hearing her over-the-top stories.

It shocked me when she agreed to meet me. I'd heard from my brother, Sedrick that she wasn't interested in seeing or talking to me. I wasn't sure why. She was the one who brought the wedding drama on herself. She was the one always getting herself into hot water. She was the one who wanted to run the streets leaving her panties on every doorstep. And let's face it, I didn't fuck Greg, she did.

Still, I vowed that today I would go easy on her. It seemed that we were so competitive; a spirit brought on by our mother. It was all about success in the Lewis family. My mother always pushed us to do better, and frowned on family who didn't measure up. It didn't matter whether it was sports, career, marriage, or with your children; it was all about who shined.

I seemed to be the one always on top, and we both

knew it. It was me who had the perfect relationship over the last three years to Rapheal. It was me who lived in a penthouse near downtown Atlanta. It was me who lived the fairy-tale life. Dominique never even had a career other than when she worked as a nurse, then got fired for sleeping with a patients' husband. Still in all, I'd made a promise to do better with my sister because I really did love her. And since she was going to be an auntie in six more months, it was best to spring the news on her now, and mend our relationship.

Our waiter stopped by the table again and asked me if I was still expecting my two guests. I just nodded, smiled, and focused on who was headed my way. My eyes grew to the size of watermelons when he got closer. His long, thick braids had my hormones jumping. I knew he would be joining us, but not so soon. I jumped up to wrap my arms around his athletic frame.

"Honey, you made it!"

"You thought I would let'cha down?" Rapheal questioned, exposing his bright white teeth.

"No, I knew you were coming but I thought your flight would've just been getting in."

"I told that fuckin' pilot to get it movin', my lady was waitin' for me."

I laughed because he'd put on his tough voice. Normally, he spoke in sensual tones, matching his charming personality. Rapheal sat down and scooted his chair as close as he could possibly get to me. Then he kissed me on my neck about six times making my panties more soiled by the minute. It drove me wild to see my man all dressed up and smelling good enough to eat. Even though he rocked a dressy linen set, his muscular arms were exposed making me want to take him to the nearest bathroom.

At twenty-nine his face didn't appear to be a day over twenty, and his physique had toned up even more due to the weight training. He had a look that was a cross between an athlete and an exotic-looking supermodel. Although handsome and sexy to death, it was his roughness that attracted most women. So it didn't surprise me that we had several pairs of eyes watching us gloat over one another.

"So, what'cha been doin' this week, luv?"

I rested my head on my man's dark shoulder. He was so damn sexy. "Nothing really. Didn't feel too good most of the week. Only left the house once since you left here last week."

"Really?" he asked, squeezing my thigh.

"Yep. But it's cool. I got to work on calling these subcontractors this week about the house."

"Yeah, that reminds me…how's that comin' along?"

"It's cool."

"That's what's up. I feel bad about dumpin' a project like that in your lap, but I really don't have the time. Business is boomin'."

He stopped and typed something into his Blackberry Curve, his second love. I wanted him to throw that phone away at times. It was always glued to his hip.

"No, I'm glad you did," I explained, giving him the eye to put the phone down. "It gives me something to do. And besides, who would complain about remodeling a house in the Bahamas, right on the water?"

"It'll be the perfect vacation spot. I can't wait 'til we Christen the place." He grinned, then slipped his finger beneath my skirt.

"Not here."

"Why not?" he asked. "It's mine."

His voice was so masculine, yet pleasing.

"What? You scared?"

Before I could even respond, I saw my twin standing in the middle of the floor scanning the restaurant. It amazed me how two people, even identical twins, could look so much alike; same nose, same slightly slanted eyes, same body features; everything the same, of course except personalities.

Her hair had grown since I'd seen her last. It was shoulder length and cut in layers, but damn she had it colored honey-blonde just like mine. I stood up and waved my hand high in the air so that she could see me amongst the crowded lunch time traffic.

Finally she spotted me and sashayed my way. I watched her strut like she'd just stepped out of a Vogue Magazine spread. Dominique never changed...so predictable, always had been. She was designer down, and rocked a Chanel jean clutch bag that I'd just seen in Neiman Marcus' new summer catalog. I wondered where she got the money to keep up with the Jones'. She didn't work last I heard. And now lived in an apartment in the heart of Buckhead.

Dominique stopped abruptly as soon as she was within three feet of the table. She glared at us like we were crazy.

"I thought it was just us," she said, with her sunshades tilted beneath her eyes and resting on her high cheek bones. Seconds later, she turned her stare toward Rapheal.

I broke her trance by saying, "I know Sis, it was just us at first. But I asked him to come because we have some special news to share with you." I leaned on Rapheal's shoulder muscle and clutched his arm like my life depended on it. "Plus, Rapheal just flew in from New York for a few hours. I thought what better way to spend the day, than with the two people I love most."

"I don't give a fuck about Rapheal coming from New York or about your special news," she said taking a seat. "Plus, I know something's up with you being this damn nice and all."

"What's up Dominique?" Rapheal interjected. "Sorry I didn't make the weddin'. Had to work...you know I gotta

22

keep my baby lookin' good."

"It's cool. No apologies needed."

"Sorry things didn't work out with you and Derrick either, luv."

"I bet you call every woman you've ever met, luv," Dominique belted. "Stop that shit. I'm Dominique," she ended sharply.

Rapheal responded with a smile. She acted as if she didn't really want to smile back, but finally gave him a little something. At least the ice was broken. I loved my man dearly. He had a way of smoothing everything over, it didn't matter whether it was family, his business connections, or with me personally. He had skills.

"Are you guys ready to order?" the waiter asked as he approached us.

"Yes, I'll have …" I started to order as Dominique's cell phone sounded.

She answered real ghetto-like. I tried to listen because she was causing quite a scene, but the waiter stared in our faces still expecting us to order. I guess he felt like we'd been at the table long enough and hadn't ordered a thing.

Finally, Dominique slammed the phone down with an attitude. "Fuckin' bill collectors!" she shouted.

"What are you having, Madam?" the waiter turned to ask her.

"Whatever my sister is having," she announced without hesitation.

I was flattered, yet, Rapheal raised a brow. "Damn y'all really are identical; eat the same thing, same car, same hair color, and some of the same jewelry," he added making reference to a bracelet wrapped around her wrist that resembled one I'd had for years.

Rapheal took charge and ordered for all of us. As soon as the waiter left, he started whispering in my ear and acting like Dominique didn't exist. He went on for several minutes while Dominique typed into her phone. I tapped him on the leg, signaling for him to include my sister in the conversation.

"So Dominique, looks like you've been stayin' in shape, girl. What are you now, an eight?"

"Six," she answered quickly.

"What about you?" Dominique asked me after taking a gulp of her water as if she weren't trying to be funny.

I had been petite most of my life, never making it past a four until I met Rapheal. They say sex makes your butt grow and mine had surely plumped up a bit. I went easy and just told her, "I'm a six now but will need maternity clothes soon. I'm three months pregnant."

Her drink came rushing from her mouth and spit splattered all across the table. She started choking and acting as if she couldn't catch her breath. It reminded me of a scene out of a movie where the actress seemed to be over-doing it. Rapheal jumped up and ran over to her rescue. I watched while he raised her arms in the air and patted her back forcefully.

I kept yelling, "Dominique, you okay…you okay."

She kept coughing while Rapheal remained by her side.

Finally, she caught her breath and excused herself from the table. I watched Dominique suspiciously as she ran toward the bathroom still acting like she was choking. As soon as she was out of sight, Rapheal asked, "What was that all about, luv? Your sister's actin' real strange."

"That's just Dominique. That's just how she is. She was born with an attitude." I paused. Believe me, she's happy for me, she just doesn't know how to show it."

"If you say so." He kissed me on the cheek. "I been around a lot of conniving women in my life, and I'm here to let'cha know your sister got some shit with her. Believe me,"

24

he added.

I kept looking toward the bathroom hoping he would change the subject before Dominique came back to the table. Ten minutes had already gone by and she was nowhere to be found. I thought about calling her but realized she'd left her cell phone on the table. I even considered going to check on her but the food arrived at the table shortly after, smelling too good for me to leave.

My cravings had already started and I wasn't even in my second trimester yet. As soon as the Lemon Pepper Shrimp and fresh asparagus hit the table, I dug in. Before I knew it, my fork had made its way over to Rapheal's plate, too. The thought of my sister kept floating through my mind. I figured she'd left the building until her cell rang, reminding me that she wouldn't have left without it.

Just like a true hood-rat, Dominique's ringer blasted loudly, an obnoxious cash register sound. It had to have been the loudest ring tone ever made. All heads turned looking at Rapheal and I. I hated being embarrassed so I reached for her phone and answered.

"Hello."

The deep, raspy voice on the other end sounded off with several instructions. I clutched my chest when he said the word, murder. What kinda shit had Dominique gotten herself into. Then he asked me a question, assuming it was Dominique. I didn't say a word. I just hung up hoping my sister knew what she was doing. The craziest part of it all was that I recognized the voice. I couldn't place it, but definitely knew the voice.

Before I could even tell Rapheal what had happened, Dominique waltzed back to the table like she hadn't been missing for the last twenty minutes. I exhaled and looked deeply into her eyes. I wanted her to know that I knew she was into some shit.

"You had a phone call," I told her with a scrutinizing expression.

"So," she shot back, and lifted the phone to check the number of the last call. "I see you're still nosey."

"I see you're still up to no good."

"Look, aren't you having a baby soon?" she asked sarcastically.

"What does that have to do with anything?"

"Well if I'm going to be an auntie, I'd like to at least be speaking to the mother when the baby drops."

"Is that a threat?"

"It's a promise," she shot back.

"Funny, Dominique." I grinned to lighten the mood because Rapheal acted like he wanted to say something. I knew he had a temper so I ended it. "Girl, you are something else?"

"Yes, I'm quite entertaining," Dominique bragged. "Speaking of being an auntie, we all thought Sedrick would be the first to make Mama a grandma, with all the bitches he fucks, but I guess not."

I smiled widely and flirted with Rapheal a bit more. I needed to get my mind off my sister's mess. She was up to something and I knew it.

"Speaking of Sed, when is he coming back to town?" she asked Rapheal.

"Well, my young soldier said he wanted a job with my company. My men work hard. Right now he's handlin' some import/export stuff for me. He should be back in Atlanta by the beginnin' of next month."

"Oh, really. Well don't have my brother in another country somewhere getting shot. The streets talk, and I heard all your business dealings aren't legitimate."

"Do you believe everything you hear in the streets? I hope not," he added, "Cause I've heard some foul shit about you."

"Whateva playa. Just tell my brother, I'm pissed. He never answers when I call," Dominique added.

"I see why."

"Fall back, playa. You not ready to go head-to-head with me."

"Wow, we got a live one," Rapheal said to me, then slipped his hands into his pocket to pull out a bundle of cash.

I couldn't stop smiling. I loved the way he handled things. I started playing with him underneath the table causing him to get excited and wiggle in his seat. Dominique's frown told us she knew what was up, so Rapheal pushed my hand away.

"So look," he said, pushing away from the table, and throwing two crisp hundreds on top of the napkin. "I gotta run, I got a few deals I gotta mash off before my flight leaves for New York tonight. You ladies, sit, drink, and catch up a bit."

"Oh yeah, what a coincidence. I'll be in New York tomorrow, too," Dominique announced.

The look on my sister's face told me she was lying. "What are you going to New York for? You never mentioned it before," I asked her sharply.

"That's because I thought I was grown," she shot back, then hit me with an evil smirk. "Look, I gotta run, too," she announced. "I got an appointment at the doctor's office. Just so you know. I might be pregnant, too."

My jaw dropped lower than I thought it could go. I wanted to say by who, but assumed she probably didn't know. I just sat with my head thrown into the palms of my hands. What was I going to do with her? She was my sister, but damn, I wanted to ex her outta my life.

Four...

Dominique

The crowded streets near the Underground had me pumped. I loved downtown Atlanta. People walked swiftly through the streets like they really had places to go and something to do. I certainly did. It was time for me to get paid. Without a doubt, I didn't play about my money. I was off to meet my money man who'd never been late when we needed to link up. Each time it was a different spot. He never duplicated. I couldn't even call him on the same phone twice. He was slick like that. I even noticed that, the more I gained his trust, he was trying to teach me to watch my back as closely as he did.

For a Tuesday, my game seemed to be off slightly; partly because I kept thinking about my lunch date yesterday with Monique. The fact that she got pregnant before me was the last straw. I wasn't sure whether I would ever commit to seeing her baby. "Bastard!" I shouted out in anger. A homeless guy heard me and shot me a look as I entered the Underground, but I brushed him off, only able to think about who could get me knocked up. I knew I had to get pregnant quick,

29

especially since I told Monique I was probably pregnant, too.

The best part of the lunch of course was Rapheal. I'd dreamt about his best feature; his big bulging arms, most of the night. I couldn't believe Monique flaunted him in my face. Her penalty should've been revealing to them both that I'd had a piece of him already, just over a year ago, and the next time he wouldn't be drunk.

My game face had been plastered on when the door opened to Jessie's Bar and Café. The scent of fresh blunts and Jamaican food invaded my nose, as *One Blood* by Junior Reid played modestly in the background. It was a quaint spot that resembled a lounge from the old days. Although it was extremely dim, damn near dark, the décor felt extra sexy, and the Jamaican beat had me bobbing my head. It was a spot owned by Yuri's friend, and was the perfect place to meet my boy since we needed privacy.

I stopped at the bar and scanned the place as if I didn't belong. The bartender watched me closely as he cleaned the same glass over and over again. He examined me firmly like he'd already decided that he didn't care for me. I had that kinda effect on people. It was my attitude.

"You looking for somebody?"

"Ahhh…yeah. But I'll wait. I don't need any assistance."

"Oh, you don't," he said sarcastically.

My voice reached a high pitch, "Let me repeat…I don't."

I commenced to sitting on the bar stool in front of me, but heard a voice coming from the back. When I turned to look, I saw Yuri standing, peeking through some red velvet curtains. He motioned for me to come to the back, so I quickly shot the bartender a nasty look and strutted back to see my employer. Of course I gave off extra hip action until I got within Yuri's proximity.

His scarred face appeared to be flushed from afar, but once I got closer it was more of an uptight expression. I never knew how to greet him so I just made a fist and pushed it his way for some dap in return. He simply squinted his face. It was crazy how Yuri always presented himself in a way which made others think he was about to spiral out of control.

He greeted me with his cold eyes and used his infamous hand gestures to welcome me into his private quarters. Before I took another step, my focus switched to his dreads. They had grown drastically since I'd seen him last, and had now resembled tiny snakes, straddling the middle of his neck. Yuri wasn't your typical Trinidadian. His parents were from the small Caribbean island of Trinidad, but Yuri was born in the states, only carrying a slight accent. For the most part he talked like the rest of the niggas in Atlanta, except when he broke out with the occasional, yuh, or gun-shot'cha, or bumboclot.

Once behind the curtain, I scrutinized the small red love seat, two plush chairs, and mini-sized coffee table. I stood in the center of the small sized area with my arms crossed and my nose turned up in its normal snobbish position. The aroma in the air confirmed that Yuri had been smoking weed, but some other substance must've been to blame for the extra glossy eyes.

"So, what's up Yuri?" I finally asked. I didn't want to sit down. I just wanted my cash.

He simply scanned my body with his eyes. Yet never once did he smile or give me a sign that I'd done a good job.

"Yuh look good," he told me, admiring my tight skinny leg jeans and three-inch stilettos; Christian Louboutin, of course.

I gave him a quick grin. "Can I get paid?" I asked meekly, while holding out my hand.

That took balls even trying to take charge of the situation. Yuri wasn't to be fucked with. The skills he possessed couldn't be purchased anywhere. It came from living a hard-core life from birth. His reputation superseded him all across ATL. And definitely anywhere on the west side of Atlanta. Yuri was known as a ruthless killer. He feared none and had been to jail countless times to prove it. Not to mention the scuff marks, and old reminisces of stitches all over his discol-ored face.

Even though he still put a little fear in my heart, I felt safe. We grew up together when my mother lived in Bankhead. For years I watched him bully our neighbors, kill those who trespassed on his turf, and put hits out on those who went against him. He used to show me and my sister love when we were growing up, making it clear nobody was to fuck with us. Sed even got paid to be a look out for him from time to time until my mother got wind of the news.

Unfortunately my step father hit Yuri's car one day. When he didn't have the money to pay for the damages, he whipped his ass thoroughly. I wasn't there to witness the beat-ing, but some girls from the hood told me my step-father was bleeding from every available hole.

Within two weeks, my mother had found us a new house off of Auburn Avenue. After we left, my sister and I would hear horror stories about Yuri weekly from our friends in the old neighborhood. I'd shake my head and grin inside, while my sister vowed never to even walk on the same block with him if she saw him again.

"Yo, sit for a sec," he ordered, in his raspy, bottomless voice.

I huffed but sat down anyway.

"Yuh did good," he said sounding like the rapper, DMX.

"Thanks, but that shit was close." I sighed.

"Yo, yuh put in work though. I'm proud," he informed.

"We got the joker good….put'em where he belonged, huh?"

I simply nodded.

Although the thick, red curtains protected us from any unwanted ears, Yuri spoke softly yet boldly. "Next time yuh gotta remember not to touch a thing."

"What did I touch?" I asked on the defensive.

"His car door."

My voice fluttered. "Well, how was I supposed to get in the car, Yuri?"

"That's for yuh to figure out," he told me, passing me a wad wrapped in red rubber bands. "Yo, just be glad he's dead."

"Wait, how do you know I touched the handle? I thought you sent me to watch him, and lead him to you?" My expression became even more inquisitive. "So, you telling me, you sent me to watch him, but you were watching me?" I pointed to my chest directly between my D cups.

"It's bizness," he said nonchalantly. He opened his arms widely, "We all gotta watch the next man in this game…know what I'm saying?"

He leaned back in the chair and locked his fingers from both hands into one another. I leaned back too, and studied him just like he studied me. It threw me off guard knowing that Yuri didn't trust me one-hundred percent. I thought since he relied on me to track down and seduce the people he was paid to kill, there was no way he'd doubt me. I guess when you're in the murdering business, no one can be trusted.

"Should I count it?" I asked, reaching for my new Chanel purse.

"It would be an insult," he stated firmly.

"No problem." I shot him a fake grin. "I trust you." I grinned again. "So who's my next target?"

"Semo. He from Allen Temple and a real thug, not like dem other pussy-ass niggas yuh been settin' up. Yo, so be extra careful."

I nodded. Just thinking about Allen Temple had me shook. The dudes from that area didn't play from what I heard. And every night I could recall a segment on the news where they discussed another senseless murder.

"Yuh hear me?"

"I hear you."

"Yuh gotta come at that dude differently… know what I'm saying."

Of course he hit me with the over the top hand gestures again, fist banging into the palm of his hand. I hated it, and wanted to grab some rope to tie his hands together.

"He hangs out at Magic City every Saturday night. Yo, get at him on some freak shit... yuh know the big tease."

His hands flew in the air with more hand gestures.

"But make'em wait 'til the next time he sees yuh. Maybe two or t'ree times. Reel'em in, baby."

I hated the way Yuri sometimes dropped the *t* or the *th* in his words; especially with the word three. He tried to be all American, but his accent was still slightly there. Yuri paused, fired up a blunt, puffed extra hard then continued.

"Then, once yuh got'em hooked, go to the ba'troom and hit me up. Yo, keep the phone on so I can hear where you headed." He took another pull. "Call out names, streets, anyt'ing to help me stay on yuh. I'll take it from there," he informed. "And just to be safe. I'ma get yuh a Glock for this cat."

"Damnnnnn, is he like that?" I asked, feeling like I'd just heard a horror story.

He took a big puff exhaling like it was his last smoke. "Yo, do I tell lies?"

First, I shook my head like an obedient child, then I listened closely as Yuri clarified the plan. It only took a few seconds for him to run down Semo's description, what cars he drove, and who he hung out with. When he told me my next job would pay five grand, I became extra attentive. I sat up straight with perfect posture liking Yuri a little better now.

"Now that that's all taken care of, I need to know why yuh hung up on me the other day?"

"What do you mean?"

"It's simple. I called yuh. We talked for a sec, then yuh hung up."

My face bawled up as I thought back. "We talked?" I questioned.

Yuri frowned.

I thought even harder. Then it hit me. The bitch Monique had answered my phone in the restaurant. She never told me she talked to Yuri. I just thought he called and I'd missed it.

"Oh, now I remember. Sorry, that was an accident," I told him.

"C'mere," he ordered.

In my opinion, we were close enough. The area wasn't but so large so wanting me to come close told me one thing. He wanted a few free feels. I obliged and moved over quickly, landing my ass on the corner of his chair. The edge was wide enough to accommodate what guys had called my ass in the past, *world's greatest rump shaker*.

"Yo, yuh gon' make some joker a good woman," he told me, smashing his blunt on the small table nearby.

"You think so?" I gloated, showing off my three-thousand dollar veneers.

"I'm surprised some joker not try to hem yuh up yet…know what I'm mean? Put a ring on that finger," he added.

He grabbed my hand searching for any sign of a ring. I did have a diamond cluster on my forefinger that I'd bought myself. Little did he know the only man I planned on marrying from here on out was Rapheal.

Before I knew it, Yuri had each of my fingers in his mouth, one at a time, sucking furiously like it was his last meal.

He started with my fingers, worked his way to my arms, then to my tits. He took his right hand and placed it between my legs, then with his left one, he forcefully slipped it under my ass and thrust my body on top of his. He was strong to be only 5'9, one hundred and ninety pounds. It was mostly muscle, compared to my soft, curvaceous body. At this point, I knew what I had to do. It would cost me my job, my only income if I didn't.

I'd only been working for Yuri for five months. Of course more and more now that Derrick was out of the picture. Overall, Yuri had been good to me, and had never tried anything sexual before. His guns and master hit list always seemed to take precedence over me. But if it was ass he wanted; it was ass he would get, because it was his money that allowed me to buy nice things, the car, jewelry, and afford the rent in Buckhead. Prior to that, I only had what I could scramble up.

I straddled Yuri, nibbling on his neck, really getting a close view of the scratches and blotches covering his skin. As my juicy tongue licked him about, he removed my sheer black, Roberto Cavalli shirt that exposed my black bra. My tits sat up extra nice with my nipples hardening and at attention. It was just like he knew what they wanted. He sucked, licked, and devoured them like they needed to be serviced. This continued for several minutes, considering he took his time like he was sculpting a piece of art.

Suddenly, neither of us could take it anymore. He gripped the sides of my hips, lifted me in the air, and yanked his long shorts down to his knees. I guess killers didn't wear underwear because there was nothing there but nuts and balls.

Quickly, I yanked my skirt up toward my waist and pushed my thong to the side.

We grinded a bit using super exotic movements. He drooled. I closed my eyes in ecstasy. It felt so good and we hadn't even officially fucked yet. I guess going without dick since the wedding had its disadvantages.

Forcefully, Yuri palmed my ass and bit my nipples. I went ballistic. I took his rock-hard manhood, and inserted it inside my pulsating pussy. He lunged his ass off the chair back and forth like he'd just been possessed by the exorcist. We had the red velvet chair moving back and forth like a rocking chair.

I went hard pumping like a horny jack rabbit- hoping to finally have an orgasm. I gave myself to him feverishly. He did the same. We pumped, grinded, sweated, and did the nasty like it was our last chance. It was magnetic how we were in tune with one another. Our breathing increased at the same time, and even our backs arched simultaneously. His head hung backward over the tip of the chair, while I froze my clit directly on the upper part of his dick. He'd found it. The spot. The spot that so many could never hit.

He called out, "Shit!" obviously not afraid if someone heard us.

So I shouted out too, "Ohhhhhh, shit!" I told him. "Right there. Don't stopppppppp! Damnnnnnnn!"

Maybe this was the one- the magic stick, the one dick with the right slant, the right dimensions to make me cum. I hadn't had an orgasm from a dick in three years-only from being ate out. I was starting to think that I was incapable.

Then, there was more hope. Slurping sounds escalated, and Yuri thrust himself deeper and deeper. My eyes rolled to the back of my head, and I hummed a strange tune.

Yuri was there. He moaned "Mmmmmmmm…so good!"

I could feel him tensing up, and his hard, black dick exploding inside of me. I never shouted, never even made a noise; his head was back and his eyes only showed the white. I thought, *what the fuck happened to his eyeballs*.

I even hit him slightly on the side of the face hoping he had not died. Yuri moaned softly confirming that he wasn't dead, but his dick was. It was slowly deflating, and so were my chances of cumming. I wanted to fuckin' scream.

Enraged, I lifted myself off of him, reminiscing about the surgery on my uterus. It all happened back in 2006, three years ago when my pussy would bleed for weeks at a time. It took the doctors about three hours to correct the problem, luckily vaginally. All seemed to go well, including the four week recovery period, until I had my first fuck, and didn't cum for the first time in life. Since then, I had to get licked to squirt.

"That was a'ight," Yuri confessed standing up, fixing his pants.

"Yeah, it was good," I said to him half-heartedly. I wanted to tell him next time –he'd have to eat me. I needed to cum bad. I started thinking about Rapheal, wondering when his magic stick would cure my disease. I imagined his thick, dark arms around me, working the middle 'til I had an explosion.

"Yuh okay?" Yuri asked, snapping me from my daze.

"I'm straight," I lied, fixing my hair with my fingers.

"I'll get at yuh by the end of the week wit' the details."

He opened the curtains for me to exit. "Until then, yuh stay sweet."

He kissed my hand like we were now an item. I didn't do light-skinned men with two-tone issues, and definitely not ones lacking the magic touch. But like clockwork, I kissed him back and walked out of there with the same strut I entered with, only with a purse full of money. I truly thought I

38

was cute and so did the two people who'd just taken a seat at the bar. Immediately after passing them, I shot the bartender another shabby look no sooner than making it to the front door. When he opened his mouth to speak, I turned my head because I didn't have time to turn nobody down. I needed to get to the airport.

"Pull your skirt down in the back," he told me.

I yanked my skirt down in embarrassment and jetted out the door.

Five hours later I had landed at LaGuardia airport in New York City with a smile plastered across my face. Walking off the plane, I reached to turn my ipod off and pull the ear phones out of my ear. I'd been listening to *I'll Take Your Man*, by Salt and Pepper and still bounced like the beats were embedded in my head. The perfect theme song. I had to laugh at myself for being so cocky.

I should've learned my lesson about being cocky 'cause that's how I'd lost Rapheal to begin with. It was me who met him first, at a friend's bar-b-que. We hit it off real good, kicked it for hours and exchanged numbers. I never got a chance to call him because the next day I ran into him again at the Black Arts Festival. But because I was bunned up with my old fling, I pretended like it wasn't me, but my twin sister that he'd met the day before.

I called Monique instantly, explaining to her what had happened so she could cover for me. Monique covered for me alright. The bitch ended up sleeping with Rapheal, falling hard for him, and stole my man. Even when I told him it was me that he met first, he just laughed and kissed Monique passionately like I was some joke, and like they'd been together for years. Even after that I wanted to hate Rapheal but I couldn't. His swagger was hard to shake.

"I gotta make that nigga mine," I told myself.

I walked quickly toward baggage claim even though I didn't have shit to claim. I showed up with nothing but a pair of sexy underwear and bra to match tucked inside my Gucci satchel bag. Within seconds, I'd made it to the taxi line, hoping to get a fast driver. Sadly, I was met with a heavy downpour of rain and could barely see. Without an umbrella, I decided to take my jacket off to my sweat-suit, cover my head, and make a run for it. Luckily, a driver was right in front of me and on point. I expected him to open my door, but the Arabian man never moved.

Gloomy was what I felt, and hoped that Rapheal would be able to cheer me up. Once inside the car he asked the inevitable, "Where to?"

I stared back into his rear view mirror not knowing what to say. I hadn't thought that far, and didn't know where Rapheal was staying.

"Gimme a sec," I said, whipping my cell from my purse.

"I don't have a second. Why don't you get out and catch someone else when you know where you're going?"

"I shouted, "Wait a second muthafucka!" while I listened to Rapheal's phone ring.

"Get out!" the driver announced as the rain beat against the windows loudly.

I ignored him hoping that he would at least move away from the terminal. I knew it would only take me a minute to get the address.

"Hello."

"Rapheal, it's Dominique…what's up honey."

"Nothing much…a little busy right now. Did you need something?"

I could tell he was a bit baffled by receiving a call

from me. We'd only talked on the phone twice, and that was when Monique was sick and in the hospital.

"Monique okay?" he asked nervously.

"Oh, I guess…Then again, I'm not my sister's keeper. I'm here to spend a lil' time with you. I got something I need to discuss with you."

"What did you say?" he asked in a nasty tone.

"I said, I'm in New York, tryna get up with you," I told him in a firm voice letting him know I was dead serious.

"For what, Dominique?"

"Whatever you like," I said mimicking Eddie Murphy's bride-to-be in Coming to America.

I was rudely interrupted by the cab driver who'd hopped out and motioned to a nearby police officer. Before I could even get my next sentence out to Rapheal, the officer made me get out, leaving me standing in the soaking rain. I tried to re-focus on Rapheal's words. I thought he asked me if I wanted to go out for a drink. That is until he repeated himself.

"Look, I'm not sure what'cha been drinkin', but I'm handlin' business while I'm here. How long you here for?"

Even with the rain pouring down on me, I put on my sexy voice. "As long as you're here."

"Well I leave in the mornin'. So have a good night."

Without hesitation, he hung up. My face reddened wondering what the hell I was going do in New York City, wet and all alone.

Five...

Monique

My morning had been perfectly planned and was supposed to run smoothly. Instead, I sat in my cousin Shawna's styling chair, fussing with a contractor instead of getting my hair cut. Each time I jerked my neck and added a smart comment, water from my wet hair dripped down my neck.

I had never been in charge of construction on a house, or a building, but I was no fool. The house in the Bahamas was a treasure. Rapheal had only paid $50,000 for the run-down house which sat on top of a small cliff. It overlooked the Atlantic Ocean with authentic palm trees and bright red roses covering the front yard. It was our vacation dream home which he put me in charge of. There was no way I could fuck it up then face him with excuses.

He wasn't a man who accepted no for an answer, and as his wife-to-be, I wouldn't either. I swirled around in the chair and rose up a bit until Shawna pushed me back down by the shoulders. She started combing my hair straight down using a rat tail comb checking out my ends. She didn't care at all that I consistently fussed, moved around in anger, and yelled throughout her small shop. The shop was naturally noisy. With three stylists, tons of clients, and plenty of gossip, any new news available could be heard there, and any business I had was always discussed in her chair.

Finally, I settled down. I had been listening patiently to so much bullshit on the other end of the receiver that I needed boots to even get up and walk around all the shit.

"Look Ramirez," I said in a voice that told him I meant business, "when my husband and I were in Nassau we told you as soon as you gutted the property, we didn't want you to hire anymore subcontractors until I approved it. Now you're telling me I owe some lame-ass dry wall guy money for something I haven't seen or approved? I'll have Rapheal call you!" **Click**.

I hung up on him because Shawna wasn't slowing down for nothing. She had dozens of clients daily, and even had two waiting on deck for me to get out the chair. The type of money she got for weaves, and lace front wigs put most salaries to shame. Besides, she must've been the poster girl for weaves. Hers flowed nicely, the way it laid flat touching the middle of her back.

"Damn girl, Rapheal really is getting it…house in the Bahamas…dayum! I hear he got so much money, he even burns some from time to time."

She laughed crazily in her signature, thunderous laugh. I just smiled and eyed the ladies underneath the dryer who stared down my throat. I didn't want any extra women chasing after my man thinking the grass was so green on my side. "Shawna, start cutting," I told her. "You keep playing in my head with that comb."

"Girl, what kinda cut you want?" she asked me, smacking her lips between words.

"I showed you. The short one on the front of that magazine." I pointed to the July issue of Black Hair.

44

"The pixie? You sure?" She leaned back and stopped combing momentarily. "I can't believe you cutting your hair. Dayum," she uttered real ghetto-like.

"Just do it." I paused getting a little nervous. "You think it'll look good?" I turned my head from right to left taking a good look at myself.

"Girl, it will. Your make-up is always flawless. And you sho got those Asian features like yo mama. It'll be fly," she added. "I just can't understand you breakin' down my door tryna get a hair cut."

"Look, I told you Dominique showed up at the restaurant the other day with the same hair color and similar cut. I need a change," I said raising my voice. "It was cute to be alike when we were younger, but not at twenty-seven."

"Yeah, I second the motion. She's my cousin...but it's gay."

Shawna laughed all loud again.

She made a few more jokes about my sister and some of her famous memories. As she joked, I thought about the time I popped up at Dominique's old house in the Conyers area over a year ago. It was a two-bedroom condo that she purposefully kept a secret. I guess because she knew we'd figure out she was a freakin' copy cat! When I walked in I saw all the same shit she'd either seen in my house, or heard me say I was getting; no individuality of her own. I mean she had the same Butternut hardwood floors, the same Persian one-of-kind area rugs, and the killer- my Egyptian satin sheets that I'd gotten from a dealer in LA. I remember her saying she wanted the web address so she could order some towels, but she turned around and ordered the exact same prints for the sheets, and the same damn comforter.

A week later the woman at the art gallery where I shopped told me that my sister had come in and wanted the Charles Burnett, *Singing In The Rain* painting that I had purchased. It didn't matter that he'd only painted fifty of them. She wanted one and persuaded the gallery owner with big cash that she needed it and to contact the artist directly.

"That damn Dominique," I said, shaking my head.

"Girlllllll, I was thinking the same thing."

"I don't know why you saying that now," I said, calling Shawna out in front of everybody. "You the one always hanging out with her and running the streets."

She pushed at my shoulder. "You jealous?" Then hit me with a laugh.

"Please." I waved her off with the back of my hand.

Instantly, she picked up her curling iron acting like she was gonna burn me. "You so plain," she told me. "Always wanna be in love. I'm tryna hang out…get my groove on." She grinned. "I love both of y'all, but let's face it, you're on lock down and she's wild'n out."

I hit her with a shy smile because I loved being on lock down for Rapheal.

"So, what's up with her messing with Yuri?"

"Yuri who?" I asked.

She stopped cutting my hair and peered down into my face.

"You know Yuri…with the discolorations all over his face. You know…the murderer Yuri, who kills anything that moves."

My eyes lit up. It was the voice I heard on Dominique's phone two days ago. I knew I recognized the voice, yet couldn't place it.

"She fucks with him?"

She hit me with the shoulders.

I showcased my discuss through my tone. "Yuck!"

"Girlllll, that's what I heard," Shawna exclaimed, in true gossip fashion; of course smacking her lips.

"Damn, my sister has gotten real desperate," I commented for everyone to hear. "She needs something to do and fast. At least when she was in her early twenties she stuck with the nursing thing for a year or so."

"Girllll that's because she worked in labor and delivery and was getting her rocks off looking at wide coochies all day."

We all laughed like crazy, but then I got serious. "Maybe I'll try to convince her to finally go back to college. I'm even thinking about going back to get my MBA."

Shawna fell out laughing. She backed away from the chair and doubled over holding her stomach. Girl…girl…girl…"

My face crinkled up. "What is it?"

"You talk about that shit like you proud. You been to college already. You got all that damn education and still ain't got no job, just like all the other college graduates I know."

I looked at Shawna like she didn't have the brain she was born with. "First off, Rapheal doesn't want me to work. Secondly, if I ever need to get a job, I got a Business Degree that will land me one. And lastly, just be glad you're getting money doing hair for now. Lord knows if something ever happens to your hands, you're finished! That's when you'll realize the importance of a college degree."

"Oh."

She picked up her Lotta-Body setting lotion bottle and sprayed near my eye like it was a mistake. I slapped her ass with a wet towel and laughed it off. I was done with preaching. The saying goes you can't teach an old dog new tricks. She was a hood rat at it's finest and couldn't be convinced. "Whatever," I ended, throwing my hands up.

She swung my chair back to the front so I could face the mirror. The cut was done, and I officially had my hair cut into short layers, resembling Halle Berry's old look. She hadn't hit me with the blow dryer yet, or curls but I saw the vi-

47

sion.

As soon as the blow dryer started, she spoke loudly trying to be heard over the noise.

"Where the hell Sedrick been at?" she asked, being nosey.

First, I pretended not to hear because of the dryer. Then she repeated herself, leaning into my ear.

"Where Sedrick been?" she repeated.

He's been in Europe somewhere for the last month. Now I think he's in New York with Rapheal. I'm not really sure though."

"Dayum. That's crazy. That's your brother. I thought all of ya'll is tight."

"Shawna, say it right," I said in frustration. I wanted her to get her grammar right. "Besides, he's closer to Dominique than me. They use to talk all the time. I guess because they're just alike. They're both hood, and they love the lime light."

Shawna broke out into a song and dance singing, *I'm So Hood*, by DJ Khaled. She kept repeating the hook, "I'm so Hood," actually sounding like a rapper. Then she hit the onlookers with, "And if you feel me put your hands up."

Those fools put their hands up and I shook my head. It was like a real show…extra funny. She reared back, bouncing and rocking to her imaginary beats then got right back into roller brushing my hair with what felt like 20,000 watts. My head was on fire so I kept squinting and moving my head each time she kept the dryer in one spot too long.

"So what you saying is he not classy enough to hang with you, huh?"

"Nooooo Shawna, that's not what I'm saying. We haven't talked much since we both left the house. Remember, Sedrick is twenty-five so he's coming into his own; it's about work, women, money, women, hanging out, women.

We all laughed, even the ladies who had no business in our conversation.

"Yeah, well he must really be busy not to show up at Dominique's wedding."

I just hunched my shoulders. For one, I'd gossiped enough. And two, it was time to get my hair curled. Shawna was famous for burning people so I shut up. She called it the quickest hand technique in town. I called it the easiest way to get burned in town.

With that said we spent the next ten minutes in silence. I simply listened to the gossip from the other ladies in the salon. They had plenty, ranging from: who had gotten busted by DEA the day before, who had Gonorrhea, or who had been fighting at the club the night before. They even started rating the ballers of the city, putting them in order from largest to smallest bankrolls.

All of a sudden, some girl who appeared to be in her early twenties started looking at me funny. I was sure by the way she examined me with her x-ray vision, she could tell if my unborn child had any issues.

"You been talking about the Rapheal who used to hang out on Monroe Street?" she finally asked me.

I looked at her with a frown. I didn't like the gossip scene at all. That's why Rapheal told me to always stay away from a bunch of chicks. They always seemed to start shit, and if you give them something to talk about, they will. Luckily, I never answered the girl. I just nodded like I had no idea who she was talking about.

Suddenly, I was pleasantly surprised. The phone rang that special ring, *Let Me Make Love To You*, by the O'Jays. It was my baby calling so I didn't even let it get to the second ring.

"What's up, baby?"

"You," he said using his sweet, sexy voice.

"I miss you."

"Me too," my honey replied.

Shawna pushed my shoulder letting me know she was done. I looked in the mirror and smiled. It looked damn good; short in the back and cut into layers everywhere else. I loved the fullness and length on the top.

"I was beginning to think you didn't love me anymore," I teased.

Of course he told me he did and couldn't wait to see me.

"When you coming home? I gotta surprise for you."

My eyes squinted hard as I listened to his story about how his boys got drunk last night, and almost got locked up at a club. He said one of his workers, named Kenny, fought one of the bouncers, and whipped his ass so good the club owner offered him a job.

"The question Rapheal, is how drunk were you?"

"Oh, luv, believe me... I took it easy. I told'cha, you got my word. I'm easing up off the Henny."

"Ummm, hmph."

I didn't believe him but got excited about my new hairstyle the more I played with it in the mirror next to Shawna's chair.

"Rapheal, guess what?"

"What?"

"I cut all my hair off just for you." I got silent for a moment just waiting for his reaction. I knew he had a fetish for long hair.

"Your hair?" he questioned slowly. "You cut it?"

He didn't sound too happy.

"Believe me baby, you're gonna love it. It's real short and sassy, makes me look more sophisticated." I stopped to check myself in the mirror next to Shawna's station. She already had some lady sitting tall, who'd hopped in her chair no sooner than I got up.

"I'm sure you're still beautiful," he told me unexcitedly. "But look, I gotta talk to you about somethin' real serious. It's been on my mind since last night."

I knew it must've been something because nothing bothered Rapheal. He sounded sorta concerned. I prayed it had nothing to do with my brother. He'd mentioned before that sometimes his work became dangerous.

"What is it?" I asked.

"You gotta check your sister."

"Dominique? What did she do?"

"She was in New York yesterday. Doing what I'm not sure. But she called me tryna hang out a bit." He got silent for a moment. "Now I know that's no crime, but I don't want her calling me unless it's about you. She too foul… you feel me, luv?"

"No. I feel you, baby. One-hundred percent. I'll take care of it."

We did our phone smooches through the phone. As he talked, I tried to act like my skin wasn't boiling, thinking about Dominique. He told me he would be home in our bed by Friday night and for me not to worry about anything.

Within those few minutes we seemed to talk about everything. He said we were going to his annual Family Reunion cookout which they had every July. I even told him about my run-in with Ramirez and the house issue. He assured me that one conference call with us all on the phone would clear things up, and that I would be able to handle it and see the project to the end.

As soon as I hung up from him, I punched Dominique's number into the phone so hard, I was positive a few keys would break. It rang then went straight to voice mail. So I clicked end and called back again. Same thing happened, so I called again. Voice mail once again. I left her a message, hung up, and called back. This time she answered.

"Damn, what do you want?" she ranted. "You a fuckin' stalker or something?"

I shouted so loud I felt the veins popping out of my neck! "I can't believe you went to New York thinking you were gonna hang with my man!" I paused and shook my head in disbelief. "Don't think you're gonna mess up a good thing and fuck my man, then tell me later you're sorry!"

"Oh, I had no intention on doing that!" she boldly told me.

"Yeah, sure. I know your kind, trick! It's just fucked up that you're my family."

"No, you don't understand. I had no intention on fuckin' your man then saying I'm sorry! Oh next time, baby, next time," she kept repeating.

She paused like she really had something else to say.

Finally, it came out. Cold. And harsh. "I *will* fuck Rapheal, and he *will* leave you!"

I stopped in my tracks wanting to find something to throw. "Oh, I forgot. Once a ho, always a ho. I should've remembered, leopards don't change their spots."

"Fuck you, Monique!"

"Bitch, you treading on thin ice!" My voice started cracking. I shouted so loud, I became hoarse. Rage oozed through my body. "You are borderline psycho! What would make you think Rapheal wants you!" I shouted, pacing the floor of the shop. "He just left your freak-ass at the airport in New York, and wouldn't tell you where he was laying his head."

I waited for my sister to respond but quickly realized in the midst of shouting, she'd hung up. All ears were raised in the salon, so it was a sure thing to hear my business on the streets within hours.

I was done with Dominique's crazy-ass and her unreasonable dreams of getting with my man. But one thing puzzled me. Why would she say… "next time?"

Six...

Dominique

I arrived at my mother's house with less than an hour to spare. It would be show time the moment Shawna called me. I'd lied to her and claimed that an associate of mine wanted to meet her. The clincher was that we had to meet him at Magic City, a hot strip joint in the city. I hyped up the lie real good saying he was part owner of the spot and that he had major paper, just looking for somebody to spend it on. My cousin was wild and crazy, and was normally down for anything so I figured she would be my scapegoat. I needed to get to the club to bump heads with Semo again.

It had been two weeks since my meeting with Yuri, so I used last Saturday night as my first chance at meeting Semo. Luckily, I got there late just as he was leaving. We eyed each other in the parking lot for several seconds, of course with him examining me like a piece of juicy meat. My focus remained on him the entire time. It was crazy how he mugged me. No doubt, I mugged him back.

Finally, he asked me to come to him, but I refused. I knew I had him going because he even sent one of his boys after me, who I blew off shamefully. Tonight would be the night, I told myself ringing my mother's doorbell.

"I could hear her prim and proper voice calling out. "Coming," she sang. "Who is it?"

I didn't say anything. She killed me, always trying to make sure she spoke perfectly, enunciating each word like Monique. The days when she spoke broken English were long gone. She was probably on her tenth English course at the community college, and had two degrees under her belt.

"Who is it?" she sang again.

"Yo daughter," I shouted real ghetto-like. I banged on the door hoping she'd hurry.

"Who?"

"Monique," I responded, trying to be funny.

I figured she would throw on her Superman cape and jet to the door.

"Dominique," she said in a solemn tone as she opened wide.

I burst through the door and brushed past her like I wasn't happy to see her either. I hadn't been inside the small house in over a year but it still appeared to be immaculate. Everything about her was perfect, the way she kept her home, the way she spoke, even the way she stood. Perfect posture was important to her even though she hadn't reached 5'1 yet. I knew height didn't matter to her. She considered herself, Mrs. Ruby P. Lewis, to be flawless and wanted her children to mimic her ways.

I finally stopped and turned as I got near the tiny, box shaped family room that was adjacent to the kitchen. Oddly my mother was standing there with her arms open.

"Give your Mama some love."

We hugged each other loosely, with her patting me on the back as if I were some fuckin' dog. She inspected me from head to toe like I looked a mess then offered me food and water like the homeless.

56

"You thirsty?"

"No Ruby, I'm not thirsty," I responded with an attitude.

She frowned when I called her by her first name.

"Well, sit down, and let me fix you something anyway. Besides I'm making your sister's favorite, chicken and dumplings."

"Why? Is she coming by?" I made sure my tone expressed that if she was- I would leave.

"No, I was just thinking about her."

I breathed heavily. Then, she gave me the once over and moved a few feet away headed into the kitchen.

"Where's Steve?"

"Working as usual, like you should be doing."

"I do work, Ruby," I shot back.

She looked at me kinda funny. "I'm not sure what you do but you look mighty shiny. Where are you headed this time of night?"

"The word is not shiny," I told her in my usual disrespectful tone, "it's fly. You see Ruby, I'm into fashion in case you haven't noticed." I took a minute to show off my True Religion jeans with embedded crystals on the pocket along with my gold, studded shirt and Louie Vuitton handbag. I even did a quick spin in the middle of the floor, followed by a quick move where I pulled my blinged out Gucci shades off the top of my head where I had them sitting. They had enough gold and fake diamonds on the sides to be the center of attention in any room.

"What I meant is…you look like you have diamonds everywhere. Are they real?" she asked in a disapproving tone.

No doubt, she hated me.

I gave up realizing my mother would never be hip. She had some features of a black woman, but mostly appeared to be mixed. She was fifty-seven and of old-fashioned Asian decent, holding onto her Asian values. But obviously she had a strong thing for black men. Maybe lusting for deep, dark, black men was our family rule. Just like my maternal grandmother, she too was a war baby. My grandmother slept with my black grandfather during World War II back in the forties. My mother was then born and moved to different countries in Asia following my father. My mother ended up moving to Vietnam and obviously waited like a loyal hooker for my father to arrive during the Vietnam War. It's unbelievable to me how she pretends to be so perfect, yet gave up the nappy-dugout the first night.

It must've been good to my pops because he moved her back to the states and seven years later she gave birth to twins. Since then, she's never worked a day in her life; not with my father, or after he ended up in the psych ward at Walter Reed hospital. Then she met my step-father, Steve, who stole her right from under my father's nose.

I started thinking about my dad and rushed over to the mantle where I knew the only picture I would ever see of him could be found. It had been there for years, and had obviously been approved by my step-father since my mother was not in the picture. I got angry because some new pictures had finally made the list; yet most still did not include me.

Pictures of my step father and Monique dominated the mantle. There was one photo of Sed, but most showcased Monique; her first day of kindergarten, her first track meet, her college graduation, and now a close-up photo of her and Rapheal. How appropriate. All about her baby girl Monique, and one photo of me from 1987 riding a beat-up fuckin' Barbie bicycle with training wheels.

Where in the hell were my memories? I wanted to shout. Instead, I looked at the woman who gave me life and cursed under my breath.

"Well," she said, "the food is ready. Take a seat right

there in your favorite chair. I'll grab a tray and bring it to you."

I just looked at her and her funny-ass shape. It was odd; ass flat like a pancake. I must've taken after my father.

"Go ahead," she pointed. "Sit down. Just give me a sec."

My mother loved to feed people. It was considered rude in her eyes to allow anyone to enter her home and not offer some type of food. I knew she meant well. Besides, I was starving, and needed to fuel up for a long night. I plopped down in my favorite lounge chair, kicked off my Giuseppe slip-ons, and sat my large, hooped earrings on the edge of the chair.

Within minutes, my mother had fixed my plate, given me something to drink, and was sitting in my face like I was an unexplainable science project. She glared for minutes with her narrow eyes while I grubbed as if she didn't exist.

"So, just what are you doing with yourself nowadays?"

"Drinking and getting high."

Her neck jerked back. "Are you serious?"

"No," I said sharply, then kept eating.

"Did you apologize to Derrick for ruining his life?"

"Did you apologize to my sick father for dumping him when he was down and out?"

"Young lady, have some respect!" she shouted.

"No! Did you?"

"Dominique, we made our amends before he died.

"Sure."

I had to keep reminding myself that she was my mother, and not a broad from the streets. She treated me as if I didn't belong. As if I wasn't worthy. At first it felt good being in her presence since the only family I really talked to were my cousins Shawna and her sister Jennifer. I'd given the rest of them my ass to kiss years ago. But now I wished that

I'd never visited.

"Ma, let me ask you something."

She gave up a half of a smile when I called her Ma.

"Go ahead," she told me.

I sat my fork down for a moment. "Have I ever done anything to please you?"

"Ahh…" she began.

"No, wait. Let me answer that. Let's see, when I was younger you never came to my sporting events but you went to all of Monique's." My voice grew louder. "And when I got a little older, I was the one who had to do all the chores, like fuckin' Cinderella while Monique got to go to dance practice four days a week."

"Watch your mouth young lady!"

"Oh, I'm watching it," I said with a smirk. "The truth shall set you free, Ruby," I said being sarcastic. "And let's not forget, I even went to nursing school and worked as a lame-ass nurse trying to make you happy. You know that's not me, Ruby; the medical scrubs, and delivering babies."

My words now sounded like the job had disgusted me, ruining my reputation. I picked up my fork and started eating again then added, "That still didn't make you happy."

Finally, my mother stopped talking and walked near the kitchen counter, still watching me gobble down my chicken and dumplings. I hovered over my food with one hand on the fork stabbing at the dumplings while the other guarded the plate. It was a familiar jail scene hoping nobody would take my plate. I hadn't been eating well and needed my strength for tonight's action.

"Why can't you be more like your sister?" she blurted out.

That was it! I threw the plate in the air. Food scattered about. "What?"

"You heard me," she said with a raised voice. "She's

classy and knows how to keep a good man."

"Mama, first of all Monique is plain, and boring…nothing much to her at all. Secondly, you only know what she tells you," I said, standing up and slipping my shoes back on. It was time to go. "Just so you know… Rapheal is cheating on Monique."

Her mouth opened wide and her jaw hung low. "You're kidding!"

"No, I'm not," I said with a serious expression.

"Have you told your sister?"

"No. And I probably won't."

I wanted to tell her that Rapheal would be cheating with me soon. I didn't care if we all had to live together. Hell, The Color Purple was one of my favorite movies anyway. I wondered what it would be like with Me, Monique and Rapheal all living under one roof. I mean Shug Avery did it, while Mister chased her around the house and about the town constantly. Ugly-ass Miss Celie never had a chance. I laughed to myself comparing Monique to Whoppi Goldberg's character.

"I'm out Ruby," I said, kissing her on the cheek. From the moment I strutted toward the front door, I could feel her disapproving eyes watching me. I stopped with my hand on the knob. "Oh, I forgot to tell you I'm pregnant," I said cheerfully.

She looked like she'd seen a ghost.

"By who?" she yelled behind me.

I laughed my ass off as I opened and shut her front door. Damn I really needed to get pregnant, I told myself.

Two hours later, Shawna and I stood inside Magic

City watching the men go crazy. The place was packed with wall-to wall dudes and plenty of booty to go around. Everything with a dick in the ATL was in the house checking out who they wanted to leave with. We stood near the bar just yards away from Semo, who had his eyes planted on me. I kept pulling an LL Cool J move, licking my lips every two seconds. The golden tone lip gloss I'd chosen seemed to be perfect and did the job well.

It was the first time I'd been able to get a close up on my target. He seemed to be about my height, with a completely bald-head. It would've been a sexier attribute if he'd been blessed with darker skin. But I guess his golden color fit perfectly with the two gold teeth centered at the top of his mouth. I watched him laugh and kick it with two other dudes who were both hefty and looked as if they could bench press three hundred pounds.

I kept licking my lips while playing back in my head everything Yuri had told me about Semo. Shawna's presence worked well. She looked as if she belonged, with thick long weave damn near down her back. She really thought she was in the place to party, and meet one of the owners. She had no idea by morning she would've been an accomplice to murder.

The DJ put on, *Turning Me On*, by Keri Hilson. The crowd went wild. Shawna started dancing like she needed to be on stage while I simply rocked sexily in place. I had to remain cool, because I knew Semo would make his move soon. Actually, I gave him no choice the way I shot him multiple *I wanna fuck you looks*.

Finally, the moment had arrived. Semo stood up and headed my way. I clocked him hard, continuing to lick my lips, while taking mental notes. As hot as it was, he wore a red and black Rock a Wear sweat-suit which fit extra baggy on his lightweight frame. Yuri had warned me he spoke extra ghetto and gave hood a new meaning. But all I kept noticing were the shiny teeth.

"Damn yous sexy," he said, walking right up on me, and grabbing my hand.

He squeezed my fingers tightly, then searched for a ring.

"Yes, I'm single," I announced with a school girl smile. I had him- hook-line- and sinker.

Semo grinned.

"I saw you over there x-raying me. You like what you see?" I smacked my lips and bent my body forward so he could get a sneak peek of my bouncy tits."

He chewed his gum faster and faster.

"Fo' sho'," he said, then nodded in delight. "Lemme snag us sum bottles."

"That's what the fuck I'm talkin' 'bout," Shawna blurted out.

I shot her an evil eye before turning back to Semo who reminded me of Luke from 2 Live Crew, just without hair. He was still chomping on that damn gum, as he ordered bottles of Veuve Clicquot from the bartender.

I know I couldn't get drunk. It was against company policy. Yuri had given me strict orders to follow, and if I wanted to get paid that's how it would have to go down. Within minutes, the champagne sat on ice and was being pushed our way across the bar. Semo peeled off nine one hundred dollar bills, slapped them on the bar, and pushed the bottles my way.

He popped the first one, pouring glasses for me and Shawna. He popped another for himself, which he took straight to the head. I sipped and danced around a bit making myself seem super relaxed.

"So, you chillin' wit me tonight?"

I froze. He'd beat me to it.

After a few seconds of saying… "Ahhhh…." I hesitated… "I don't know."

"Don't be scarrrrrred," he joked, getting close up in my face. "I won't bite," he told me. "Fo sho."

"Ahhhhh…I'm not scared." I watched his moves skeptically tryna make it all play out the right way. "Let me see."

Semo was a straight-up country bamma. He was authentic though…one of those hot bamma's from the south…the ones who gave us a bad name. He just kept nodding his head and saying, "Fo sho," while I was thinking, even though I hadn't asked him a damn thing.

"Let's do it," I said hesitantly as if he hadn't fallen right into my plan.

He lifted his bottle in the air like he was celebrating our departure.

"Hey, gimme a minute," I told him. "I gotta break the news to my girl." I pretended as if Shawna would be emotionally distraught if I left her in the club alone.

"Do yo thang, sweetness. Fo sho."

"We gonna run to the ladies room," I announced, pulling Shawna's drunk- ass by the collar.

When we got to the ladies room, I simultaneously told her I was leaving with Semo just as I was texting Yuri. My text was brief yet clear.

Got'em…leaving club now.

I turned to Shawna, gave her the keys to my car, and told her not to drink anymore. My car meant the world to me, so a drunk driving crash wasn't acceptable. I poured her drink down the sink along with mine, and reached into my purse for my lip gloss. With each pucker I kissed into the mirror thinking about how Step One had worked perfectly.

Shawna stumbled my way. "Bitch, where is the owner? I thought we came to meet'em," she slurred.

"Bad news Shawna." I gazed into her eyes, grabbing her by the shoulders.

"What?" She looked concerned.

"He saw you out by the bar, and changed his mind. Too much weave. Sorry boo." I snapped my fingers and pointed to the bathroom exit.

Shawna got completely silent. Might've been the first time I'd heard her quiet in years. By the time we made it out of the bathroom, Semo's friends were standing near him at the bar. One guy had his keys in his hand while the other played around with his fat gut. He kept trying to do the unthinkable…tuck a medium-sized polo shirt into his tight-ass pants.

"Let's roll," Semo said, slamming the last bottle on the counter.

"I'm out," I told Shawna, then headed to the front door.

Semo followed me. Then someone followed him. I heard him mumbling behind me, yet remained afraid to turn around. It seemed as if a monkey wrench were being thrown into my plan.

I stopped when I got to the front door. With one turn, my eyes met Semo's. My paranoia kicked in when I saw one of his boys follow behind us. "He's not going too, is he?" I stopped in my tracks, and positioned myself to eye them both. "I don't do threesomes." My arms crossed sassily.

"Oh, he just my man. We'll have privacy when we need it, Sexy."

Semo gripped my ass hard like he'd known me for years.

I rushed out the door into the parking lot with my hands in the air. "No. No No. No," I protested. "I barely know you, and now you think I'm getting in a car with you and him, so I can be on the ten o'clock news tomorrow morning. Just call me tomorrow," I announced, pretending like I was walking away.

"Hey. Fo'real though…slow yo roll. Gimme a sec."

Semo took his boy over to the side, said a few words, then took the keys out of his hand.

"This way," he announced, walking in a different direction from his friend.

"I looked at his big friend who was shaped just like Barney. *See ya fat-ass*! I thought inside.

Nonetheless, we walked swiftly, alone, and through the crowded lot. When Semo flicked the alarm on his key, I saw the lights blink on a white Lexus LS. It wasn't what I expected for the reputation he carried, but it looked good enough. When he opened the door, the vanilla air-fresheners hit me in the face. I smiled and melted into the butternut seats.

"So, where we headed?"

"You wit' me, a'ight."

"Yeah, I'm with you, but I don't know you at all. I gotta at least tell my sister who I'm rolling with or where I'm going. See," I said, reaching across his shoulder to show him a picture of Monique on my phone. "She kinda wild…might come looking for me."

"Damn, fo'real, she look good, too. Tell'er she can link up wit' us, too." He laughed.

"No…serious, it's what we do. We never go places with guys without letting the other one know. You might be a killer."

I grinned.

"No shit. That's wassup," he said, typing into his phone and turning the wheel at the same time. "I gotta shoot my girl a text too, since I won't be home for a while."

"So where we going?" I repeated.

"You tell me. You worth the Marriott or the Days Inn?"

"Funny. I'll tell her I met this nice guy named Semo and if anything happens to me…have the police investigate the Marriott."

"Fo sho."

We both laughed as I typed. Then Semo gripped my leg. "We gon' do real good together, shawty.

In white Lexus LS tag # MNY176. On hwy 75 headed 2 Marriott.

I wanted to ask which Marriott, but figured that would raise a red flag. So I chilled and listened to his loud- ass music. It was some ole' off brand Atlanta based artist who Semo claimed he managed. He talked about that shit all the way down Highway 75 until we turned on Andre Young Boulevard.

"I'm sorta hungry. You think the hotel will still have room service?"

"No doubt. We gon' lay at the one downtown on Peachtree."

It was confirmed. I texted fast.

Marriott Marquis on Peachtree

That fool didn't even look my way. He was texting, too. He had the music jumping and his foot heavily on the pedal. Suddenly, the dreadful CD ended, and Semo turned the volume down and asked me to come closer. He had me gripped by my neck and pushing me toward his lap. I wasn't 'bout to give him no head.

"I think I know your girl," I announced, hoping he'd loosen the grip.

"Why you say that?"

"I know this girl who used to do hair with me who messed with a guy name Semo. She light-skinned, right?"

"Nope. Not it."

"Good, cause I really dig you," I flirted. "So, when we get up in this room you just might get the royal treatment, and not the one night only treatment."

"Oh shit! Now that's what the fuck I'm talkin' 'bout! Fo sho."

He got anxious, drove faster, and hopped on Peachtree Center Avenue. He started clapping, singing, and twitching in his seat. I took a quick second and rubbed him all in the middle. He loved it! And his shit hardened within seconds. I let my hand cascade all over his hips and upper leg area feeling for a piece. I stopped finally, licked my lips and sent another text.

3 mins away. No sign of a gun, yet.

When we pulled up to the hotel, Semo was pumped. He hopped out, handed the valet the key and walked in front of me like I wasn't even with him. Anxiously, he rushed past the front desk. My mind started tripping. Was he gonna check in? Maybe get a key?

"Hey, where you going?" I called out.

"My lil' cousin works here," he announced. "I get a room here every Saturday night. I texted him already, told him I was coming… let's roll," he said, holding the elevator door.

My mind went ballistic. Of course I thought the worse. Was he gaming me? Just as I had been texting Yuri, he could've been texting someone to set me up. I got nervous instantly. Sweat beaded up on my forehead just as Semo moved close to me. He wrapped his arm across my shoulder and I panicked with each movement he made. Surely there were about thirty chill bumps that covered my arm.

Then when the elevator stopped on the 5th floor, I froze. When it opened there was a young guy, in a bell cap uniform who looked to be in his early twenties standing by the room directly across from the elevator. He gave Semo some dap, then a quick manly hug. He handed off the key and told him he had to get back downstairs to work.

"She a hottie," he commented after checking out my back-side.

I exhaled. Maybe I would live to see the next day.

We both rushed inside the plush suite with Semo falling flat on the bed and me kicking off my shoes. My heart was still pounding, yet I had to remember everything Yuri had taught me. For one, I was sure not to lay my bag down unattended.

"I gotta pee," I lied.

I rushed into the bathroom and sent the next message.

Room 512- Hurry!

It worried the hell out of me that Yuri never responded to any of the messages. He never said that he would, but it seemed necessary because of the way we pulled this hit off. I even began to think about the horror stories people had spread about Yuri's past. Whether he was being a stick up boy on the streets, selling drugs, or giving somebody two shots to the head, he kept his untrustworthy stature. Cut throat was what they called him. Some said he would turn on his mama if he had to.

The knock at the bathroom door startled me.

"Hey baby, you gettin' ready fo Daddy?" Semo asked.

His voice deepened and sounded even more psychotic.

I fumbled around with my purse, pushing my phone to the bottom, underneath my junk. At that moment I wished Yuri had followed through and gotten me a gun. When I opened the door, to my surprise Semo stood completely naked in front of me stroking his dick. I couldn't back down, so I pranced from the bathroom sexily and walked like my feet had touched a run-way. *Come on, Yuri,* I prayed inside.

I did a freaky trot over near the king-sized bed, and started taking off my clothes slowly. I figured a striptease act would buy me a lil' time.

Semo sat on the edge of the bed with his dick pointing starkly to the ceiling, and his mouth wide open. All I saw were his shiny gold teeth and saliva drooling my way. He was ready. And me, I was desperately waiting for back-up. Slowly,

I started with my shirt then inched out of my jeans, twirling them in the air for several seconds. It was clear my moves were stiffer than normal, considering my attention remained on the door. I still hadn't figured out how Yuri would enter the room. We'd discussed the possibility of him taking me to a hotel, and he'd consistently told me, "I got it."

He got it, I thought to myself. *He got it. C'mon Yuri!*

I kept dancing seductively. Once I got down to my bra and panties, my hips swayed from side to side. "You like," I asked giving him a good view of my ass.

"Fo sho," he hummed. "Yous fuckin' exotic lookin', baby. You got some Indian in you?"

I laughed. Every man wanted his chick to have some Indian in her. "Far from it. I'm black," I said proudly. "My mom's got a little Asian in her, so some of it has rubbed off on me. But tell me...this looks like a black girl's ass, don't it?"

I bent straight down, touched my toes then grabbed the back of my ankles. I figured I'd given Semo a heart attack because he reared back on the bed holding his heart.

"Damn, baby! C'mere," he motioned.

I moved closer, kissed him, then told him I needed to grab a condom from my purse.

I rushed over to my purse that sat on the floor near the night stand. Quickly, my hands nervously snatched my phone, never pulling it out of the purse. A comment was there. It was Yuri. Oh hell, I told myself.

It read; **Watch yuhself!**

I gasped for air, lifted myself off the floor, and announced to Semo that I wanted to treat him to the best blow job he'd ever had. "It's gotta be dark."

"Oh, hell yeah!"

I enticed him as I started turning lamps and lights out around the room, of course inching my way to the door. Just three feet from the last light, I reached, hoping to make the room completely dark. But I stopped abruptly when the door flew open. One by one, Yuri and his two boys filed in. They looked like the militia on attack as they bust up in the room. Yuri had a silver nine millimeter in his right hand, coupled with a mean strut and an evil grimace on his face. From the corner of my eye, I could see his boys standing guard near the door with two pistols that couldn't be made out.

Semo was helpless.

"Yous a muthufuckin' coward!" he shouted, rising up on the bed.

At first, I thought he was talking to me. But he was talking to Yuri and staring at the silencer attached to the barrel of his gun. All I saw were gold teeth and iron. Semo sat up straight not showing any fear. His eyes quickly darted around the room. He looked as if he was about to move until Yuri fired.

The entire scene seemed to play out in slow motion. Semo's body jilted backwards while blood splattered about. Instantly, I vomited. I'd done some cold shit in my life, and had set up many for Yuri, but never seen him kill anybody in cold blood right before my eyes. Then I thought about the silencer. It had indeed softened the sound when the gun fired but I couldn't help but wonder if someone on the same floor had heard the noise.

Without hesitation, Yuri hopped up onto the bed like a certified killer. The sound of his gun being cocked again frightened me even more.

"Hit'em again," one of Yuri's boy's shouted from behind. "No witness baby!"

Inside, my heart pounded like a drum. Yuri monitored Semo's chest as it rose slowly, then down, even slower. When it didn't rise again, I swallowed hard. He was done.

Yuri gave up some type of victory hand gesture while a

bowel movement almost slipped from my ass. I was so damn nervous I could barely walk.

Between the smell from the vomit and my panic attack, I remained frozen. Yuri tossed me my purse and my clothes, while ushering me swiftly to the door. We took the back exit stairs two at a time, with me in the back, still half-naked. We stopped momentarily in the hollow stairwell as they all screamed, "Put your shit on!"

My eyes kept blinking like they'd been programmed to do so. I remained frozen.

"Yuri, where'd you get this slow bitch from!" one of his boy's shouted.

Hearing somebody call me the word I hated most snapped me from my spell. I slipped my pants on, then yanked my shirt over my head. Yuri was talking and giving instructions the entire time. All I heard was the end.

"When we get to the bottom of the stairs, we'll exit by the back part of the lobby. Follow me slowly," he paused. "Act normal," he said eyeing me. "And don't say a muthu-fuckin word no matter what." He ended with, "Trust me… yuh home free."

I simply nodded even though I knew the police would be waiting at the bottom of the staircase to handcuff us all.

Seven...

Monique

I woke up to the birds chirping and the sun shining. Even my white crinkled sheets made me smile. It was a beautiful September morning; mainly because my man was finally home, and we'd made love half the night. It didn't matter that I was almost eight months pregnant, stomach protruding, and fat forming around my neck. Rapheal claimed my loving was good and had reminded me that he loved seeing me pregnant, carrying his seed.

It was a good thing having him home. Although we lived in a fabulous penthouse in Lindbergh, which overlooked the city of Atlanta and Buckhead, most of the time I was lonely. That was something you couldn't put a price on. It troubled me that I had family, yet always stayed away from them. Rapheal told me not to worry, he was all the family I needed; my daddy, my lover, my friend, my man.

When I rolled over and realized he wasn't in bed, I hopped up, threw on my favorite terry cloth Pink robe, and rushed to find my man. I'd become overly insecure lately. Rapheal blamed it on my hormones; I blamed it on him. He was rarely home, maybe three to four times per month.

He'd just missed my thirty-two week check up where I had my sonogram that showed our beautiful baby girl. It was upsetting that I didn't have him or my mother to share that moment with. She was out of town with my step-father, and of course calling Dominique was out of the question. We hadn't spoken in over two months, since that day at Shawna's. I guess telling me she wanted Rapheal hit a nerve, ultimately severing our relationship.

When I walked up on Rapheal, he was sitting in our tan, suede chair on his cell phone, but ended the call immediately when he heard me coming. I paused, not even saying a word, yet he sat confidently in his black wife beater and black Joe Boxers as if he'd done nothing wrong.

I crossed my arms and glared out of our oversized six by eight foot window. It was one of the best features of the penthouse, and had been the place where Rapheal and I shared our hopes and dreams for the future. Today it seemed the place where he told me lies. He must've been reading my mind because he grabbed me by my waist and pulled me close, giving me my morning greeting.

"What up, beautiful?"

Normally his infectious smile would flatter me, causing me to overlook anything he did or said. Not today. "Who was that?" I asked worriedly.

"Who?"

"What are you, an owl? You know who. On the phone."

"C'mon, luv. That was my mother. She asked about you," he said with his puppy dog eyes. "Why you been gettin' yourself worked up so much lately?"

He smiled warmly showing his perfect teeth, then pulling my body on top of his.

"This what we gotta go through the whole time you pregnant? Maybe you need to get'cha self one of those hot

74

stone massages at the spa. I'll pay. How much?"

I didn't answer. On the real, I was content just being in his arms. The feel of his muscles made me feel safe, and the smell of his body had me feeling a little horny.

"You know you my only concern in life? Right?"

He squeezed me tightly hoping to get a response out of me.

He repeated himself, "Right?" then kissed me softly on the lips.

"When you taking me to Louisiana to meet your mother?" I asked, then grabbed the back of his head. I loved fondling with his braids; especially since he had a fresh set.

"As soon as she gets settled in her new place."

I kissed him dead on the lips. He knew he had me. Within seconds, I acted like a hundred and forty-two pound baby. Although I'd gained weight he held me like I was weightless while I whined about what I wanted him to fix me to eat. Damn, I loved his fine chocolate-ass.

After our second love session of the morning, Rapheal finally decided to whip us up a meal. We sat in the living room devouring our gourmet brunch. His mother was a southern lady, and had taught her only son well. He'd prepared some type of tangy grilling sauce, mixed with green peppers and onions, to smother our grilled chicken. Then he passed me a bowl of cheese grits which looked like Bobby Flay had cooked them himself. Both my stomach and waistline expanded just from the smell.

Rapheal knew I was enjoying my food by the way I licked my fingers and pulled my tender chicken from the plate. We were watching my favorite movie, The Five Heartbeats on the flat screen, and laughing between bites. We were having a great time, enjoying each other's company when I got hit with the news.

"Listen, this week I need you to lay low, luv. I got a lil beef goin' on with some folks from Pittsburgh," he revealed, never even taking his eyes off the television.

"Beef?" My brows crinkled. "Pittsburgh, Pennsylvania?"

"No. Right here in our backyard," he said, flipping the channel. "Pittsburgh, Georgia," he added nonchalantly.

Instantly, I took my feet off the couch. "Rapheal, why would you have a beef with some people from Pittsburgh?" my voice grew louder. "You're not in the drug game. You're not out in the streets. You're a business man, right?" I questioned with a menacing stare.

I hopped up, walked over to the granite countertop, and slammed my plate down. As usual, he maintained his calm demeanor, but never turned to face me as he spoke. The television had his undivided attention.

"A business man I am…but you now I'm originally from the streets. That's where I got my start…so you know niggas jealous."

Rapheal finally looked me in the eye. I refused to take my fixed stare off of him. I needed answers. "So people being jealous of you is enough reason to make me stay in the house?"

"I'm not sayin' that!" he said with frustration.

He sat up, hitting the off button on the remote.

"I'm sayin'…people talk. They assume I'm gettin' my money illegally, and now they got my name mixed up in some shit. It'll be cleared up real soon. Trust me," he said with confidence. "Until then, I gotta make sure you safe."

Once again, this should've been a case where I hated Rapheal for a moment. Instead, we locked lips, and melted into each other's arms. Luckily, he was spending the night at home. He had already broken the bad news that he had to go out for a couple of hours. But I'd already planned for a lazy day alone, and a long night wrapped around his fine body.

Rapheal ended our kissing session, and headed off to the showers while I straightened the kitchen a bit.

Minutes later, the house phone rang which told me it was either my mother or Shawna. They were the only two people who had our new house number. I told Shawna she would be cut off if she gave it to Dominique. I rushed over near the end of the granite counter top to grab the cordless off the receiver.

"Hello," I answered in my usual happy housewife tone.

"Hey, sweetie," my mother said in her high pitched voice.

"Hey, Mama. What's going on?"

"Ahhh…just got a few things on my mind," she announced.

Oh boy, I said to myself. I knew that meant trouble.

"Listen, I heard some things about Rapheal I don't like." Her delivery quickened and she spoke a mile a minute. "I've been humiliated enough with your sister's drama and can barely face my friends now. As much as I brag about you, it bothers me when I hear things. You know Monique…"

"Hear things like what, Mama?" I snapped. "And from who? Your friends don't know anybody that Rapheal knows."

"Well, Dominique told me something a few months ago that has stuck with me. I never said anything to you…just tried to ignore it. But now one of the neighborhood girls mentioned something about …"

I cut her off abruptly. "I don't want to hear it," I said firmly. "Don't you get it? This is all Dominique. Whoever told you something was sent by her. Believe it!" I shouted. "I don't wanna hear anything about my man!"

"Okay, now don't be a fool," she preached. "You're my daughter. You are beautiful, articulate, and intelligent. But don't get so comfortable that you don't pay attention anymore. Just watch out, baby." Her voice softened. "You know you're my favorite. Besides, we don't need anything else to cause a disgrace to this family."

My mother's words cut me deep. That's all she cared about, her reputation. She wanted the world to think the Lewis' were perfect, just like her mother raised her. It was all false, just like my whole upbringing. I told her I was about to take a shower and got off the phone in a hurry.

A half an hour later, I found myself laying down the rules for Rapheal. Lately, he'd been coming home extra drunk. For years, he drank, had a good time, yet always stayed sober enough to get home safely. Strangely for three weeks straight one of his boys had been bringing him home, because he'd gotten so drunk he couldn't make it to the front door.

My speech took about ten minutes flat. Afterwards Rapheal was out the door, and I had my feet kicked up on the base stand of my comfortable rocking chair. I was in our baby's nursery eating a bag of Lay's Bar b que chips, gazing at the hand painted designs on the ceiling. I pretended as if my mother's words hadn't bothered me. Under normal circumstances her medaling would've been ignored, but Rapheal had been acting a little suspect lately.

Trusting my man had always been important to me. In so many ways I followed in my mother's footsteps about appearances within my relationship. She'd cheated on my father big time. She knew it, but still pretended like she met my step-father after my father died. What bothered me the most was that my mother had a big mouth, and if anything really happened with me and Rapheal, she'd spread the news quicker than I could scratch my ass.

I sat partially overjoyed at the progress we'd made on our daughter's room. We'd chosen a calm lavender hue which complemented the pink and purple borders around the top of the ceiling. The crib was in place along with the singing mobile, one-of-a-kind wall art, special ordered hanging accessories, and all the other bells and whistles that came along with decorating a nursery.

Shawna messed up and told me she was throwing me a baby shower the following month. She'd chosen October 3rd, but I told her that was the date I was probably going to the Bahamas for the final inspection on the house. I was pushing for closer to the end of October, giving me enough time to look good and fat for my shower pictures.

As I sat thinking about who my daughter would look like, or if she would have any of my partially Asian features, my cell rang. I hopped up, rushed toward my bedroom, and grabbed the phone. I recognized the number, and smiled instantly.

"Sed," I answered excitedly.

"What's up, Sis," he blared into the phone.

"Oh my, God. I miss you so much. You just forgot about us," I said just happy that he was on the phone. "The last time we talked you said you were coming home in two weeks."

"I know...I know...I know," he kept saying.

"So, what's up?" I asked sensing that something was wrong.

"Sis, I gotta talk to you about something. It's important."

I blew imaginary air through my mouth. "I hope it's not about Dominique."

The tone of his voice changed. "Naw. That's not what I need to talk about. But I did talk to Dominique a few times last week," he revealed. "She told me y'all got this stupid beef going on. But that'll all end soon. We fam and fam stick together, right?" he asked as if he really meant he and I.

"Yeah, Sed…we fam, but what did Dominique tell you?"

"She said you were jealous of her. And…"

He stopped mid sentence.

"You know what…I'm not gonna add to this shit. Forget what she said." He paused momentarily. "You pregnant, she pregnant. Y'all should be shopping together instead of arguing. She told me she's only two months behind you."

I got quiet.

"So, what is it you want to talk about?"

"Aw, Sis," shit gettin' crazy out here!"

"Out where?" I asked Sed. My blood pressure felt like it was rising. Too much drama for one day.

"I'm in Miami for the moment…just got from some small town outside of Germany. I think I'm coming home next week though. I can't take this shit no more."

"Take what shit?"

"Man, I'm tired of lying," he whined.

"Lying about what?"

"I know you don't really wanna hear this. But Rapheal ain't right…"

I listened with deep concern while he told me some of what was going on. The conversation became real tense and I all of a sudden wasn't feeling too good. I grabbed my stomach underneath the bottom and rubbed it in a circular motion. I'd had one alarming call after another.

I breathed into the phone heavily. "Look Sed, let me talk to Rapheal about this?"

"Naw, don't do that. You tryna get me fired!"

"No, I'm not. You family. I just need to get to the bottom of it," I told him. "I gotta go. I don't feel too good, Sed.

This is too much," I ended, then closed the phone.

After I hung up, I started thinking about my brother. Then I thought about his words, trying to decipher if they were true. Would Rapheal do that? I rushed to the kitchen to find myself a ginger ale. We kept our refrigerator stocked with plenty; mostly to settle Rapheal's drunken stomachaches. My own stomach churned badly, far worse than being drunk. Too much stress had been put on me for the day, and it wasn't even five o'clock yet. If things weren't already bad, a knock came from the door. I didn't feel like accepting any deliveries but I knew I'd ordered tons of baby stuff.

I got to the front door and took a look through the peep hole. My gaze on the two men seemed to magnify as I moved my eyes around quickly. The badge held in the air caused me to frown right away. No reasons stood out as to why they would be at my door.

Different scenarios ran through my head. Of course the scenes from movies when the police showed up to reveal that your husband was dead. My first thought was to rush to put on some more appropriate clothes. My second thought was to deny the officers entry. Then I froze.

"Yes, how can I help you," I sang loudly with my ear against the door.

"Are you Monique Lewis?" one of the officers yelled with major base in his voice.

Without hesitation, I half-way opened the door.

The expression on my face-priceless.

"Ahh… yeah that's me," I said through the small crack in the opening of the door.

"Miss, no need to worry. We're here just for information," one of the two white officer's said. "Really, no worries," he added in a softer tone.

I guess my terrified expression couldn't be hidden. The officer with the soft voice made me feel more at ease. He

81

looked to be in his early twenties and related more to me than the other guy. I closed my robe up even tighter, still thinking about going to change. Would I be taken down for questioning? I wondered.

"Can we come in?" the taller, older officer with the thin moustache asked.

Under normal circumstances, I would've said no. However, they had me so scared I wanted to give them all the cash in my purse and the keys to my car.

"What's this all about?" I said, finally allowing them inside.

"This is a pretty nice place," the older guy said nodding his approval of my spot. "I'm Detective Barnes." He extended his hand.

"Thanks," I said softly. "I'm Monique…" I stopped. "I guess you know who I am…"

His partner had a cigarette in his hand. "Mind if I smoke?" he asked.

"Sure. Go ahead."

I watched him light his cigarette with one of those cheap 7-eleven lighters. I felt so uneasy after seeing them looking around and taking notes.

"How can you afford all this? I mean it's you and your boyfriend, correct," Detective Barnes asked after circling my living room.

My senses went off. Was this about Rapheal?

"Ah…yeah. It's just us two. My boyfriend owns an import-export business. The money can be good at times." I smiled proudly.

"Ahhh I see. Importing what may I ask?"

"Clothing mostly," I shot back. "Hats, scarves, watches, and other accessories for the most part."

"Oh, I see. Does he know Sean Brodis aka Semo?"

I shrugged my shoulders. I'd never heard the name before.

"Do you know him?"

My head shook rapidly from side to side.

"Do you know him?" he repeated.

They flashed two pictures in my face. One of him alone, and one of him coming out of a club with my sister. Instantly a lump formed in my throat.

"You sure you don't know him?"

"I've never seen him," I pointed. "But that's my twin sister Dominique."

"Your twin...huh," they asked in unison as if they didn't believe me.

The situation was getting worse by the minute. They both shot each other questionable looks just before I decided to interrupt.

"No seriously. I'm Monique Lewis and she's Dominique Lewis. I know we look identical in the face, but just look at the hair," I announced, pulling strands of my hair. "You can contact my mother if you'd like. She has our birth certificates."

"No need. We can just go down to the station if need be."

The lump in my throat wouldn't seem to go away.

Detective Barnes studied the photo for several seconds. He would look at the photo then back at me.

Damn, I said to myself, I knew we looked more alike than most twins, but this was some serious shit that Dominique had me involved in.

"Do you know where we can find your sister?" the younger detective finally said.

Even though I'd never dealt with a street dude, I knew the code...never snitch...never give up any information. But Dominique had dug her own grave years ago. I didn't hesitate, "She lives in Buckhead," I said, rushing over to my small, antique-looking desk in the living room.

"You mean Bankhead?" Barnes questioned.

"No, not that neighborhood. I said Buckhead, the nice part of town."

"Wow, you both live pretty good. Does she have a job?"

My shoulders hunched. I snatched a piece of paper off a note pad and scribbled down her address. "I haven't seen her in months. Unfortunately we had a falling out. Is everything okay?" I questioned. "I mean, she's not in any trouble is she?"

"Not sure," he told me. "What we are sure about is that Semo is dead, and his cousin who worked at the hotel where he was murdered should be able to identify the young lady he was with prior to the murder."

"Oh my," was all I could say. I held my chest firmly.

"Semo was already under investigation so this case is pretty tricky," Barnes added.

My face squinted slightly and my antenna went up. Dominique was always into some shit. I hoped for her sake she'd just met the guy at the club when the picture was taken and that she'd gone no further with him.

Whatever I found out on my own...would certainly get told.

"Can I have your card?" I asked, ushering them to the door.

Eight...

Dominique

What a life! I couldn't believe I had resorted to a stake-out. The private detective thing wasn't my style, but watching their every move had become necessary. Really an obsession. Sitting in front of my sister's apartment building wasn't my idea of the good life, but this had become routine for weeks. I assumed my life would be different by now. The assumption was that I would be living in the lap of luxury. Instead, my days were spent spying on her bitch-ass, and on the run as a result of Yuri's high profile killing.

My purpose was clear; to watch their routines...then strike when they least expected it. Like a boring–ass housewife, Monique only left her building for groceries, doctor's appointments, or over to my mother's house sparingly. My mother had told me Monique would be leaving for the Bahamas soon, but hadn't told me the date yet.

Now Rapheal, his comings and goings proved to be a bit more tricky. He left out at all weird hours of the morning, and some nights didn't return. He caught planes, trains, and rode in different, expensive automobiles daily. One thing was for sure. Every time he showed up at their spot after a night out, he was pissy drunk.

I sat back thinking about how he was at his weakest when he drank. Little did he know that's when people step to you. Rapheal was well known in the city, and plenty of dudes probably wanted to rob him, better yet see him dead.

The thought of murder made me think of Semo. His murder had been blasted all over the airways. The streets hummed with she said this and he said that; of course from people who had nothing to do with anything. The only words that bothered me was hearing that the Allen Temple boys wanted to talk to me. Somebody told them that he left the club with me the night Semo was murdered. Shawna told me in her shop it was rumored that the police were looking for three girls. At first I fought the idea until more rumors spread about boys from Allen Temple looking for me.

I snapped from my thoughts when I noticed a car behind me as I pulled my 525 BMW away from Monique's building. With a quick adjustment of my rear view mirror, I was able to get a better look. It was a black Crown Vic…reminded me of a police car, but the windows were tinted, signaling thugs. Unfortunately, the car was definitely following me.

I clutched the wheel tightly, never taking an eye off the vehicle that turned right along with me. The pace of my heart beat quickened, and confusion set in. It could've been either Semo's crew looking to retaliate, or the police. The question remained, which one was the lesser of two evils.

I'd heard from some of Yuri's flunkies that some of Semo's folks had been looking for a girl, but they had no idea who the girl was, only a physical description for now.

If the police ever came at me, I was ready. Whatever questions they threw my way, I'd plead the fifth. Yuri had schooled me good. He told me to say, "Fuck no! No sub-poena- No questions!"

86

The thought of a potential chase had me pounding on the gas pedal. I hit the corner of Piedmont Road going sixty in a thirty. They were still directly behind me. For mid-day traffic, it was light. Too light. I needed witnesses, protection for what was about to go down.

Out of the blue, the Crown Vic sped up, cut me off and managed to ride directly beside me. My eyes damn near popped from my head. When the tinted window rolled down, I ducked and swerved to the right.

The officer held out his badge, and instructed me to pull over with his finger. There were two of them, both white, so I hoped they didn't want to pull a Rodney King on me. Slowly, I pulled into an abandoned parking lot where a rundown cleaners sat. As soon as the car stopped, I reached in the glove box and pulled out my registration.

The first guy walked over to my window and leaned inside. He was a young detective who I'd immediately concluded was my age. He wore a pair of loose jeans, an old-ass navy blue Members Only jacket from the 80's and a pair of black Ray Ban shades. I kept smiling at him, hoping he would be my ally.

"You like the fast life, huh?"

"Was I speeding?" I asked shockingly.

He looked back at his partner who stood behind him, not cracking a smile. "I'm Detective Carter, and this is Barnes."

He pointed to the other guy who I'd decided I didn't like.

"We have some questions for you to answer, little lady," Barnes said to me bitterly.

"Oh, you need a subpoena for that," I sassed.

"No we don't," he shot back.

I got nervous. He seemed so confident about what he'd said. "What kind of questions do you want to ask me?"

"Some important questions," Carter answered. "We got a homicide we're investigating. You're not in any trouble. We just need your help." He smiled widely.

"Okay shoot."

"No…no…no. Not here," they chimed in unison. "Follow us to the station," Barnes uttered, then took off toward the driver's seat.

Carter was still in the same spot gazing into my face. I could tell he was feeling me but I had no intention on fuckin' with a broke cop. His eyes told me to comply, but my heart said remember Yuri's words.

"How long will this take?" Breath fluttered through my tightened lips, as I waited for the answer.

"No more than thirty minutes," Carter replied.

"Let's go. How far?" I asked with a concerned look.

"Just follow me," he said, banging on the top of my hood, like he'd made a crucial deal.

He hopped in the passenger seat of the Crown Vic and they took off. I figured they didn't have nothing on me if I could drive myself to the station. Hell, at any moment I could've turned off, and hit the highway going in the opposite direction.

As I trailed slowly, hesitantly behind. I grabbed my cell, to call Yuri. "Shit," I shouted when I heard the operator saying the phone was no longer in service. I hated how Yuri changed his number like he changed his underwear.

By the time we arrived at headquarters I'd become extra antsy, practicing how my answers would be delivered. I would pull a Monique on them, talking real proper like I had some sense. Then I told myself, naw, I'ma be me.

When my car door opened, Detective Carter was right there to greet me. There were tons of cops walking back and forth from the building, talking and mingling about. I stood out like a sore thumb simply because they all had nonchalant expressions while my disposition read guilty. Carter led me to the front of the police station and up the stairs to the main lobby. I strutted uneasily behind, sticking a piece of gum in my mouth, and still reciting my potential responses in my head. It seemed unheard of to be questioned without hand cuffs, but I continued to follow him until we got to interrogation room A. It was a small room with a two-sided window.

"I think I need a lawyer," I blurted out as soon as he opened the door.

"Now do you?" Carter asked suspiciously. "Have you done something wrong?" he asked calmly.

Without hesitation, I answered, "No," as if he'd offended me.

"Come inside. Let's talk. Then if you feel you need a lawyer, we'll let you call one."

For some reason Carter made me feel at ease. If he hadn't been white, I would've slipped him my number. Carter scooted to the far side of the small table, and I took the chair on the other side.

The bright lights in the cramped room shone down on me as if I were guilty already. Seconds later, Carter started pulling out several photos from a large brown envelope. The setting just didn't feel right.

I frowned. "You sure I don't need a lawyer? 'Cause you told me it would just be a few questions to help you figure out your case. This is looking more like a set up," I warned. "You pulling out pictures and shit."

"The questions are easy and clear. These are just some

photos from our surveillance. How many times had you met Semo when you were at the club in this outfit?"

He pushed the picture my way. I swallowed hard. It was me following Semo the night I left with him headed to the Marriott.

"I had only met him once." My answer was sharp. "That night," I added.

He showed me a few other pictures of Semo taken in other places. There were several guys in the photos too, none of which I'd seen before.

"Do you know this guy? This guy? Or this guy?" Carter pointed.

"No. No. No," I said quickly.

"What if we told you we have other pictures. Other than the ones we showed you?"

My eyes lit up.

"Go ahead. Show me," I said boldly. "I've seen this scenario before," I said, chomping down on my gum. "I know I've never been with him anywhere other than talking to him outside the club." I stood up, causing my chair to make screeching sounds across the floor. "Can I go now?"

Carter got up, too. "Let me check. There's a guy coming down who worked at the Marriott. We need you to participate in a line-up, then you can go."

My heart stopped beating, and all my blood rushed to my head. I felt faint, flushed and could barely breathe. "Line up? I never said I would stand in a fuckin' line-up!"

Just as things got heated, Barnes walked in and whispered into Carter's ear. The more his lips moved, the more faint I became. "What is it?" I asked frantically. "Tell me now, 'cause I'm leaving."

Within seconds Carter announced that the guy was unavailable to come in for the line-up. But that maybe it would be a good idea for me to retain a lawyer.

I wasn't sure what that meant, but it didn't look good for me.

"Miss Lewis, just know that cooperating is the best thing you can do for yourself. Accessory to murder is a serious charge," Barnes said in a grave tone. "And first degree murder is even worse. You could land in prison," he added with a smirk.

I never flinched. I simply crossed my arms.

"You're free to go," Barnes said to me, taking a long puff of his cigarette. "Just don't leave the state. We'll be in touch," he added with a devilish grin.

I snatched my purse off the table with an attitude, thinking about the fact that I was gonna be late meeting Yuri.

As soon as my feet hit the pavement, I was on my phone dialing Yuri. I knew he would go postal. His pet peeve- never be late. It didn't matter whether it was a hair appointment or a meeting to give a dude in the streets two shots to the forehead.

For fear of the Allen Temple boys, I'd been staying with Yuri most nights. I was getting to know the *real* him well. Talk about temperamental- he was like a little spoiled kid, kirkin' out at any given moment. Obviously he was missing a few french fries from his happy meal.

He thought we were a couple, but little did he know he was being played. I needed a safety net and he provided that. We fucked three times a week at least, and even though his dick couldn't make me cum, his head game was right. Yuri ate pussy like he was sucking the meat off a chicken bone and made me cum each and every time he went down south.

He even taught me how to perfect my head game. He said it was all about skill and had me practicing every night.

For me, it was a chance to get ready for Rapheal. I knew when the time came, I would put it on him so bad, there would be no returning to Monique.

I hit end and tried Yuri again, hoping any numbers I had for him would work. All were disconnected. Suddenly, my phone rang. It was an unknown number so I pressed no. I drove like a bat out of hell with my hand both on my cell phone and on the wheel. With each street I hit, I pressed on the gas even more.

The phone rang again. Unknown. "What the fuck?" I shouted.

"Hello," I snapped.

"Where the fuck yuh at?" he asked me slowly and furiously, sounding as if he were gritting his teeth as he spoke.

"I'm almost there," I said nervously. "I tried to call you but you changed your fuckin' number again."

Yuri remained silent for several seconds.

I used that time to rotate my hands, slipping on my wig. I thought about saying something else, some more slick shit, but decided to wait on him to speak.

"Almost not good enough," he finally said. "The courts should empty soon. I'm on the corner of Central and Courtland."

"Bet, I'll be there in ten."

"Five. No less," he ordered.

Dayum!

He hung up.

Nine...

Rapheal

Steppin' from the limo in Miami always felt damn good. *Me- I'm a bad boy*, I boasted. For sure, my swag was on. It had to be because I knew all eyes watched me from inside my showroom. The sign above that read C.J.'s Exotic Cars made me smile inside.

I had been doin' big thangs and was makin' big paper. When it came to snatchin' up a hot car at the lowest possible price, I was the man. The car business was like takin' candy from a baby, but only when things were bein' ran the right way. From the looks of things, Sed wasn't on his job. After scanning the outside lot, it was clear they hadn't sold many cars for the week, and not one customer was in sight.

I moved to the center of the lot, and took a few steps back…just to get an aerial view of what we had. Eleven cars seemed to be the count. My eyes quickly zoomed in on the two silver Aston Martins, a Maserati GranTurismo; a big seller, and the Lamborghini Diablo.

I shook my head in disgust. As soon as I started walkin' toward the front door of my establishment, the expressions changed on my workers. I could spot their grumpy mannerisms through the huge front glass. They knew shit wasn't going to go over smoothly. I stopped abruptly next to the Maybach which was closest to the front. My hands ran smoothly across the hood like it was a special commodity. Indeed it was the hottest around, and one of my bestsellers.

When I finally made it inside, my small staff of three were seated in the showroom surrounded by two shiny Hummers and a F1 McLaren which we'd had for weeks. It was clear that things were tense. I'd gotten the call from Sed about some agents takin' pictures of the car lot and how nervous they were about the new shipment on the way.

Their faces said it all. Lisa, the only female worker sat in a high back, leather chair slidin' back and forth across the marble floor. Charles, the manager of the Miami location had his arms crossed, never even moving to wipe the sweat from his forehead. And Sedrick, my man Sed, my family, my homey; he sat like a dog in training waiting for me to speak.

I expected more from Sed than the others. After all, Sed had been with me for over two years, and was my right hand man. I expected him to handle problems more effectively. His only job was to travel to the different locations keeping the managers in check, and handlin' the importation of the cars. Simple.

"Lisa, what's the reason for the sad face, luv?"

"Oh, I'm good, Mr. Rapheal. I'm just trying to figure out if we need to pack everything up and be out of here by the time the shipment arrives."

"I don't believe that's necessary," I replied, makin' sure not to seem bothered by the news.

"Look-a-here. Everything's still under control," I announced, entering their little circle on the floor. "I got some folks workin' for us in Commerce, so I made a few calls. They gonna take care of everything," I said confidently. "Don't sweat it," I told everybody with a hardened tone.

"Everything is good. You got my word."

"Man, everything is not good," Sed blurted out. His voice roared above every other sound. "You come in here with your sharp looking gators on, and your expensive-looking suit. "Man, this is not a legitimate business! Things are going sour!"

"So, you got it all figured out?" I asked him calmly. "You wanna run thangs?"

"Naw, man. C'mon, why you going there?"

"You don't seem to want to take direction from me anymore. This is my establishment. This one, and all the other ones where you've worked."

"Man, I know that. I opened up all those spots for you! All nine of'em!"

My blood began to boil. He was tryna play me in front of my workers. I was known to always keep my cool, lettin' them know I wasn't a street boy, but a businessman. "There's never been any financial risk to you. You get your money every week whether I make twenty dollars, or fifty thousand."

"Man, shit gettin' too hectic, that's all I'm saying. I ain't 'bout to do no time for you."

Sedrick had gotten way too hyper. He bounced around airing his frustration as he whined. "Calm down," I said, in a softer tone.

"You say you got it covered, but at the Baltimore shipping doc the other day, I thought we were done. The customs guy was actin' all strange, then he reviewed the paperwork over and over again. Man, they on to us. I'm telling you! We gotta end this. Trust and believe."

"So, what are you sayin', nigga? You backin' out on me?"

I took two steps in his direction.

"What I'm saying is you gotta know when to fold'em."

I clenched my jaw, then threw jabs from one palm to

the other.

"Oh, so it's like that?" he asked me with his chest poked high. "I thought we was fam! All I'm tryna do is tell you what's up."

Sed was Monique's brother, but I wasn't gonna let him ruin my business. "Oh, we are. But you know how the sayin' goes. Family will bring you down."

"That's what I'm talkin' 'bout. Dawg, you my brother, but I see you tryna bring a nigga down. I can't let you do it!"

He kept shaking his head back and forth like he wasn't gonna work another day. It got heated.

"Nigga, I made you!" I shouted, backin' him into a corner. "You think you my only soldier? Step down!" I told him. "Give somebody else a chance to make this good money. Where else can you make twenty thousand a month?"

Sed couldn't speak 'cause I had him by the collar and jacked up against the wall with my fist holding his chin hostage. He was at least forty pounds lighter than me and much shorter than my six-foot-four height. There was nothing he could do. He kept squirming tryin' to escape my hold, but I made sure to stare him straight in the eye.

"After all I've done for you, this is what I get?" Charles finally spoke for the first time since I'd been in the buildin'. "Rapheal, man," he said softly in his usual light voice. "The shipment is on the way. The truck driver just called and left a message to make sure we make room so he can drop the cars." His voice was squeakier than usual.

Even though we needed to make a decision, I kept Sed pushed up in the corner on lock down. In my heart, I knew he was only one problem. The customs department was known to be sneaky. They were probably watchin' us hard, trying to build enough evidence before they made their move. I thought about packin' up all our shit and movin' the eleven cars we had on the small lot to a hide-out spot. It would all have to be done within the hour assuring that we moved out before the new shipment showed up. It was just more evidence stacked up against us.

But then there was the issue of losing over $600,000 just like that. I had to make shit right with Sed. He was my boy. I needed him. He was the only one who could be trusted to handle the real business, and more than anything I needed him on camera accepting the shipment, not me.

As soon as I let go of my grip, Sed started fixin' his clothes like his attire really mattered. He was a rough neck and never dressed to my standards.

"Look-a-here man, we didn't have to go there. Let's settle down and think quickly." I dug into my pocket while I thought of the best choice of words. We need this shipment simply because we paid for it all up front."

I counted out what I owed Sed for the week; fifty crisp hundred dollar bills. "Look man, you my boy."

I even rubbed him on the head like a father would his son. Luckily, he loosened up.

"Man, I know. This shit just been botherin' me, man. I can't go back to jail. I just thought this was my one good lick."

"What'cha mean, thought?" I questioned. "It is," I said confidently. "You just need to trust me," I told him, then held out my hand for him to hit me with some dap.

"All these cars comin' in are pre-sold," I lied. "By the end of the week, you can be outta here. And we'll lay low from the east coast. Just work the mid-west where everything is cool."

Sed didn't answer me. He simply nodded in agreement. Strangely, he wouldn't look me in the eye either.

Shortly after, he followed me outside to the front lot. Charles had just informed us that he'd called the driver again to get an updated estimated time of arrival. Twenty minutes was what we were working with. I didn't want to be seen, didn't plan on being involved, so I made my phone call, too.

It took about thirty minutes for shit to really start popping. Lisa had the blueprint plan about how many days it would take to move any remaining cars to another location. Me and Sed laid out our plan for any cars coming on the next shipment.

Just about the same time that my ride pulled up, Sed started sweatin' and actin' all panicky. I shook my head at how the little nigga was startin' to be a liability.

I took out my cell just as I shook Sed's hand goodbye. Unfortunately, Yuri's phone went straight to a pre-recorded message. *Damn, the number had been changed.* I'd only called on him once before to handle a tragic situation for me. Other than that, our relationship was shallow. He bought cars from me on a regular, and I stayed clear from him other than that. I had to get his number I told myself, walking toward my ride. I knew he'd been waitin' for the new Ferrari to come in.

For Sed, the wait was finally over. Just as I opened the passenger door to the Porsche, the huge eighteen wheeler pullin' a car carrier turned the corner to my spot. The first two cars to catch my eye were two black Maybachs. My brows crinkled as I thought about giving my German connection $50,000 extra for both. He was supposed to come through with a supply of four Maybachs. I had four dudes lined up all on the east coast ready to splurge, lacin' my pockets with $80,000 each. That was steal considering the cars retailed at $400.000.

The price was decent for me too, considering I only paid $20,000 per car, and sold it for $60,000. I'd have the VIN #'s switched before they were put on the ship comin' my way. Many hands were in the pot, but they all got their cut. It all worked out, and became a win-win situation for everyone.

Sed should've been watchin' the shipments, countin',

or makin' himself useful. Instead his eyes were fixated on me.

I shot him a scornful smile as I hopped into her car. He frowned, probably wantin' to say somethin', but the nigga knew better.

"What up, luv?" I asked her and kissed her on the cheek.

She didn't speak, only shot me a gorgeous smile. Within seconds, she revved on the gas of the red convertible Porsche Boxster I'd gotten her, and zoomed off the lot.

CARBON Copy CARBON Copy

100

Ten...

Dominique

The Smokey and Drake Peterson trial proved to be the most talked about trial the city had witnessed in years. Brian Townson better known as Smokey had charges stacked against him including King Pin charges, while Drake his right man, stood trial mostly for murder. Drake had been Smokey's enforcer for years, the same as Yuri operated for anyone who had the right amount of money to afford his flawless services.

The way the story played out made perfect sense. Drake had a dozen people tied up into his bullshit. About four King Pins from different hoods were all connected with Smokey and stood trial as co-defendants at the Fulton County Courthouse. Problem was; word was out that Drake had been cooperating with the D.E.A. Informants assured Yuri that Drake would eventually testify, blessing the courts with step by step accounts.

Smokey wasn't having it, and decided to spend his last to have someone contact Yuri. It only needed to be said once. He was definitely a man about his business. Payment was made, and both Yuri and I were on the scene.

I stood on the curb in an inconspicuous sweat-suit,

dark shades, and a jet black wig with curly tresses touching my shoulders. My job appeared simple; watch for anyone associated with the high profile case. I'd been dropped off twice within the last hour as Yuri circled the block, making sure he wasn't getting set up, too. Careful was his middle name.

Before I knew it, he was back, ready for an update from me. It puzzled me that he chose his yellow Maserati for such a task; the S version at that, a one hundred and thirty-five thousand dollar car. I assumed we wanted to be less noticeable. The engine seemed louder than most, and the color stood out like a sore thumb. I knew it was his favorite color, but the vehicle was catching every open eye on the block. Still, Yuri appeared unbothered, and I certainly wasn't gonna question his judgment.

I had already showed up late, fuckin' around with those corny-ass detectives. Even though that situation was beyond my control, Yuri still looked at me cock-eyed like he wasn't satisfied with my job performance.

I hopped inside the car quickly. "Nobody came out yet," I informed. "Must be some serious shit going on in there."

"A lot of snitchin'. Muthufucka's!" he yelled, then banged on the steering wheel.

He obviously took his job personally. I watched him twitch in his seat, and make crazy facial expressions as he slipped into deep thought. He played around with his dreads that had been growing like crazy, and mumbled death threats under his breath. Yuri didn't know Drake from a nigga in the streets, yet he was pissed as if he'd done something to him.

Suddenly, he stepped on the gas without warning, hurried to the next corner on Central Avenue, and whipped a u-turn in the middle of the street. The car revved louder than I thought it should have. Yet I remained silent. Yuri whipped into a tight spot, parking within four yards from the front of the building. It was a good view from where I sat. It was now a waiting game.

Minutes turned into an hour while we sat patiently, listening to the loud music. Yuri played Bob Marley's greatest hits on the highest volume possible until he turned it down for one of his mysterious phone calls. Minute after minute we watched bystanders file out of the busy building until the area seemed deserted. I breathed heavily through my lips hoping to smash Drake. I needed the money badly.

Suddenly there seemed to be some action. My head popped up, noticing the extra movement. Reporters scattered about looking to interview anyone leaving who had valuable information from the case. I saw Renee Starzyk from Chanel 7 news giving me a sign this had to be the people from Smokey's case. It was like a three-ring circus, but an act I needed to join. I hopped up, pulling my shades far down on the bridge of my nose.

"That's him," Yuri announced in an underhanded tone.

"Where?"

My head swiveled from right to left searching the rapidly disbursing crowd.

"There," he pointed with his scruffy hands. "Right there…with the Dodgers baseball cap on his head, and his hands in his pocket. That's that muthufucka!"

My adrenaline pumped hard. At first I couldn't pin point the dude. Then I got it. His face was on my radar. Drake walked quickly, but luckily toward us, just on the opposite side of the street. He never looked up, just behind him, then forward again.

I hopped out tugging my jacket tightly until I could get it zipped. The weather changed drastically, and the wind had picked up as the late afternoon rolled around. Fall had never been my favorite season, but in this case made people move about faster than usual.

Luckily, my outfit wasn't going to attract any extra attention. It wasn't the normal form fitted ensemble. I wore a black, two-piece, loose fitting sweat-suit, and a pair of black Nikes just in case I found myself running for my life.

My strut became swifter as I followed my target down Pryor Street and into the entrance of an underground parking lot. I hoped like hell when Yuri decided to follow me he had a mechanism that would quiet his damn engine. Surely if he didn't, our cover would be blown.

Our operational plan had changed from before. Yuri instructed me not to get into Drake's car. He told me to fast talk him, make him think he knew me. "Improvise," he'd instructed. "You gotta do him in the lot."

I wasn't ready to witness another murder. Already on the detective's radar and possibly being called in for a line-up had me super paranoid. But in my heart, I knew if the time came, Yuri would never allow Semo's cousin to make it to the line-up. I sucked up my thoughts, breathed heavily, and walked faster trying to keep up with Drake.

Suddenly, he stopped once he heard my soft footsteps coming behind him. The garage was mostly empty with the exception of a few cars so any noise seemed to echo to the third power. He turned, glanced my way, but saw nothing. I'd managed to hide behind an old black Camero. Within seconds, Drake was on the move again. He jetted up the staircase in the corner of the garage making his way to the second floor, with his hands still in his pocket.

I followed like I had a team with me, one foot drudgingly behind the other. So much heat had come my way from the other murder that I'd become a pro. Unexpectedly, Drake's alarm from his car key chirped. I couldn't let him get inside.

I called out to him, "Drake!"

He stopped, looked at me funny, then moved faster to

his car. I guess snitches had to have the ability to move fast.

"It's me, Charlene." I waved with a fake smile.

His eyebrows crinkled. He had to have known something wasn't right. But most men pulled stupid moves, when pretty women were in their presence.

"I met you with Smokey before. Remember?"

"Naw."

Quickly, he reached for the door handle.

"Wait," I grinned sexily. "Smokey said thanks for looking out. He wanted me to give you this money," I announced, looking into my purse. I kept acting as if I was out of breath as I looked. "I almost missed you," I told him nicely.

Drake eased up a bit.

"So I met you before?" he asked, waiting for me to grab the money.

"Yep. Smokey your boy, right?" I announced since he was still pretending to be down with Smokey.

I kept scrounging around in the bottom of my bag hoping like hell I'd hear Yuri's engine roll through.

Meanwhile, Drake got antsy. I was taking too long. My luck had run out.

"Where did you meet me?" he questioned.

He opened his car door with a suspicious look on his face, but luckily he still stood outside the door. "Ummmmm," I mumbled trying to think on my feet.

The first shot sounded. It was music to my ears as it flew past my shoulder and penetrated the upper part of Drake's chest. I watched him grab his heart letting out a loud painful moan. Then Yuri stepped into view looking like death on a stick. Instantly, my eyes focused on the gun he held down by his side. He had the piece pressed up against his trademark, long shorts. For the life of me, I couldn't figure out why Yuri wore shorts year round. I shook my head waiting for his next move.

Before I knew it, he hopped across a parked car with speed, like something from a Steven Seagal action movie. His face showed no remorse and no sign of fear. His gun was perfectly aimed toward the middle of Drake's forehead. For a split second, I watched my mentor search the parking lot for witnesses.

My eyes blinked. I spun around and darted behind a parked Ponitac Grand Am, knowing what was next. Drake was supposedly a big man on the streets but had turned into a complete pussy. He pleaded, "Naw, mannnnnn, naw! "

"Yuh talk too much!" Yuri uttered ruthlessly.

"C'mon, man!" Drake cried.

"Yuh dead now boy!"

Yuri walked directly up on him firing off three more bullets, two of which ricocheted off Drake's car. I wasn't sure who panicked the most; me or Drake. His eyeballs rolled to the back of his head as the final bullet exploded inside his temple.

Before I knew it, Drake's body jilted, fell to the ground, and slumped over proving that he'd snitched for the last time.

I clutched at my chest, trying to absorb what had just happened. Yuri acted like I didn't exist. "Man down," he boasted to himself.

He took off running in his favorite brown loafers. My mind remained in a daze as I watched the flaps on his faithful shorts swing from side to side. I struggled to keep up with him as he skipped the stairs headed to the bottom level. As soon as we made it to the bottom, the sight of the Maserati made me smile. I had no air left in me. Just one more minute of running would've left me behind with some explaining to do.

Within minutes we were safely inside the car, and had

jetted from the parking garage without paying the fare. Yuri burst through the flimsy, white gate, and within less than a minute was on Highway 20. I looked over at Yuri thinking, damn I'm really tied to this crazy muthufucka now!

Eleven...

Rapheal

"**R**emy VSOP is a motherfucker!" I shouted extra loud, stumblin' from my Bentley coupe.

My boy Kareem had driven my drunk-ass home in the coupe, and passed the keys off to Terrance, my doorman. They knew he would look out even though I had no idea where he would park my car. The fellas all laughed as they watched me stagger inside the revolvin' doors to my buildin'.

"Don't throw up on those marble floors," they joked. "And don't sleep in the lobby this time," Kareem added.

He knew he was the only one who could talk shit to me, or comment on my past alcohol melt-downs. Kareem was my road dog and the only true friend I had. He understood that I was a ladies' man, and didn't want to spend a lot of time kickin' it with the same sex. He showed up occasionally; especially when I needed him, and other times stayed out of my way. The other jokesters just hung out from time to time drinkin', and that was it.

I started to respond to their laughter, but saw Terrance rushin' inside behind me.

"Mr. C., you okay?"

He grabbed my arm to help keep me steady.

With a quick snatch of the elbow, I fired, "Mannnn, don't touchhhh me, I-I-I-I'm g-o-o-o-o-d," I slurred.

"No problem, Mr. C. Just wanna get you safely upstairs."

"I-I-I'm G-o-o-o-o-d," I repeated.

He started to say somethin' else until we both heard a familiar voice.

"I'll take it from here," I heard her say.

I thought my brain had been fried from all the alcohol and now the hallucinatin' had kicked in, until I heard Terrance say, "I'm glad you're here, Miss Lewis. Mr. C looks like he needs a little help gettin' upstairs."

I couldn't even look my baby in the eye. I thought my late night out with the fellas would go unseen. Monique was supposed to be in the Bahamas. Why was she here? Spyin' on me maybe? "I thought y-o-o-o-u left e-e-e-earlier," I began.

"Missed the flight," she said quickly.

We started off walkin' side by side toward the elevator, until Monique fell behind. I was conscious enough to know my lady was pissed because she wouldn't let me look her in the eye.

I started makin' excuses, "Luv, I swear this is it. No more drinks," I slurred. "I-I-I-I...," I started to say, when I felt her soft hands touch the lower part of my back. Believe it or not she was guidin' me along, helpin' me make it down the hall.

My head pounded like crazy, and my stomach felt like a bottomless pit. I needed somethin' to eat, and somethin' to help me focus better. The more I stumbled down the hall, the more it seemed like the walls were closing in on me. Soon, we'd made it to the elevator and waited for the doors to open. Monique kept a slight grip on me but didn't want to talk to me at all. I knew my body reeked the smell of strong alcohol, but damn, my baby was treatin' me foul.

When the elevator doors opened on the twentieth floor, we walked in slowly with me lookin' for somethin' to grab onto. I could barely stand up and the sudden movement had me feelin' even worse.

"This is it," I slurred. "No more drinks. You got my word," I added.

Monique turned her head and rushed off onto our floor before me. Not even a second went by before we were at our door, and Monique had her hands in my pockets, takin' my keys. I wanted to tell her to use hers, but decided against it.

When the door flew open, I made a b-line to my favorite oversized chair. I flopped down on my back and watched the room spin like an online virtual tour. It took a second for me to even throw my leg up on the ottoman.

"I need some food," I moaned. "Can yo-o-o-u fix me somthin', luv?"

No response.

The room spun as I asked her again. "Luv, can you…"

The sound of Monique fumblin' around in the kitchen made me feel like there was hope. She said nothin', but I knew she would come through. Within seconds, I heard the sound of her footsteps clankin' against the marbled floor. She stood above me poppin' the top off of what sounded like a soda can.

"Drink," she ordered.

I lifted up to find her standin' over me with a ginger ale in her hand, and stomach lookin' larger than before. I wanted to tell her she was gettin' real fat but could barely focus.

"Sit with me," I said, extending my hand into the air.

She pushed my hand back and out of the blue dropped down to the floor. Her hands softly caressed the bottom portion of my pants; punishin' my crotch area. It seemed to be

111

her focus as she sat beneath my dick on the living room floor. I could only see the top portion of her head but felt all her moves. I wasn't sure whether it was her foreplay or the after effect of the champagne and Remy that had my balls on fire. Whatever it was, when Monique yanked at my pants, I found enough strength to pull them down without even liftin' my head.

I was sprawled out with just my shirt on, waitin' for her next move. Next thing I knew, Monique was stroking my weapon like she'd never done before. Her touch seemed rough, but felt extra good when she took the first lick. She seemed to tease, which aroused me even more. I bit at my lip, with each lick, and squirmed around on the chair. My eyes were closed tightly as the sounds released from my mouth, "Oooohhhhh."

I laid back droolin' like a dog in heat as she took all of me in. She was deep throatin' me like she'd never done before.

"Uh…uh…ohhhh." I moaned, grabbin' onto her hair.

I glanced up to see what alien had taken over my baby's body. She seemed horny the way she bobbed and slobbed. She sucked me off rapidly like a chick from a porno movie.

I kept squirmin'.

She kept suckin'.

After a couple of minutes, it seemed like my high was going away…just the light-headedness remained. I was horny. Ready to fuck for real.

I tried to grab hold of Monique's side to push her back a bit. I needed to get up to service her for a minute. But she wouldn't stop. I was goin' ballistic. I fell back when I felt the veins in my dick jumpin'. I squeezed my butt cheeks tightly tryin' to hold on.

"Oh shit…oh shit!" I tightened. "Damn girl…ohhhhhh

hell yeah!" I shouted, then lost full control.

I grabbed her head with force, pullin' her closer. And refusin' to let go. As soon as I released my thirty-five babies, Monique slowed her jaws. Her clutch had loosened but she remained still.

Damn, she swallowed for the first time.

I continued to lay back on the chair pantin', and watchin' Monique with a close eye. "What the fuck got into you?" I asked.

She had her head face down on my shit, leavin' only the top of her freshly done hair-do for me to see. She seemed to be nursin' my piece which had gotten somewhat hard again. My hormones were ragin' and I wanted a piece of her bad.

It only took a second for my shit to get rock hard again. My veins in my dick got extra antsy lettin' me know I was ready to fuck. Without hesitation, I sat straight up and pulled Monique from the floor. She resisted but my strength overpowered her.

"C'mere girl. I want you now," I told her.

Just like that, my senses went off. A pillow fell to the floor. A pillow that fell from her shirt. The shit had me puzzled, but like a typical man, my dick didn't care. It wanted to be in denial.

Monique jumped to her feet, pulled her shirt over her head like she was ready, too. When her boobs released, I fell back in amazement. I lay still though, tryin' to focus. Her hair was the same, her complexion the same, but she wasn't pregnant. Hell, she didn't have the same sized tits. Right then and there I knew I'd gotten myself into some shit.

"What the fuck? Dominique!" I yelled.

She lunged onto me, wet pussy and all, never givin' me the chance to escape. All I could do was turn my head away from her attempted kiss. She had her legs wrapped around me tightly, provin' *no* wouldn't be taken as an answer.

I couldn't think. I couldn't talk. My dick was doin' it all for me. Before I knew it, I had plunged myself into Dominique and was fuckin' her in all positions. I had'er up against the wall, knocking down all of our expensive paintings. We grinded hard, alternatin' from the floor to the wall. It was like somethin' I'd never experienced in my twenty-nine years.

Soon, I had Dominique in the air, pullin' her thick legs over my shoulder like the pussy was really mine. On average, I bench-pressed more than she weighed, so I knew I could hold her as long as I wanted. We started by the window with her ass pressed against the glass, then we moved to the kitchen counter where Monique had made me my favorite lemon cake. I knew my actions were foul but I couldn't say no. The sex was wild!

"Is this what you always thought it would be," she asked me between breaths.

I ignored her and thrust deeper. Sweat dripped from my ass and onto the cold floor. I had to admit she was a better fuck than her sister but a trick was a trick.

She started screamin', and actin' like the exorcist had her soul.

"Fuck me, Rapheal! Oh shit....C'mon baby, that's it. That's it."

Her ass cheeks moved with speed as my dick met each hit.

"Oh, hell, I'm gonnnnnna cum!" she screamed. The shit was good to us both. I knew holding on was out of the question. I grabbed her by her hair wonderin' if her new cut was a wig or if she'd really gotten it cut like Monique's. Next thing I knew, Dominique's body shook, and I quickly nutted inside of her.

Damn, I said to myself pushin' her off of me.

My demeanor changed quickly. "What the fuck, Do-minique. Why?" I'd found some of my conscience. "Why'd you do this?" I paced the floor with my limp dick swingin' back and forth.

She laughed.

"Oh, I did it by myself, huh?"

"You came up in here pretendin' to be my woman."

"I am your woman," she shot back with assurance. "You just don't know it yet."

"Man, get the fuck out," I said, holdin' the sides of my head. My headache was back, and strong. Adrenaline pumped through my body as I tried to figure out the best solution to my problem.

"Look, Monique is in the Bahamas, so let's just sleep on this and hook up tomorrow. I know this was all a big mis-take, but we can't let this get back to your sister. Ever!" I added.

"Huh! That's a fuckin' laugh. As soon as I get to my car, I'm calling her. She needs to know."

"C'mon now, luv," I begged.

"Tell me one reason why I shouldn't," she asked me.

Dominique looked deranged…reminded me of the fatal attraction bitch who fell for Michael Douglass. "Okay, Dominque, let's talk about this," I reasoned.

"Rapheal, here's the deal. You've got something spe-cial." She paused. "No! We've got something special," she said lowerin' and then raisin' her voice. "You just made me cum. That's rare, I gotta have you," she warned with a bizarre grin. "And you dark… extra chocolate just the way I like my men."

She moved close, rubbin' her hands up and down my forearm. "What's the tattoo about?" she asked me.

I looked at the long black sword. "It's just somethin' I wanted when I was younger."

"And what about the fuckin' initials. C.J., who the fuck is that?"

My brows crinkled. The chick was going crazy. "It's the initials of my sister who passed."

"Oh, sorry to hear that shit," she shot back. "But we can always replace those with mine," she said as if she was dead serious.

"What I gotta pay?" I asked with a more serious expression.

"Pay. Who, me?" She pointed to herself. "The only thing you might have to pay is child support."

She laughed, then grabbed a Granny Smith apple from our fruit basket off the counter. "Umph, so good…these are Monique's favorites," she said, as she took a big bite.

Now I wasn't the type of brotha who was into callin' women bitches, but Dominique was a certified bitch. I was startin' to hate her even though she'd given me the best fuck I'd had in years.

"Let's be reasonable," I said moving closer to her. "We're not havin' no muthufuckin' children together." Emphasis was put on the word 'no'. "What do I have to pay for you to act like this never happened?" I asked her in my most severe tone.

Dominique seemed to be gettin' nervous. My eyes were blood shot red, and my voice seemed to switch between pitches. It was a no brainer that I was angry. She'd set me up and I felt like some shit for bangin' her out when I knew she wasn't my woman.

"I gotta run boo. I'll see you tomorrow so we can discuss our relationship. Oh…and one last thing. The dick was much better tonight than a year ago when you were drunk and I did you in your own bed."

Instantly, my face changed colors. "Get the fuck outta here," I remarked, as if her words couldn't be true.

116

"No, really. I even slept underneath the bed once Monique came home." She grinned devilishly. "But just think, now I'm on top. She'll be on the bottom."

And just like that she grabbed her purse off the counter and jetted to the door. When the door closed, I banged myself in the head wonderin' if she would really call Monique. And most importantly, how did I attract a stalker and psychopath all in one?

Twelve...

Dominique

As I drove south toward Stapleton Gardens near the bright blue water, I started thinking about my new man. Everything about him stuck with me…his well defined arms…his touch…his smell…his swagger. I was shook. The fact that his mid-section was ripped made me want to stop the car and finger myself.

It had only been three days since he'd made love to me, and honestly, he'd been on my mind twenty-four hours each day. After all, he knew how to make my juices flow. He made me cum, so I was forever indebted to him. He'd been calling me like crazy leaving all these messages about how we needed to talk. He said he'd talked to Monique and all was good. "It needs it to stay that way," he warned on his last message.

I grinned inwardly thinking about his dark, chocolate, sexy-ass, and stepped heavily on the gas. The hot sun beamed down on my skin as I drove with the windows down, my signature shades covering my eyes, and my left arm hanging out the window. The temperature in the Bahamas had gotten up to 89 degrees which seemed perfect for an October afternoon. I mostly drove at a decent pace since the road had thousands of pot holes, and my senses were clueless about how to get to *my* house.

After glancing down at the directions, I knew the house wasn't much further. By the time I took two rights and one left around a wobbly bend, I found myself driving down a narrow road with mid-sized beachfront homes. I started hating instantly, thinking, *if the bitch's pussy game was right, she might've gotten a bigger house.*

When I pulled up to the front of the stucco built home, I slowed the rental car drastically. Envy immediately took over. The shit was right on the sandy beach and reminded me of the perfect Mediterranean home. Hibiscus plants hung from the porch while pink roses and small palm trees lined the driveway. The fact that there wasn't a car out front puzzled me.

Quickly, I pulled ahead and parked a few houses further up, near the end of the street. By the time I hopped out of my Hyundai rental and proceeded up the street, I'd convinced myself it would happen. *Monique would have to die.*

The fact that Rapheal had been stalking me via voice messages confirmed that he wanted me. I never answered only because I wanted to stay focused. But tonight, he'd hear from me. And I would soon sleep in his bed where I belonged.

I crept near the front, hoping no one would see me. As I monitored what was going on to my left and right, I thought about the location. The neighborhood reminded me of an elderly suburb where nobody came out after lunch. Boldly, I treaded along the side of the house with a clear view inside. My head shook with hatred. *What a shame, still needs work*, I boasted inside.

When my body leaned to peer through the big beautiful windows, my entire ass hung from my tight, jean booty

120

shorts. I felt the air wince by as I remarked, "Umph…Miss Perfect don't even have curtains yet."

Although work still needed to be done, I couldn't help but imagine me and Rapheal in the house together, just the two of us, doing our thang hourly. I could see that tile covered the entire house. A few throw rugs were in sight, and no carpet at all.

My head suddenly did a double take when I noticed a side door which looked as if it led to the kitchen. It was worth a try, I told myself. Security didn't appear to be an issue like back at home. As luck would have it, I turned the knob and the door quietly opened as if it was fate.

The smell hit me in the face. It was that wet, island smell, like you'd been at the beach all day. With one foot in front of the other, I stepped on the terracotta tiled floor and moved along like a hungry snake on attack.

The kitchen didn't have much of a décor, mainly white appliances, all pretty basic if you asked me. Unimpressed, I moved down the short hallway headed toward some furniture.

When I saw her, a funny feeling came over me. She was sitting in the open area with the patio doors wide open. Her feet were kicked up, as she flipped through a magazine and listened to the sound of the waves rolling toward land. The view of the ocean was amazing- the best I'd ever seen in person. The bitch had the nerve to have on all white-like she was pure. It was a long, flowing maxi dress that straddled her ankles. It was the one that hung on the mannequin at the White and Black Store back at home. It had been passed up by me weeks ago, but would surely get purchased by the end of the week. The thought of her sitting there like she didn't have a worry in the world angered me.

I stood opposite her, near the front door, out in the open for her to see me. She never looked up. The moment seemed surreal as the Bahamian air filtered through the open sliding doors. I stood quietly, examining the décor of what I assumed was the living room. The house was sparsely decorated, nothing more than an L-shaped oversized sofa in the family room area, a few coffee tables and cheap-looking throw rugs. There wasn't even a T.V. in sight. You could tell that work was still being done on the house from the way screws and paint brushes were still laying around. There were even a few ladders scattered about. It still smelled like fresh paint but for the most part, the house seemed about eighty percent complete.

"Ummm …ummm," I uttered in an annoying sound, trying to clear my throat.

Monique paused just after spotting me. The diameter of her eye balls tripled. Her mouth fell open like she wanted to speak, yet nothing came out.

"Surprised to see me?" I asked with a smirk, then removed my shades with a quick yank. I gave her a few seconds to digest my presence while I played with my shades.

Her eyes showed concern, but she still couldn't speak. I watched her rise from her chair, throw the Black Enterprise Magazine off to the side and face me hesitantly.

"How did you know I was here? And how'd you get this address?" she asked in a fearful tone. "What do you want?"

My face portrayed that I'd lost any sense I was born with. I wanted her to ooze with envy as she took a look at my half shirt that read BAHAMAS and my daisy duke booty shorts that showed off my thick thighs and voluptuous ass.

"I came to settle something with you."

She clutched her stomach as if my words had caused her some pain. I sensed her anxiety and decided to stare at her protruding gut.

"Get out Dominique!" she shouted my way after giving me a firm stare. "You should've asked to come here first.

This is my home with my husband."

"Whateva, bitch! You're not married; especially not to my boo," I said, with a quick roll of the eyes. "Besides, there's something we need to discuss. And now," I added, sitting my shades on the edge of the sofa.

"You don't understand," she warned, "I want you out of here. Rapheal told me what you did."

"Oh, did he?" I responded with sarcasm. "What exactly did he tell you?"

"That you came on to him," she said in a matter-of-fact tone. "You are nothing to him. And now nothing to us," she said spitefully, rubbing her stomach. "I don't want you anywhere near us."

"You know…I hate to toot my own horn…but I stole your man."

"No! He turned you down!"

I laughed crazily. "I had his ass. Tattoo and all. My initials will replace the one's there now. That C.J. tattoo will say D.L. soon, baby!"

Her eyes widened like she didn't believe me. "This bitch don't think I'm capable," I told myself angrily. *They never think I'm good enough!*

"No, really…I did. I fucked him good," I repeated. I needed to get my point across.

"Just like you stole my hairstyle," she shot back. "That's ridiculous, Dominique. I mean it's just like mine. Why would you do that? Can't I have anything to myself?"

"No. Nothing. Not even Rapheal." I had my head moving nastily and my eyes rolling childishly. "I'll tell you where I fucked him…in your kitchen, right next to your Granny Smith Apples." I laughed crazily. "Drunk dick is the best." I smiled.

Her face tightened like she believed me. It felt good to see her saddened for a change. It also felt good to see her fat, oversized and developing a light, black ring around her neck. She didn't look clean, I gloated. Finally, I was the better twin.

"You know you've always had the best of everything," I began. "The best clothes, the shoes, the best friends, the best hair texture…. And always had the most love from our mother. She never tried to make me happy. It was always you." My pitch grew higher. "Monique, Monique, Monique, Monique," I kept repeating. "Well, it's my time to shine."

"I need you to leave, now!"

I laughed crazily. Even in a time of desperation she still spoke in her usual proper voice.

"Little Miss Perfect," I said, moving meticulously toward her.

Monique started backing up attempting to exit the room from the back patio. The outside area was only two to three yards within her reach, so I had to think fast. My sister may have been naive about a lot of things but she was on to me. Her face had turned flush and her body language confirmed she would make a run for it. I couldn't allow it. She couldn't make it outside for fear of witnesses. She had to be done... right in her home and left for dead.

I took a few steps forward, then watched her take two steps backwards. The room had become completely silent except for the thunderous sounds of the waves banging against the tides.

My only sister eyed me skeptically as all my anger and hatred toward her over the years ignited.

"What do you want, Dominique?" she moaned, while breathing heavily.

"Rapheal," I said, placing stress on each syllable as I spoke. "And we need you gone," I told her looking like a psychotic woman who needed to be committed. Really I did, I laughed inside.

My tone was flat and emotionless, as I told her, "This

is it."

It was apparent the pressure had gotten to her. Her face was sunken in and the stress was evident. She held onto the bottom of her stomach and jetted toward the door.

I lunged forward, grasping the back of her dress. It was a small piece of fabric, yet just enough. Instantly, Monique's weight titled her body backwards. Legs first, she was in the air and within seconds fell flat on her back. I stood directly above her head with the sides of her cheeks clutched between my ankles.

"Going somewhereeeeee?" I sang in a crazed voice.

She started sniffling like a fuckin' baby. "Dominique, this is your niece I'm carrying. Help me! I think I'm hurt," she whimpered.

"I'm sure you are, pumpkin." I blew quick kisses through my tightened lips. "Whata shame…whata shame…whata shame."

She looked at me with tears in her eyes. "No seriously Dominique…I think I'm in labor." She whined some more before screaming. "Call for help!"

"Oh, I'm a great nurse. Remember? You told me so yourself!" I laughed like an evil witch.

"I'm begging you!" she pleaded. "This is my child we're talking about," she sobbed like a baby.

Whateva. I was so unbothered by her pleas. The bitch started breathing quickly through her lips sounding like she was sucking up air. She even made me think she was gonna deliver at that moment. Her legs were wide open and knees straight up in the air. She really thought she was in a hospital bed, straps in all.

I had seen enough women go into labor during my years as a nurse to know we had time. Without further hesitation, I jetted down near the bottom of her feet, which straddled the sides of her waist. A quick confirmation was needed.

She had on white panties which were soaking wet and blocked my view.

"Bitch, you went into labor. Your water broke," I said with attitude, realizing she was about to give birth. With one big yank I had her panties down to her feet, and to my surprise saw my niece's head crowning.

"What the fuck?" I said out loud.

My plans had to continue, I kept telling myself. It seemed like everything was happening so fast. And so wrong. Monique breathed like mad, doing all that bullshit people learn in Lamaze class. But no matter what she'd learned, I saw her frown each time a labor pain hit her where it hurt. This was serious. But I still had time, I told myself. "No babies would be born on my shift," I kept chanting obnoxiously. Monique would have to die quickly, and I'd decided the rest was outta my hands.

My conscience took my mind through a whirlwind. My sister. And a new baby. My sister and a new baby. I kept thinking those same words as I watched her give off one big push. With Monique on the floor unable to move, I thought about what I would use to kill her. I'd bought rat poison from the local store before heading to the house, and had a knife in my purse. A gun no doubt would make shit certain, but I was without fire power.

I stood up searching for Plan B while Monique grunted and pushed again. It seemed like nothing was around, and I had become more and more frantic. Then my eyes darted across the room. A brown extension cord, obviously left by someone working on the house, caught my attention. It was my only chance.

Monique saw my movements and started hollering from the floor. "Oh nooooo… Dominique, nooooo!" she cried in between words. It seemed like a pain would hit her wimpy-ass every thirty seconds.

I looked at her with pity. How could I have been so jealous of such a wimp? I asked myself.

In a dash, I'd made it back to my same position with the thick extension cord in hand. It was wrestled around my wrist on the ends and extra tight in the center. As soon as my body lowered above her head, she squirmed and held her stomach all at the same time.

"C'mon Dominique! Not this!" she yelled. "Not this. Why? Why? Whyyyyy?" she wailed uncontrollably.

I pushed the crotch of my jeans closer to her face hoping she could smell the remaining stench of Rapheal.

"Noooooo," she cried out again.

I wasn't sure if the shouts were from the labor pains, or from the fear of dying. Neither mattered to me. She always said I was no good anyway.

Just like that I wrapped the cord around her neck and pulled tightly with all my might. Her eyes looked up at me revealing a very sad story. If they could've spoken, I'm sure she wanted to know the reason. Why did our relationship get to the point of one murdering the other? I didn't have the answers, but I did see her eyes start to roll to the back of her head as she gasped for air. She fidgeted around trying to break free from my grip, but none of it made me loosen my hold.

I started counting...trying to help me stay focused. One...two...three...four...I must've been slipping on the job because Monique managed to raise her arms a few millimeters from her head only to dig her fingernails into my bare arms; I'm sure an attempt to pry my cold-blooded hands from around her neck.

I kept tugging, without a drop of emotion, sensing her strength was no match. It did dawn on me that every time I looked in the mirror I would see Monique. My sister. My twin. The woman I wanted to be. She started heaving....then coughing. It started a little louder…then lower… then slower…then barely.

Her voice shattered as she lost more breath. "Dominique, n-o-o-o-o-o," she stuttered softly.

"Oh, yes," I said like a trained killer.

Her sounds became more and more muffled as the life was being sucked from her soul. "H-e-l-l-l-p," she tried to say as her voice lowered and gave out at the same time. I watched as she took a long breath and pushed with all she had left.

Minutes passed, and I found myself sitting back on the floor wanting to smoke a cigar. I took a long, deep breath and smiled wickedly. I asked myself, *would Rapheal and I keep the house? And most importantly would we keep the baby?*

Thirteen...

Rapheal

Life hit me up with one piece of bad muthufuckin' news after another. I was fired up... ready to whip ass. The feds had me locked down well past the forty-eight hour limit. And in a local run-down Vegas jail cell at that. Shit had gotten real hectic. And of course exposed all snitches. But no matter what, I had to try Monique again. It was no time to be fakin' for the fellas, she had me on edge. I had called her countless times, for two days straight, and couldn't get her before the Feds confiscated my phone. Now that I had been released, I hoped like hell she had called.

Walkin' across the busy street to catch a cab, I braced myself for the worse. I dialed, and just like before it went straight to voicemail. I went off yelling and actin' hood all in the middle of the street.

"Monique, where the fuck you at? What the fuck?" I added in frustration. I knew my demeanor had changed and I needed to flip back to the man I really was. So my script flipped quickly. "Did I do somethin' wrong? I mean...luv, we can work this out. Just gimme a chance." My voice had softened and I ended with a heavy sigh. "Man, call me."

I hung up and massaged my pounding head. It was crazy how something inside had me convinced that Dominique revealed everything…bit by bit; probably even how long we fucked. What other reason would she have for not answerin' my calls? It seemed like my life had spiraled out of control. Monique was ignorin' my calls. Dominique was ignoring my calls. And the feds were monitorin' my calls.

"What the fuck?" I asked myself, rushin' to a nearby pay phone. I had so many calls to make, but not from my cell which was probably tapped by now.

My first call was to, Ansar, the only one of my Vegas workers who hadn't gotten picked up like the rest of us. When he answered, he seemed hesitant like talking wasn't an option. I made it fast, told him where to meet me, and hung up to hail the approachin' cab. "Aye," I yelled, like the driver had to stop.

He stopped alright...In the middle of the highway. The Polynesian man rolled down the window before unlockin' the doors and gave me the once over. My braids hadn't been freshly done in days, but my jeans and polo styled shirt made me look decent. Instead of commentin', I studied him too; placin' more interest on his out of style Kango hat. I shook the door knob with my hand, but he still wouldn't release the lock. He opened his mouth ready to fuss until I flashed a c-note in his face. The sound of the locks poppin' made me shake my head. I hopped in sayin', "The Wynn."

He pulled off speedily, makin' my head hit the back seat roughly. No complaints were needed. I'd already been through hell. I laid back, allowin' my mind to recall my two day gruelin' interrogation. It was me, Cole, the Vegas manager, two salespeople, and of course Sed. They drilled us like crazy in hopes of somebody punkin' out. Cole ended up being that punk.

They wouldn't say exactly what he told, but his information gave them the ammo to hold us longer than usual. All I kept thinking about were the records and tag # data he stored in his computer. It had names, addresses, phone numbers, and specific dollar amounts of what cars were sold in all locations. Luckily, he didn't know the procedure for switching the VIN #'s, nor how my motor vehicle connections were involved.

I sat back and took a deep breath watching the sun go down. Vegas was a real slick city at night, and at its best when lit up. My mind eased up a bit at the sight of all the beautiful hotels that lined the strip; especially when I passed the Monte Carlo, my favorite gamblin' spot. The crap tables seemed to be callin' my name, but I couldn't gamble at a time like this, I told myself. Shit was fucked up. Real fucked up. I had to figure out a way to get all the cars moved off the lots in Chicago and D.C. before the agents were onto me completely. They used the scare tactic telling us all if we gave up information about our overseas connection, they'd reduce our time. I knew it was bullshit, but Sed listened way too intently.

From my experience, he smelled like a snitch. I felt it. But I still left his ass in there to fight off the Feds. They actually locked his little skinny-ass up and booked him. He was caught on tape so nothin' would help him for now. I lied, told him bail money was on the way. On the real, I wanted the nigga to get used to the jail life.

When I pulled up to the Wynn, Ansar was waitin' outside the lobby doors like a trusty assistant. His face wore a troubled look as he looked around nervously. "It's cool," I uttered, walkin' past him swiftly. "Nobody is followin' me. I'm the best at this."

"You sure about that?" he questioned, in his thick Arabian accent.

"Trust. You got my word," I said, gettin' my swagger back.

"Look, use your I.D, get me a room," I ordered, handin' him a bundle of cash.

No sooner than he left my space, I found a spot near one of the specialty shops to make that call again. I whipped out my cell noticin' I had twenty-five messages, but nothin' was more important than Monique. It rang two times and went straight to voice mail. "C'mon baby, I'm sorry," I whined. "If you just call me back, I'll explain everythin'." I hit her with one plea after another while pacin' in a circle. The moment I hung up, it hit me. Rule #1, never admit any wrongdoing.

"Fuck, fuck, fuck. I'm slippin'," I fussed to myself, watchin' Ansar come toward me with the key.

By the time we made it up to the eighth floor, a million thoughts had rumbled through my mind, and I'd given my boy twenty different things to do. When we walked inside I took in the view and started plannin'.

"First, order up some bottles," I instructed. "If they got VSOP you know what to do. What'cha drinkin'?" I asked like I expected him to get drunk with me.

Ansar just shook his head real fast like a puppet as he dialed and started orderin' my drinks. Seconds later, he hung up and started askin' me a bunch of stupid homo shit.

"So, we going back to the lot?"

"What'cha think muthufucka?"

I shook my head. It was poundin' so hard that no type of codeine or anythin' else would help me. Only solutions to my problems. "Look, I need you to take these numbers here, go down to a payphone, and call my folks. Tell'em to abort. They'll know what that means. Now, don't fuck that shit up," I warned. "While you do that, I'll handle stuff from here." I paused and checked to see if he was gettin' it. "Got it?" I confirmed.

He shook his head all crazy again, got up, and headed to

the door. Just as he was leavin', my drinks arrived. "Don't even let that muthufucka in here!" I shouted. Just put the shit on the table. Grab a hundred for'em," I yelled out, pullin' my dirty shirt from over my head.

Just like that the door shut, and I was alone. Alone to think. Alone to work. I rushed over to the hotel phone, which I knew wasn't tapped to organize movement of the remainin' cars. Secret locations of course. My last bit of money was tied up in the cars since the Feds had frozen my accounts. Until that money came back, I'd have to sell off some of my hot engines to make ends meet.

I thought about my initial instructions to Ansar in the elevator, tellin' him to hook up with the girl who registered the VIN #'s on cars through the Nevada motor vehicle. Her testimony would kill me if they got to her, so she had to be paid off and sent away. No paper trails I hoped. The only part about my businesses that made me feel at ease was that none of them had the same name. The big boys would have to investigate like hell to locate them all, unless Sed sang like a bird.

In the meantime, I took my liquor straight to the head, and headed to the shower. I was already feelin' the effects of the alcohol as I stripped, leavin' myself but naked and racin' to the shower. The water was hot and steamy but gave time to contemplate how things would fall. And who they would fall on. Sed troubled me. "He just might be the weakest link," I mumbled to myself as the water beat down on my back.

The pressure was strong and would hopefully cleanse the stint of jail off my tiring body. I'd only been locked up once in my life time. Nearly ten years back. Bars weren't meant for a suave nigga like me, I bragged. With each scrub I thought more about Monique, and the other woman in my life. Then it dawned on me, C.J. hadn't gotten back yet with my clothes. She wasn't number one in my life, but she was just as important.

I hadn't talked to her since she arrived to bail me out. She was down like that. When the Feds told her no bail was needed, she never left the premises. It wasn't until I got out, and instructed her to get me some clothes did she leave. It was strange that C.J. hadn't made it back to the room yet. When I washed the soap from my forearm, my eyes gazed at the tattoo. Her initials always took me back to what we were supposed to be. It never quite worked itself out, but she understood. I grinned a little thinking about how true she was to me. The fact that she could roll in any situation always turned me on.

Hearin' the sound of my cell startled me. I figured I'd talked C.J. up. Maybe she was downstairs wantin' to know the room number? Quickly, I stepped from the shower soakin' wet, and reached for my Blackberry on the sink. I got nervous when I saw the number. If she was callin' me, maybe Dominique hadn't said anythin'. "Monique," I said, with a little hope in my voice. "Why you callin' from your mother's house number. Why haven't you been answerin' your phone?"

I shot off question after question not giving her a chance to speak, but somethin' told me to stop. Sobs sounded through the phone. A cry that said somethin' was wrong.

"Ahhhhhhhh, my baby!" Mrs. Lewis cried out.

I grabbed a towel, wrappin' it tightly around my waist wonderin' what the hell was goin' on. "What's wrong? What is it?" I asked anxiously. Her tone frightened me.

"Oh my God, Rapheal," she moaned like she was dyin' a slow death. "She's goneeeeee," she cried. "She's really gone."

It felt like my heart stopped. "Who?" I asked, afraid to hear the answer.

"Monique, Monique, Monique," Mrs. Lewis repeated. "She's dead!"

BY AZAREL

I dropped the phone fallin' back onto the toilet,
wonderin', what the fuck had happened.

Fourteen ...

Dominique

When I pulled up to the church there wasn't a parking spot in sight. It was puzzling to me how she'd pulled such a crowd. She never shined like that when she was living, yet plenty of high-dollar cars dominated the curbside just behind the hearse. It was the first week of November, just three days after Halloween, so most of the trees had already lost their leaves. I decided to double-park under the large oak, thinking, who would challenge me? After all, it was *my* sister's funeral.

Luckily, 11:00 a.m had finally rolled around. The anticipation had caused me to miss a lot of sleep. It had been fourteen long days since Monique's body was found by the Bahamian authorities, followed by another five days just to get her corpse brought back to the states. My mother's initial call to the police, and her constant nagging tipped them off, ending with a declaration to find her killer, and her baby's abductor. It was all over the news that an American woman had been killed in the Bahamas and her baby was missing.

It was weird how Monique's boring-ass still got all the stardom. Her murder was plastered all over every headlining news show; more than JonBenet' Ramsey and the Anna

137

Nicole Smith catastrophe. Even our family had gotten much attention from the media over the last few days, that Nancy Grace wanted both me and Ruby on the show. I declined instantly. Just my luck, someone from the Bahamas would be watching and say they saw me in the airport, or on a flight leaving the Bahamas, then I'd have to kill their asses.

For me, it had been a weak of constant pretending. I showed up at the funeral home to help my mother make arrangements, but stayed away from everyone mostly; even Yuri. It was tiring having to cry real tears, and get choked up every time someone new came around. So, I started acting as though I couldn't take it anymore, and told my mother the doctor had put me on strict bed rest. She believed me, of course. And since I was six months pregnant, it was best if everyone left me alone to mourn in peace.

As soon as the double doors opened, and an usher handed me a program, I became the center of attention. The whispers started, and the eyes roamed. My first reaction was to check my wig. I patted the back, making sure it was on extra tight. If it came off by mistake and people saw that I had the same exact haircut that Monique had gotten just a month ago, it might've raised a red flag. Secondly, I checked the position of the pillow stuffed deep inside my spanxs. I had the full body armor on; which covered up to the upper part of my stomach. I couldn't afford to have the pillow exposed beneath my knee-length black knit dress.

For the first time in years, I looked like a conservative housewife with a loose fitting dress. I wore my short bob wig swooped in my face a little, but still rocked my signature sunshades. I opted for a dark, black pair, the darkest I could find. My eyes needed to be covered at all times to hide the deceit, so the large oval shaped lenses worked well.

I saw them all rushing toward me in the back of the church. It was Shawna, Jennifer, and a few girls from my old neighborhood. They looked like a swarm of groupies ready for attack especially my cousin, Jennifer who had her arms spread wide.

"Where have you been?" Shawna asked with deep concern, and smacking her lips between words.

"I been around." I took a deep breath like I needed a moment. "I just needed some time to myself...you know this is a big loss for me," I sniffled, then pulled a handkerchief from my black, dressy clutch bag.

"And what the..." she stopped mid sentence inquiring about my pregnancy with her eyes.

"I know I shoulda told you," I said apologetically. "But we'll talk about it later. Not here in front of them," I pointed, seeing that the females were coming up on us.

They all crowded around me in a semi-circle throwing out condolences so my performance had to shine.

"Anything you need. I got you," a friend of my sister's commented.

"This is so hard," I revealed in a soft tone. "We- were – so- so- so- close," I uttered, getting choked up between words.

Jennifer took her hug even though I didn't hug her back then Shawna rubbed my back in a circular motion, and ushered me along.

"Girl, this is terrible. I know how you must feel. I know y'all had your ups and downs but she really loved you.

"I don't even know how to feel," I said, making my way to the front.

"One thing is fo' sure... you shoulda told me to do your hair. That wig looks terrible," she remarked.

I just burst out crying. So she got off my hair.

"Don't you think about nothing," she said, moving people out of her way with a wave of the hand. "Jennifer, grab her some water," she instructed her sister. "You come on up here and sit with your mother. She all messed up."

"No. Not yet." I stopped. "I want to pay my respects."

"Girl, you do that with the family. You'll get another chance just before the funeral actually starts. Let those other folks see her now."

I glanced over to my left and saw the long line waiting to view the body. Correction, waiting to view the picture of Monique sitting on top of the silver casket. Her body had been held too long, and from what my mother said, made her unable to have an open casket.

"I'm going to the front," I announced. "I gotta see my sister."

My entourage froze. They knew my suggestion wasn't a good one, but followed me anyway, mouths open and hands in the air. I waddled through a few pews making my way to the left side of the church. I wasn't waiting in line to see my immediate fam. I bypassed them all. Plus, I wanted everyone to notice the way I treaded along. It was that walk that said, yes, I'm pregnant. Of course I played it up real good. By the time I made it to the front, I'd given four fake grins, and three *fuck off* waves to people I didn't like.

They watched me closely. Some mugged me like I was a hand-me-down. Little did they know I wanted them, too. I started with a mellow rub of the casket, then switched into a soft cry. My cousin Jennifer stood on one side of me while Shawna rushed to the other side.

"It was always just the two of us," I wailed. "It should've been me Monique, it should've been me." My over the top sobbing was causing a big stir in the church. It was exactly what I wanted.

I turned slightly for everyone to see me clearly, followed by a quick clutch of my stomach. Frightened faces stared on. Most didn't know what to do. My mother stepped from the pew on the first row and hurried to my side.

"Don't make a fool of our family name up here, girl," she gritted in a low tone through her teeth. "Now sit down," she ended coldly.

"I can't. I can't go on," I cried, kneeling toward the floor. By the time I landed on my knees, I was covering my eyes and could feel my mother pulling on my arm. She smiled at everyone in the sanctuary, like everything would be okay.

When she whispered, "You hardly even liked your sister," I was shocked. Outdone. Why would she go that far? In a church? Dayum.

Suddenly, she pulled me up forcefully, signaling the help of my cousins. Together, they rushed me over to the front row and sat me down like they were handling a fragile package. At that moment, my world changed. He was in the house. The house of the Lord. When I saw him sitting on the front row like his world was shook, I got angry. I felt betrayed as I studied his saddened eyes. I watched closely as a few of his boys consoled him with pats on the back, and words of encouragement. Kareem, his friend that he hung out with most, was right there pumping him up, and doing most of the talking.

I stopped crying instantly. My focus had changed. I needed to make a statement, so I stood up daringly. Unfortunately, my mother's hand on my shoulder pushed me back down. "Don't you embarrass me, missy," she informed with her finger shaking all in my face. "Grieve at home," she told me harshly.

Whateva. She got ignored, so my focus could remain on Rapheal. He had his head down just above his lap, and never even looked my way. It seemed as though he was crying his eyes out like the grieving husband on the front row. Right then and there I'd decided if he didn't acknowledge me, our business was gonna be aired as soon as they started the eulogy.

"Look at him," I told my mother, "he's over there crying his eyes out and has been cheating on Monique all along." I crossed my arms and twitched my lips showing my anger. "Just think, he got your son locked up for doing some shady shit, and now he can't even be here for the funeral."

"We'll have none of that foolishness at a Lewis funeral," she announced. But her body language said something differently when her eyes darted over to Rapheal and gawked at him suspiciously. But within seconds, her shameful stare was back on me.

"Enough is enough, Dominique," she said through clenched teeth. She tried to keep her tone low, but her anger showed clearly and her voice screeched. "You have ruined everything you've ever touched. You never really loved your sister, or me for that matter. So sit back, remain quiet, and prayerfully the rest of the world won't figure out what a disgrace you are to this family."

My mouth hung open. I got teary eyed, *for real*, which was rare for me. All I ever wanted was for somebody to love me. This was my mother, the woman who gave me life, and she was taking life from me without even knowing it. Well that was it. I knew she hated being embarrassed, so embarrassment was what she would get. I hopped up holding my stomach and put my voice on volume ten.

I shouted standing above her, "Ruby, all I ever wanted was for you to love me. All my life you've treated me like sloppy seconds. Your stuck-up ways made me the nasty, uptight person I am today. It was all about Monique." I dragged out her name making sure to point to the picture on the casket. "But guess what?" I leaned over into her face. "She's gone!" I made sure to point to the casket again. "Probably happy to be away from you!"

"Dominique, I don't think you're feeling well," was all she could say, as she checked her surroundings to see who watched from behind.

"I'm all you got now. Me and your grandbaby," I said, rubbing my stomach and glancing over at Rapheal who had his face balled up. He stared me down like he wanted to shoot me dead right in the church. He even moved around a bit like he wanted to intervene. I dared him to say something. I would blast his black-ass and the whole church with details from our late fuck session at his apartment where he seduced *me*.

I turned back to my mother. "If you don't want me around, say it. I'll leave you alone. But I'm sick of you praising Monique in my face. Face it," I said, grabbing my clutch off the bench. "Monique's baby was stolen. We'll probably never see her again. But this one you might," I ended, walking toward the back of the church.

As soon as I started walking, lots of commotion filled the air behind me. I dished out more tears, enough to win any Academy Award category as I paced myself down the aisle to make it all look good. There was tons of yelling behind me, mostly comments of concern, although some were nasty remarks from my older aunts and uncles. With all the commotion going on, I almost missed the sweet sound of Rapheal's voice coming from behind.

When I turned around, he was standing there in front of me with a confused look on his face. "We need to talk," he said, trying to bring up the bass in his voice.

"Of course we do," I told him. "Plenty of plans to make…situations to work out," I sang sweetly.

I moved a few steps further into the vestibule since the funeral was about to begin. I saw the pastor up on the podium, realizing this was all real. Most people were taking their seats with the exception of Shawna and Jennifer standing up in the second pew, waving for me to come back and sit down.

Turning my back to them, I spoke slowly to Rapheal,

so that he was clear about what we needed to do. "Rapheal, I'm either moving into your spot, or you into mine. Which is it?" I asked with the most serious expression my face could form.

He spoke through his teeth, as he looked around nervously. "Man, you crazy as hell. Something is really wrong wit'cha. I mean really," he repeated. "I've been callin' you for weeks Dominique, since you left my place. You never returned one call. And now you're here, the day of your sister's funeral saying we're movin' in together."

"I take it that's a yes."

I grinned my famous grin.

"No, it's not a yes," he said, angrily with his hands stuck deep into the pockets of his expensive looking black pants. "I've lost my woman and my child all in the same week. Can you cut a brotha some slack?"

I grinned again. Little did he know, he did have a living child. A child that only I knew the whereabouts. The authorities said a baby girl was born, and that she was stolen before the paramedics arrived. Technically, she wasn't stolen, just taken by the rightful owner. I smiled as I thought about going back to claim my child when the time was right.

Rapheal seemed frustrated as his eyes stared me up and down. "What's this with you pretending to be pregnant again. Are you gonna seduce somebody here at the church?"

"Funny," I said, then shot him a half-ass, rapid smile. "I am pregnant, Rapheal. Just not this far along. I did this whole pillow thing again to protect your image." I frowned but put emphasis on the word *your*. "I'm only three weeks pregnant with *your* child, but if people think I'm much further along they'll never think it was you. So pay me." I threw my palm in his face.

It seemed like he fell for my white-lie. He didn't say it, but his forehead crinkled as he looked around the church try-

144

ing to see who watched us. I had to be on point; able to fool them all. My mother thought my pregnancy was two months behind Monique, so if I was going to bring Monique's baby back to the states and raise her as my own, my timeline would have to work.

Just thinking about having our child at home with us made me think back to her birth. Because I'd cut so many unbiblical cords in the hospital, cutting my nieces was no problem. I just had to make sure that Monique's blood stopped pulsating so that no complications would occur. The hardest part was finding something to hold the cord in place, so that it wasn't jumping around when I cut it.

I remembered like it was yesterday how Monique had slipped into a state of unconsciousness as soon as the baby was born. I ran faster than ever to boil some water, hoping to sterilize the scissors I'd found on her coffee table. When I cut the cord and held Ronnique in my arms, chill bumps filled my skin. It was the proudest moment of my life. I smiled inside thinking how I'd named her a name chosen by the inspiration of both me and Rapheal.

"Man, I'm out," Rapheal announced.

I guess he was tired of me gazing off into thin air. Besides, the choir started singing, *I'm Going Up Yonder* from the front of the church. The service was on the way, and people had started noticing us even more.

"So look," I said, moving closer to him. "Let's discuss the rest over dinner. Your treat…okay." Without warning, I kissed at him softly, but he stepped back avoiding my next move. "I'll give you one more chance," I warned hatefully.

"Is that a threat?"

I started hitting Rapheal with shifty eyes letting him know he was facing a time bomb ready to explode. I wasn't to be fucked with and was ready to show off. "It's not a threat luv, it's a promise," I said in a sadistic tone.

"Look, not here."

"Not here, luv," I mimicked. "Then where!" I shouted, making all heads turn to the back of the church.

He didn't think it was funny. He seemed to be processing all that I'd said to him. Not only did my man's frustration show, but his attention diverted. I followed his eyes making sure he wasn't watching another bitch. Then I saw him. He looked better than I'd ever seen him in a pair of black slacks, a red button down shirt and a colorful tie.

"Yuri," I said surprisingly.

He walked up to us both, not really saying much to me, but giving Rapheal some dap. My thoughts started doing flips in my head. The first idea was to pull my stomach in, but the pillow still made me look fat. All of a sudden, I felt Yuri's hands on my shoulder as he asked Rapheal why he hadn't called him back.

My eyes bulged. I was confused. "You know each other?" I asked.

"No doubt," Yuri announced. "We do a little business together every now and then. How you know Dominique?"

He posed the question to Rapheal. It was his turn to get me back. *Oh shit! I told myself.*

"Her sister was my lady," he said sadly.

I wanted to kick Rapheal in the nuts. He wasn't gonna keep disrespecting me, talking about the past.

"So Yuri, thanks for coming," I said, trying to hide my belly. "I didn't think you knew where it was," I said nervously.

He didn't respond. He didn't make a move. He just worked up one of his killer expressions, then glued his eyes to my belly.

"What the fuck is this all about?" he asked me with a disapproving stare.

Rapheal snickered. He quickly gave him another pound

146

of the hand, and walked back to the front of the church, leaving me with some explaining to do.

Just as I started to explain, a man walked in alone, resembling me a lot. His features so familiar. Scary enough to make my problems with Yuri seem small. He called out my name, making me melt. All my memories fluttered back into my mind causing me to feel ill.

"They told me you were dead," I said to my father.

He just smiled. "I never died beautiful. Your mother just killed me in her memory and yours."

Dayum- all kinds of shit was about to hit the fan.

Fifteen...

Rapheal

 Two weeks had rolled around since the burial of my girl. The bad dreams kept happenin' daily, mostly in the mornings when I was alone. She would always be standin', with blood drippin' near the foot of my bed, askin, beggin' for help. It drove me crazy not understandin' why it all happened. I had called every contractor I knew in the Bahamas and had even given their names to the police who were investigatin' Monique's death. Nobody had any clues. And no one had seen anythin'.

 It all had me shook. At night I drank myself silly, and thought of ways to finagle the sale of my remainin' cars. That was my second issue. It was workin'- just not as quickly as needed. Cash flow was tight for everybody; especially me. I'd already met with Mr. McNair, and given him a $10,000 retainer. I was sure his legal services would be needed within a matter of days.

 At least one dude in the Atlanta area still had money to blow. I watched him turn the corner like he was in a high speed car chase. His boy on the passenger side held onto the handle inside the roof of the car as they came to a speedy stop

right in front of me. I'd chosen a parkin' lot where the old
A&P used to be off of Highway 20. For this transaction, we
needed privacy.

His dreads shook like snakes as he exited the 98
Corvette and signaled his boy to take off. It never ceased to
amaze me how hood he looked. He had on an oversized
hoodie, a pair of dirty Levis, and Timbs that didn't even have
laces. Me on the other hand, stayed suited up, just minus the
tie today, like a business meeting was about to begin. I even
had a fresh set of braids which had grown over the weeks and
now straddled my neck.

He walked up to me, seeing me leanin' on his new
ride, and shakin' his head in the process. He did a few wild
looking dances, and examined the vehicle from a distance.
My focus remained steady on the black backpack swung over
his right shoulder. I'm sure it was where my money laid.

"Wassup, Man."

"Not too good," I told my client.

"Look like yuh livin' lovely, if you ask me."

"Nah…looks are deceivin'," I told Yuri, givin' him
some dap. "That's how niggas get locked down. People see
what they got and start spreadin' lies."

We both laughed while he examined the soft leather
seats of his new red Ferrari. I stood back away from the sports
car as Yuri walked completely around the perimeter of his
new purchase. I knew he liked what he saw, 'cause he kept
bobbin' his head.

"612 Scaglietti. Boy, yuh come through! This the
sweetest Ferrari out!" He banged on the hood of the car
showin' his excitement. "How's the system?"

"80 watt sound system with a sub-woofer," I bragged.

"Damn nigga! Yuh know I'ma be playin', *Kill the
Bitch* by Sasha." He bobbed his head even though the music
wasn't on yet. "That's that good Caribbean music…yuh know

what I'm sayin'," he said openin' the door, and hopped inside to crank up the system.

I gave up a tiny laugh just to save face. Wasn't nothin' in my world funny anymore. I just wanted the money. I started checkin' my watch, givin' him a sign we needed to be goin'. Look man, it's yours now," I said proudly as some sound I'd never heard came blarin' through the speakers.

"No doubt boy, it's sweet," he said hoppin' out the car and takin' his backpack off his shoulder. "This car straight, right?"

"It's just like the other you got from me." A frown spread across my face.

"Nah, man...I'm just sayin', I know a few people who been gettin' into some shit with the police behind hot cars. When I spend my money with yuh, I know I'm not buyin' from the dealership otherwise I would spend double, but I gotta know my paperwork is in order so no shit will come back to me."

I folded my arms nervously wishin' he'd just pass me the backpack. "Yuri, you good man. No worries. All the paperwork is in order. Everythin' is in the glove box. As usual," I added with confidence.

"Bet. No heat comin' to me then no heat comin' to you," he grinned, while tossin' me the backpack. "Sixty thousand it is," he said proudly. "Yuh wanna count it?"

"Nah, man. All I need is a ride. I got my folks up on Pride Street waitin' on me."

"Hop in," he told me, while examinin' the chrome on the side of the door.

I rushed to the passenger side and I got in slowly. Bad move.

Within seconds, Yuri had started the engine and zoomed off even though my door wasn't completely shut. I just gave off a sigh-didn't want to appear too soft. But the fact remained Yuri was wild. I was strictly about makin' money.

His next question puzzled me. He asked, "When you gon re-up?"

"Oh, ummm….," I stuttered then held onto the door handle as he hit a sharp turn. "I just need 'bout three weeks. My manz over in Germany takin' a break for a minute. He'll be back in touch soon. But damn, man. You got three fly-ass cars already. What'cha gon' do with another one?"

He downshifted as we approached the red light, but ignored my question. It seemed like he was thinkin' about how to respond. Within a flash, the light changed, and Yuri sped through the gears…shiftin' like a suicidal race car driver. …second…third…fourth….fifth gear. We were speeding through the streets and catchin' every available eye. Even ones from a passin' police car.

"You neva know why I might want another car. Maybe just to look at it."

He smiled devilishly.

"Don't worry. I got you. This new baby here will keep you wet for a minute. Turn right here," I announced quickly.

Yuri stopped abruptly and hit a sharp, fast turn. I grinned showin' him my pearly whites. Hopefully he thought everythin' was okay. I knew for a fact if Yuri suspected any heat comin' from the Feds he wouldn't buy.

"I got an associate, he wanna get a lil' somethin'. He just tryna get his paper right."

"Stop right here. It's just over there where I need to go," I said, clearing my nose from the smell of burnt tires. "You make the sale. I'll give you the commission. Twenty percent," I said. "If you can get him to buy from my existin' fleet, I'll give you twenty –five percent."

"Damn, what yuh tryna do, boy?"

"Man, I'm movin' to Miami in a few months. I'ma still do my thang down there, but I need to push these cars. Know what I'm sayin'?"

The tone of his voice changed drastically. "Yeah, I got yuh," he said, reachin' into his Timberland boot, and whippin' out a .38 snub nose revolver.

"Whoa, whoa, whoa…What the fuck, Yuri?" I had my hands slightly above my chest like it was a stick-up.

He held the gun low and remained calm.

"Yuh know those sneaky bastards watchin' us from there." He pointed to his left.

"Man, those my folks. They just waitin' on me," I told him fearfully, trying to calm my increasin' heart rate.

"Cool. Yuh just saved a life."

"What'cha self man. Don't catch a gun charge ridin' around with that piece."

"I got plenty."

He grinned real crazy-like as I stepped from the car. My Blackberry had been vibrating constantly since I had gotten inside. When I scrolled down to see who'd been callin'…it was C.J. She'd been callin' like crazy, ready to move into position #1. She wanted to come to ATL, but I told her no-I would be movin' to Miami permanently within two months.

Hold tight. I texted her.

Then I went over to shake hands with my boys as Yuri sped off doing a wheelie in the middle of the block.

Shocked, was all I could feel walkin' into the lobby of my building. Several suitcases lay in a neat circle around Terrance's countertop where he checked visitors in, and kept his miniature log book. It was a small desk with more height than width, which he normally kept extremely clean.

The flags were up, and the signs that somethin' was

wrong made me want to ask him anyway. There were travel bags on the opposite side of his desk, and about three to four boxes that lined the wall all labeled with different rooms; kitchen, bathroom, livin' room, baby's room, written in big bold, black letters with a magic marker.

Terrance was a frail, scary type dude on any average day. But today his eyes seemed to pop from his head, constantly shiftin' from right to left as I drilled him with questions. He tried diligently to get me to look in the direction of the mailboxes over to the left. I didn't at first, for fear of what I would see. There she was, sittin' on a huge ottoman, where visitors normally sat, filing her nails. Problem was…she wasn't a visitor… 'cause I didn't invite her. Yet she stared me directly in my face as if I had.

Dominique sat in a relaxed state, with her legs crossed, exposin' all the skin between her upper thigh and her thigh-high boots. The wig was off and her hair revealed. It was a strikin' replica of Monique; same hair, same facials, and today even the same calm spirit.

She looked sexy in her above the knee flared jean skirt, and tight fittin' brown sweater, but that wasn't enough to get her upstairs. Or her truck load of belongings. Besides, I wasn't drunk. I just needed to think…quick.

"I'm sorry Mr. C.," Terrance stuttered. "I wasn't sure what to do. She said she lives here now, but you didn't give her a key yet."

He was really looking for confirmation, but wouldn't outright ask for fear of losin' his job. We'd discussed Dominique's last trick the day after she pretended to be Monique. Terrance was fully aware of what happened and vowed to watch my back a little harder in the future.

I really wanted to calm his nerves, so I cleared my throat. "It's okay Terrance, I'll take it from here."

"Yes, Terrance, we'll take it from here," Dominique

said, standin' to her feet. She grabbed her duffle bag from the shiny marbled floor, and a few Macy's bags underneath the large ottoman. She threw them all over her shoulder just before struttin' my way. I thought about how she would get handled when she got closer to me. Instead, she hit a hard left and headed straight to the elevator, leaving both me and Terrance with our faces on the floor.

In a complete state of shock, no words would release. I just froze.

"Terrance, have my things brought up to our apartment," Dominique said casually then disappeared around the corner.

Her voice was so pleasant. She sounded so sweet. The bitch had planned on killin' me, I was sure. I knew she didn't have a key, but I needed to figure everythin' out. I looked at Terrance. He looked at me. Before I knew it, my feet were runnin' in her direction. I told him to put her things in a storage room downstairs until I figured out what to do.

When I caught up to Dominique in the elevator, she was still filin' her nails. Her expression confirmed she was a disturbed woman, so I wanted to craft my words carefully. Everything moved in slow motion. It felt like the longest elevator ride in history. Finally, we made it inside the apartment and I darted straight to the kitchen. I started talkin' slowly as I poured myself a glass of Hennessey.

"So Dominique, what are we gonna do?" I asked, swishin' my alcohol around in the glass. I refused to give her eye contact…and didn't want to make her feel at home.

"Well for now," she said slowly, "I'm going to get comfortable," she told me takin' off her earrings and placin' them on the table next to the couch.

She'd dropped all her bags in the middle of the floor, and started movin' about the livin' room like she was really home. Her actions seemed so at ease, but on the real she worried me. I was even afraid to go to the bathroom for fear she'd burst the door open and cut my nuts off. The chick was out of her damn mind and I knew it. I downed my drink, and grabbed the bottle for another. My mind rambled, wonderin' what my next move needed to be.

"Are you gonna come out of the kitchen?" she asked me kindly.

I played around in the refrigerator searchin' for a Red Bull to add to my drink so I never lifted my head to answer before she spoke again.

"Do you hear me, honey?"

I had my back facing her, but thought, "Oh shit, she called me honey." I froze again tryin' to figure out the best way to throw her out. Then all of a sudden her mother came to mind.

I closed the door and turned around with a smirk on my face. Forget about the undressin' in slow motion. Dominique was standin' half-naked in the middle of the floor, just three yards from me, with nothing on but a matchin' hot pink panty and bra set, and a pair of high-heel boots.

I took my drink to the head as my heart began to race.

"I hope you're not angry?" she asked me seductively. "I didn't bring everything… so there's no sexy night clothes tonight."

She ended by sticking her finger in her mouth and suckin' on it rapidly. The bitch was serious and the fatal attraction shit was progressively gettin' worse. I really wanted to open my front door and start throwin' her shit down the hall like fast Frisbees. Instead, I remained still, scared to come from the kitchen area. Her sex was so good the last time, my fear was that I'd start to want it more and more. Ain't gon' lie- I'd dreamt about it; especially the way she rode me like a bull. But I couldn't, I told myself shakin' my head back and forth.

Besides, the fact that she was standin' there looking like the spittin' image of Monique made a weird feelin' come over my body. I had my hands behind me, flat down on the counter holdin' my body up. My senses told me one thing while the little devil on my shoulder said another.

"You're a lucky man," she told me, while fondlin' with her breast.

I had to admit, her bra made her look like she had cleavage for days, and every time she pulled her nipple out for me to see, my dick got harder. She started squeezin' the tip of one of her large nipples then pulled it near her mouth and licked it like a snake. It was turnin' me the fuck on, no doubt. Before long, she had fingertips doing a dance inside her panties. They were halfway down as she made her first move.

"C'mere," she said softly, while her pointer finger did the beck and call movement.

I didn't move, so she kept masturbatin' right in front of me with her head titled back. She moaned erotically lettin' out super freaky sounds, "Ahhhhhh. Oohhhhh. Fuck me right here," she begged. "C'mon baby. Come to Mama."

My mouth stayed open for so long, I started droolin' like a baby. I moved away from the counter mesmerized by her foreplay. I knew she was dangerous, but maybe hittin' it one more time wouldn't hurt.

She asked me again, and I obliged, "C'mere."

"We shouldn't be doin' this," I said, takin' baby steps toward her.

"You got a fantasy?"

I grinned, just as my dick pulsated even more. It was so hard that it started to hurt.

"What's your fantasy?"

"I got many. But we can start with the ass."

I headed her way ready for attack when the doorbell sounded.

"Don't get it," she begged, rushin' up against me, and summonsin' my hand into her wet panties.

We stood facing one another with my dick bulging through my pants and rubbin' against the upper part of her stomach. The fact that she was much shorter made me want to lift her in the air right then and there. Then the door bell sounded again, followed by five repetitive knocks. My brows crinkled. I recognized the knocks. It wasn't Terrance for sure. "Who is it?" I shouted with a worried expression.

Then the banging intensified. "Police, open up!"

I panicked, stepped away from Dominique like an alien was at the door. I took my time goin' to the door hoping my manhood would sense what was going on. I saw Dominique runnin' off to the side to throw her clothes back on as I asked them, "What's this all about?"

Their next response had me shaking. I didn't want to go down to County, so I opened up without hesitation. "What's this all about?"

They hit me with the badges, high in the air, burstin' through my place like the militia. There were three of them, one in uniform, and the other two in plain clothes. "Can…" I started to say, but was cut off by the younger officer.

"Sir, sit down," the older gentleman ordered, pointin' toward my dinin' room table.

It took less than two seconds for me to comply.

All three of them rushed toward Dominique, but they still talked to me from a distance. "I'm Detective Barnes, this is Detective Carter, and this is Officer Stewart, the older gentleman announced. He seemed to be runnin' the show and actin' like Columbo all at the same time.

"You know why we're here, right?" he asked Dominique.

She didn't say a thing which was rare.

"Surely you knew this was coming," Barnes continued.

"Hmmph," was all I heard her say.

The next set of words had me all fucked up.

"Dominique Lewis, you have the right to remain silent. Anything you say can and will be used against you in a court of law," Barnes began, while the thin officer whose name badge read T. Stewart cuffed her. The rest of the Miranda rights began to sound like background music to me as I sat freaked out with my hands in my lap. I couldn't believe this shit was happenin'.

"You have the right to talk to a lawyer and have a lawyer present with you during questioning. If you cannot afford a lawyer, one will be appointed for you if you so desire. If you do choose to talk to the police, you have the right to end the interview at any time."

When he paused, I looked into Dominique's watery eyes. It was fucked up that she was going to jail for me. Somehow they must've thought she was involved with my car shit, and was takin' her in. Maybe they thought she knew somethin', and could possibly be a witness to turn on me like some of the others. Whatever the reason, they had her hands behind her back, cuffs on, and readin' her the last part of her rights.

"Do you understand each of these rights as I have explained them to you?" Barnes added.

She nodded.

I sat speechless.

Everythin' moved so fast. I just couldn't put all the pieces to the puzzle together. I wanted to ask questions, but the disapprovin' looks I got warned me not to.

"So we're gonna head downtown Missy where you can call your lawyer. But we are gonna do a line-up tonight," Barnes concluded, shufflin' Dominique to the front door.

When they got close to walkin' pass me, the younger officer who'd identified himself stopped and asked, "You got some identification on you?"

"Uhhhh…"

"Either you do or don't. We can always finger print you downtown to figure out if you got any alias."

I slowly moved my right arm to my back pocket leaving the right on the table for them to see. I didn't wanna become a statistic, gettin' shot up; 'cause they thought I was reachin' for somethin'. I pulled my ID from my wallet slowly and laid it on the table.

"Rapheal Coleman," Barnes said sarcastically. "You got a lot of shit going on with you." He paused… "How about you don't leave town either?"

I showed my agreement with my head.

They started talkin' about how long they'd been watchin' my place, and my every move. They even gave condolences for the death of Monique. Suddenly, they were on the move again.

As they headed to the front door, I let everythin' they said marinate in my brain. I remained glued to my dinin' room chair, lost in my own place-afraid to move.

"You're one helluva guy," Barnes commented to me on the way out of the door. I didn't understand his comment but knew it must've been a compliment 'cause he grinned from ear to ear.

Dominique was pushed ahead and out the door, but I'd gotten one last look at her. Her glassy eyes troubled me. She wasn't the Dominique I once knew. She'd softened. A lot. I should've been delighted to see her go, but wasn't. I had to help her, so I could help myself.

Once the door closed, I sprung into action. I first rushed toward the kitchen where I'd laid my Blackberry, still wondering how they'd connected Dominique to me. I snatched the phone up, and started dialin'. I needed to dump the remainin' cars even if it meant burnin'em.

After calling the first guy, I thought about callin' Ansar. I clicked end on the call and saw that a text had come in. I opened it, thinkin', more money more problems. It was C.J. The text read:

```
    B there soon- headed to Atlanta.
Just so u know-I played 2nd base 4 years.
I'm moving in until we both move back to
Miami. See ya soon. C.J.
```

"Dayum!" I shouted, throwin' the phone across the counter.

Sixteen...

Dominique

"**D**ominique Lewis! Dominique Lewis!"

Subconsciously, I heard my name being called, but refused to open my eyes. My sudden state of depression had me giving up all hope.

The voice soon became clearer. It was deep, sincere, and soothing as he called out again, "Dominique."

I hopped up off the thin mattress and glared at the bald-headed officer strangely. It was Officer Reynolds who reminded me of a black Santa Claus. He was cheesing in front of my cell, rubbing on his thirty-pound stomach like he needed to burp. He had about fifty keys on a big ring that he always swung back and forth, as he opened the door to my cell.

"You're outta here, sweetie."

"Me?" I asked like I didn't believe him.

"Yes you. You made bail. You got a job to do."

He smiled. And I said nothing.

It had to be true if it was coming from Reynolds. He'd been my friend for the nearly seven days that I was in.

He had looked out real good…giving me extra phone time…food from his house…and an extra pillow to lay my head.

"I'm out for real?" I asked one more time, following him out of the central cell area and over to the discharge area.

He laughed hard, making his overlapping belly rise even more. "Yes, you're leaving," he said. "Don't forget all the stuff you promised me," he reminded. "I can't wait to see you on the big screen."

"I won't forget," I said, hoping I'd never see his big ass again.

I felt relieved that someone had actually come to my rescue. In my heart I knew it was either Yuri or Rapheal. I had called them both, so at the moment either would work. I needed plenty of support since I'd been charged with conspiracy to commit murder. Semo's cousin indentified me in the line-up without any doubts. He gave details about what time he saw me at the Marriott with Semo, what room we were in, and how long after that he was shot and killed.

I played it off to a tee-saying that maybe it was my sister. But it didn't work. In America you're guilty until proven innocent. I was booked, arraigned and went before the judge; unfortunately with a court appointed lawyer. When I called Rapheal he told me he'd send his lawyer over, and I'd be out soon. Yuri on the other hand didn't make things easy. The first time I called him, he didn't want to talk…he even pretended not to know me. When I called him again the number was changed. So, I didn't know who put up the $25,000 bail amount.

It didn't take long for my release to be processed. Reynolds claimed he pushed things through. I'd already changed back into the same, dirty, dingy jean skirt, and pullover sweater that I'd been locked up in. And my short cut had lost any curls it had, and smelled like it needed a wash.

"Take it easy," Reynolds called out as I waited for the iron gate to open, releasing me into the open area where families waited.

"Can't wait to see you on the big screen!" he shouted as I stepped out a free woman.

At first I chuckled inside at how even in my depressed state I could come up with some bullshit. I'd told Reynolds I'd just been cast into Tyler Perry's new movie and that the hotel thing was a big mix up. I gave him fake dates, titles and everything about when the movie would be released and how he would get shout outs for looking out for me. Thinking about all I'd said was funny at first until I adjusted my vision.

"Shit," was all I could say when I saw her standing there. It felt like my heart had dropped into my belly. Immediately, I turned away from her then took off down the hall in search of a bathroom. The only thing that came to mind was toilet tissue. It was the only thing that could be used in place of a pillow. *I had to be pregnant*, I told myself.

It didn't take long for me to work my magic. By the time I waltzed out of the bathroom, I had three rolls of tissue stuffed into my panties, and my mother was right there at the door staring at me strangely. She eyed me from the top of my matted hair down to the bottom heel of my boot.

"When did you cut your hair like Monique's?"

"A few days ago," I answered feeling like I needed my shades to hide my deceit. I especially wanted my favorite pair that had been missing.

"Who did you kill?" she asked me sharply.

"I didn't kill anyone," I said, making my voice sound like I was offended. "It's all a lie. They trying to set me up."

"Ummm huh. Sure."

Her gaze wasn't a good one. It was disbelieving and followed by a nasty frown.

I skipped the subject. "How did you know I was here?" I asked inquisitively.

"Rapheal told me. He sent me. It was his money," she added angrily. "Definitely not mine."

She turned her back on me, and walked toward the red exit sign. I followed her swift movements wondering what she was thinking and if she had suspicions about the hair cut. I wanted to ask her where Rapheal was, but she opened the door too fast and stepped into the wind.

"It's freezing out here," I said, bursting through the double doors of the precinct. I crossed my arms and rubbed them continuously trying to drum up some heat. The wind blew rowdily, proving that some real bad weather was approaching.

My mother didn't comment nor did she look back to see if I was keeping up. She rushed off down the steep steps, and out into the street headed toward what I assumed would be her car. Hell, I didn't know 'cause she wasn't saying shit to me. She could've been trying to leave me.

I focused on staying warm, rushing swiftly behind her. At least she had on a short black, pea coat which appeared to be warm. The weather had changed drastically. It normally didn't get too cold in Georgia until Christmas actually rolled around. But it already felt like forty degrees or below had settled in on the city. With just a few weeks to go before Thanksgiving, I knew I needed to unpack my box of coats at Rapheal's.

Finally, my mother slowed her pace and crossed a small, narrow street where five cars were packed one behind the other. I recognized her Honda and ran toward the passenger side. Luckily, she opened up and I hopped in rubbing my hands together briskly back and forth.

As soon as she started the engine, I turned on the heat. "So Ma, you talk to Sedrick?" I was trying my best to be nice.

"No."

"What about Shawna? Does she know I was locked up?"

"No."

It was clear she didn't want to talk. I watched her focus on the road like a rooky driver pulling from her space with both hands clutched to the wheel. Besides, I'd turned up the radio to hear what they were saying about the upcoming storm. While they talked about the hurricane warning, I stared out the window up into the dark sky. It was getting darker by the minute and the rainfall had just started. Even though it could've been dangerous, it seemed like perfect thinking weather. I sat back and weighed my life options.

After riding in silence for the first ten minutes, I tried once again to strike up a conversation asking her when Rapheal informed her I'd been locked up.

"Yesterday," she announced like I was bothering her.

"And when did he give you the money?" I added.

"Today."

"So, did he say when the lawyer would call me?"

"Not sure."

"Damn, Ruby!" I shouted. "What's with the one word answers?"

"I'm trying to concentrate, Dominique," she told me angrily. Hurricane Monique is headed our way."

"Damn, they named the Hurricane Monique? How appropriate," I said underneath my breath.

The wind was kicking up a notch and the sky had progressively gotten darker; just like my mother's spirits. It seemed the mention of Monique's name put her into a deeper funk. She was still holding onto the wheel tightly and looking straight ahead. She appeared to be too afraid to even look off to the side. Or maybe she just didn't want to face me.

I felt kinda bad when I saw tears streaming down her

right cheek. I wanted to console her, but in our family we never did any of that. Or at least I was never taught, or got it from her. For the first time since we'd been in the car she took one hand off the wheel and wiped her tears. The rain started coming down hard almost a sign that more tears would be coming from my mother's eye's.

"Ma, I know it hurts," I said softly. "But we gotta let time run its course.

"The police called," she uttered real slowly and in a softer tone.

"Which police?" My eye brows wrinkled up scarily.

"The Bahamian police."

"Oh," I said like it didn't bother me. "What did they say?"

"They said that the investigation has been going well, and that autopsy showed skin underneath Monique's fingernails." She paused getting more emotional. "She must've fought off her assailant."

Without further delay, she burst into tears and pulled her head closer to the wheel. I wanted to tell her to pull over because the wipers didn't seem to be working too well. Instead, I asked a stupid question, "They say anything else?"

"Yeah. The baby is still missing. But they're certain she was born alive."

I saw her getting choked up again just as she got off at the downtown exit. We'd never discussed where she was taking me so it was time to break the news before she made the left turn headed to my apartment. "Ma…"

She cut me off. Her words stung me like a violent bee.

"When did you last talk to Monique?" she asked me suspiciously. Gladly, she never looked me in the eye.

"We had lunch before she left for the Bahamas."

"Oh, you did?"

She looked surprised. I turned to look out the window.

168

"That's funny," she said in a weird tone. "I talked to her the day before she died and she said you guys hadn't spoken in over a month."

It turned out that my mother had caught me in yet another lie. I was tired of pretending, especially about Rapheal. She was headed in the wrong direction and I needed her to turn around quickly before we both got caught in the storm. She would find out sooner or later that Rapheal and I were indeed a couple.

"Ruby, turn around," I told her. I don't live at my old spot anymore." I hesitated. "I live with Rapheal."

She turned to look at me like a monster had taken over her body. Her eyes were no longer on the road. The car slowed drastically, and the windshield wipers started making a loud, irritating noise.

"Dominique, Rapheal doesn't want you. He was in love with your sister."

I took her comment as a challenge. "He does and I can show you better than I can tell you," I shot back. "My stuff is there now. Why do you think he bailed me out?"

She hunched her shoulders but still didn't turn the car around. We were less than two miles from his place so I'd decided I would walk if she didn't make a u-turn. "Ruby, just be happy for me," I said, turning half-way around in my seat to face her.

"You're one sick girl. But guess what, I don't care. You're not my daughter she said. I think you had something to do with your sister's death."

My breathing damn near stopped. Her suspicions obviously ran deep. "Ma…I mean Ruby, that's a terrible thing to say," I said sadly. That was it. I wasn't calling her Ma anymore just to appease her.

Just then my mother hit a u-turn in the middle of the street and the champagne colored Jeep Cherokee turned

169

quickly behind. It had been following us jumping in and out of traffic since we got off the exit, but now had me worrying like crazy. The pouring rain made it difficult to make out faces, plus the fact that they kept a good distance behind.

"Ruby, listen, I think somebody is following us. So when you drop me off in front of the door be careful," I told her.

She never flinched. She simply remained in a daze, driving like someone else had control of the wheel and her soul for that matter.

When my mother stopped the Honda in front of the door to Rapheal's building, I searched from the car for Terrance frantically. The only person I could see through the pouring rain was a worker polishing the marble floors with a steam cleaner. I looked to my left noticing that the Cherokee had stopped several yards behind us. Their lights were on, but nobody moved. I didn't have an umbrella or nothing to cover my head. "Where's Terrance?" I screamed.

My mother turned her head robotically toward me. She looked like she'd been possessed as strands of hair stuck straight up on her head.

"Get out Dominique," she told me like those were the last words she'd ever speak to me again.

I wanted to fuss. Argue to the end…but people were watching me from behind. I thought about the Allen Temple boys. I thought about Yuri. I thought about the Atlanta based detectives, Barnes and Carter. Then I thought about the Bahamian Police. I took it all in and realized most likely, it was the Allen Temple crew.

Within a flash, I jumped from the car, running like hell into the building. Debris flew from everywhere making it difficult for me to make it to the front with ease. When I pulled on the door, the force of the wind hindered me even more. "Shit, Shit, shit," I said using my hands to shield me from the pouring rain. I kept my good eye on the Cherokee that remained in place, while my mother pulled off not giving a shit if I made it inside.

Finally, I was in, and the heavy door shut forcefully behind me.

I kept looking behind me all the way to the elevator making sure no one ran up on me. When the doors opened, his presence startled me. Terrance was getting off and shot me a shady look. He appeared to be standoffish like he didn't want to speak. However, I couldn't worry about that petty shit. I had bigger fish to fry but have his ass checked later by Rapheal.

As soon as I made it to the twentieth floor, the door to Rapheal's was opening slowly. He opened the door gradually with a drink in his hand. "I need one, too," I told him, brushing past him and into the penthouse that smelled of fresh Lysol and Pine-Sol.

"Who cleaned the place?" I asked casually.

"That's not important," he said to me.

"Oh." I shrugged my shoulders. "What is? Me?"

I grinned and flipped off my boots.

His face was sunken in like he'd had a rough day. And from the looks of things he'd drank a half-bottle of Hennessey all alone. The T.V. was up high blasting the updates on the hurricane. It seemed like the water had gotten harder and was now beating against the window roughly.

"Terrance called you, huh?"

"Of course. That's his job," he said in a disturbed voice.

I couldn't help but notice how sexy he looked in his long, tan silk robe. It had his initials and securely hid his fabulous abs the way he was tightly wrapped up. I figured I would get comfortable and we'd enjoy the rain together; especially if all the lights went out.

"I need a shower bad," I said, pulling my sweater over my head."

"Uhhh, that's probably not a good idea."

"And why not," I barked. "I'm wet!"

"My lawyer called," he announced skeptically. "I'm glad I was able to help..." He paused. "But you know your case had nothin' to do with me Dominique."

"And."

"And." He repeated. "We never discussed you being here. When you left, I thought I'd gotten you caught up in some shit and wanted to do my part to get you out of it."

He stopped completely and glared at the flat screen. It showed images of a small town being trashed by the storm. Shit was flying everywhere and looked scary on screen. Just then thunder sounded. I jumped, moving far away from the window.

He didn't care if light-poles started crashing through, he wanted to get his point across. He moved closer to me, moving all my things back into one area. The area near the door.

"But it looks like you got yourself into some mess." He paused again and looked toward the long hallway leading to his bedroom. "I can't get involved with dudes on some re-taliation tip. I heard about Semo," he ended, looking at me funny.

I didn't know what to say and could've been bought for a penny. Suddenly things got worse. A petite, dark-skinned woman looking to be in her early thirties waltzed from the bedroom area, with a robe on that matched Rapheal's. It too had initials. Initials that read C.J.

"What the fuck is this, Rapheal?" I yelled like a mad woman.

"This is C.J," he introduced.

"Why is she here?" the tramp called C.J. asked in a serious tone.

"Don't worry. She's leaving," he had the nerve to say, then grabbed C.J.'s hand. "It's a bad storm out, not really safe for anybody."

She mugged me hard. I mugged her back. Little did he know, she was going, not me. I belonged, I told myself just before everything went black. The lights were out leaving me and C.J to battle in the dark.

Seventeen...

Dominique

Spread eagle was the position of my legs pressed against the edge of the mattress. I was ass-naked, on my back, laying across the bed. As the sunlight made its way through the small windows inside Yuri's bedroom I could only smile. My nipples had hardened and were perked up directly to the ceiling. He was bent down, knees on the floor with his tongue flirting with the hairs on my treasure.

"Go 'head. Eat it," I stated seeming impatient.

"Like this," he teased. Yuri lifted his head for a split second then took a long stroke ending with a flicker of my hungry clit.

"Yessssssss," I hissed like a snake, making a nice arch with my back. "C'mon, Yuri. More," I begged, then grabbed the back of his head.

His dreads felt rough, almost the feel of a brillo pad. But I didn't care. I wanted tongue. His tongue. He hadn't even done much yet, but I got horny just knowing he would make me cum. Licking was what Yuri did best, and had gotten good at it over the last few days. Before I knew it, he'd grabbed me roughly by my thighs and pulled his morning

175

feast closer for him to eat. He dove in tongue first, sending me into oblivion.

I shouted loudly as he gave it to me with long, thick stokes and fast, sucking movements. Instantly, my body got to moving around in a jittery state 'cause I couldn't control my movements. Every lick felt extra good and almost erased all my problems for the moment.

"Uh…uh…uh, shit!" I yelled showing my pleasure. My breathing intensified and I kept raising myself off the bed. "Ohhhhh… yes…yes…" I lifted my left leg high in the air and Yuri clutched the bottom of my ass sucking like he needed to get all the chicken off a bone.

"Ahhh…ahhh, it-it-feel-feels so good-Yuri," I stuttered, feeling my body start to quiver. Juices exploded-he never gave up- only pulled me closer. "Oh yes…fuck me," Yuri!" I shouted as he dove deeper. I meant with his tongue but he must've took my words literally. He flipped me over yanked me downward as he plunged inside me trying to balance himself from the floor.

I fired my ass back up against his dick, taking all of him in. I was surprised at how Yuri was working his shit and how good his piece felt. Maybe this was the day. Maybe he'd hit the spot. Sweat poured from our bodies as we fucked like two horny jackrabbits…fuckin' at top speed.

"Get in there damnit, get in there!" I shouted, backing it up harder than imaginable.

Just like that Yuri exploded, with his body going into a state of shock. He remained stiff while I kept pumping, hoping I would explode, too.

Finally he gave out, fell back on the floor with a wide grin on his wet face. I got an instant attitude and hopped back on the bed, pulling the red sheet over my aching body.

When Yuri got off the floor, I watched his naked butt cheeks tighten as he stopped, yawned, and placed his hands high above his head. He had his back turned to me as he grabbed his cell, and scrolled down to check messages. He grunted, making negative remarks about a text he read. Every time he flexed, sweat dripped down the side of his small, but muscular frame. It was the first time, I had seen him completely naked, and the first time we'd slept cuddled up throughout the night. Normally, he wasn't a cuddly type nigga. I really wasn't either. But it seemed like I'd settled for sloppy seconds.

We had the craziest relationship. I'd call, he wouldn't answer. When he did answer he would confirm if he was staying at his place for the week. I was surprised we'd hooked up after he pulled the ultimate diss, not showing up to bail me out. I guess it was all good 'cause he came through and I'd been chilling with him all week since Rapheal kicked me out his spot.

I felt lost, not on top of my game anymore. Rapheal had me in a place I didn't wanna be. I hated to admit it. But the feelings were real.

I was in love.

In love with Rapheal.

Yuri jetted back onto the bed shortly after I'd made the bleak revelation to myself of falling for a cheater. Rapheal no doubt had always made it seem like he was off limits; a one woman man. Yet, he was anything but that. I had never loved anything in my life. At least never felt like it.

Yuri hopped back on the bed and played around with my backside after seeing me turn flat on my stomach. Pretending to fall back asleep would keep me from round two, which was useless, and allow me to think about Rapheal in peace. I was heated. Fired up... that he dissed me for a lame bitch named C.J.

My mind flipped back a week earlier to the night when she appeared in her silky robe. When she showed up out of nowhere. I took it easy at first, thinking she would be the one leaving the penthouse. It reminded me of a reality T.V show where emotions were high and you assumed the other girl was being kicked out of the house. When Rapheal gave me a look that said I would have to leave, I went ballistic. The electricity went out as a result of the hurricane; and so did my lights. I completely blacked out, jumped on Rapheal's back, beating him in the back of his head until he was able to pry me off. It was understood by my irrational behavior that nobody would sleep peacefully.

I breathed heavily as I rewound the events step by step while Yuri kept rubbing me firmly with his rough feeling hands. The feeling caused me to ease up but it couldn't make me forget. When the truth came out, C.J. told me she'd been fuckin' Rapheal for nearly four years, all along while he dealt with my sister. "Damn, bitch don't you have any morals?" I remembered asking her. She blew me off and clung to Rapheal's shoulder. I vowed to get revenge for Monique. Cheating on her with anyone other than me was a major violation.

She would pay, I told myself as Yuri yanked me by my neck like a rag doll and asked me what I was thinking about.

"Nothing," I lied.

"Something's on yuh mind. Speak."

"No really," I said, closing my eyes and allowing my mind to go back.

Throughout the night it was revealed that Rapheal had major ties to C.J. He had two businesses set up in her name, she had two fancy cars, compliments of Rapheal, and was planning on getting married. I remembered asking him boldly, "If life was so great with C.J., why was my sister your main lady?"

C.J blurted out. "I can't have babies."

It shocked the shit out of her when I revealed that I

was pregnant with Rapheal's child, too. Her eyes lit up, asking, "What are you gonna do about it, Rapheal?"

She was angry and I felt good knowing I had one up on him until he told me, "We'd get a blood test done just to make sure it was his."

After that, I sighed like his comment didn't bother me. It seemed like I'd been pretending to be pregnant for months. In Rapheal's mind, he obviously believed what I'd told him at the funeral about being two months pregnant. But really, I prayed daily some of his semen had slipped to my ovaries.

We all ended up sleeping in chairs until the morning shone through the windows. Immediately Rapheal had my things taken downstairs, and had a caravan ready to take me back to my spot. My mind shot back to the same Jeep Cherokee that waited out front. Luckily, the occupants were asleep and I made it out of there alive. I had the cabby drop me at Yuri's fearing for my life. The last thing I remembered was calling Rapheal back and telling him we would be together whether he wanted to or not.

I know I had one up on C.J. since she was incapable of conceiving. And I also had one up on her because of Yuri. I just needed to break the news that I wanted her done.

Yuri was still in phase three of massaging my back, and slipped his fingers in between the crack of my ass. He was like a race horse when it came to fuckin', just couldn't hit it in the right spot.

Out of nowhere he flipped me over, told me that he wanted me to be his lady. I was shocked 'cause he never had a main bitch in his life. But when he started talking about how he wanted to protect me and how he wanted to take care of the Allen Temple boys, I couldn't say no.

"No worries," he said, "Even if we gotta do dem one by one, they'll be handled."

"Ummm hmph," I uttered, obviously liking what I heard.

"Is that a moan 'cause yuh want some of this?"

He pressed his hardened dick against my leg.

"No Yuri," I whined. "I wanna rest for a minute.

For the first time in months, I felt safe. He went on talking about what he'd heard on the streets about Semo's retaliation and how it wasn't gonna work. The way Yuri talked, it was like we would be the next Bonnie and Clyde.

I wanted to tell him about my new hit, C.J., but I didn't know why I would say I wanted her done. He interrupted, telling me about our next mark.

He looked right into my questionable eyes then repeated his name again. Everything stopped. Even my heartbeat.

I felt like I wanted to puke when he said, "Yeah, he gotta go. Rapheal did some dirty shit."

There was no reaction from me. I just leaned back further on the bed and pressed a pillow forcefully over my face. Allowing Yuri to see my true expression would be a terrible mistake.

"Yo, what the fuck yuh doing," he said abruptly, snatching the pillow from my grip. He swung it hard, long, and it landed on the dresser making a glass frame crash to the floor.

"Why'd you do that?" I asked with a slight attitude. My body rose up and I found myself sitting on my butt.

" 'Cause you flakin'!" he shouted.

"What the fuck does that mean!"

"It means yuh not on your game. Yuh gettin' soft just 'cause yuh know the nigga." He paused for a few seconds, staring me down. "It's all on yuh face Dominique."

"I'm just not feeling it," I admitted. "He's the father of my sister's baby."

180

My voice fluttered and I got all emotional on him, grabbing his shoulders. I started ranting about how my mother was hoping the Bahamian police would eventually find my niece and of course wanted her to have her father in her life. Little did he know my mother wasn't speaking to me, or answering my calls. But it sounded good to Yuri. He listened briefly, mostly warily before rendering his decision.

"Yo, he sold me some cars that weren't legit and now the shit is bringing me heat. I warned that nigga to have his shit together, but he didn't listen. Now he gotta be dealt with."

My eyes bulged, assuring him that I had no idea.

"Yeah. The Maserati, Ferrari…everything I've ever got from the nigga. Yo, he knew his shit wasn't in order like he portrayed. Now if I drive the shit and get caught, that's my ass."

"Damn, Yuri, that is fucked up. But you gotta kill him?" I questioned. "He's gonna be a father soon."

All of a sudden he pulled away from my embrace. He showed no emotion. "Man, that shit ain't my fuckin' problem!" he shouted. "He still gotta go!"

"But why?" I pleaded like a four year old.

"It's principle." He froze and shot me a harsh look. "Yuh in or not?"

A lump formed in my throat. I knew if I said no, there'd be hell to pay. "Yes," I said in a softer tone. "You know I'm in."

I grinned with an artificial smile as he gave me all the important information about how it would go down. He was more precise than ever before, giving step by step instructions to make things go smoothly. Inside, I'd gotten sick. But I remained wide-eyed and kept nodding like I was really paying attention to what he was saying. Deep down inside, I wondered if I would really go through with it.

Eighteen...

Rapheal

For a Wednesday mornin' my street buzzed with energy. People walked the block along with the many service trucks that either swept the grounds or kept the building in tip-top shape. A huge trash truck blocked my view as I pulled up to the gate to exit the garage beneath my buildin'. When I pulled slightly past the gate, a car with two younger men were pullin' in. I pressed on the brakes, abruptly bringin' the old '98 Camry to a complete stop. Watchin' my back had become a habit. Nothin' was safe anymore. I eyed the dudes thoroughly for a few seconds. They checked me too then used their code to pull into the garage.

Slowly, I made my way out onto the street and hooked a right turn passing the front of my buildin'. Terrance wasn't on duty. It was the older white guy Fred, who stood out front showin' he wasn't as sharp as Terrance. I waved to him casually as I passed by then whipped a u-turn to circle the block again.

He looked at me and frowned almost askin' the question everyone else would want to know. Why was I sportin' a Camry? Little did they know, the Bentley had been put away in an old girlfriend's garage, and Ansar had picked up my other cars in the middle of the night. He was and had been for days in charge of disposal. Word on the street was that the cops had locked up a few people that I'd sold cars to on routine traffic stops. It was confirmation that the VIN number situation must've been uncovered by the Feds. I had called my motor vehicle ladies, but none returned my calls. It was clear why.

The customs agents, Feds and the local police were all apparently hip to my car ring, so riding legit was crucial. I'd picked up the silver Camry from a dealership just days before and paid the five grand on the spot. There were just a few more things to take care of to liquidate all the businesses.

It would all play out well if I kept things intact, I told myself hoppin' onto a street where I could finally do 55 mph. I still kept thinkin', everythin' would be fine and really no big deal as long as I kept myself out of jail. Startin' up a new company in another six months wasn't the big problem. I would hire all new front men, get my paper right to get at least six new hot off the assembly line cars, and get shit poppin' again once the smoke cleared. I would just have to find a few good women all over again with good credit. As usual, I'd have them put the businesses in their name, so if shit got rough they'd take the heat.

No sooner than I started thinkin' about women my cell rang. With a quick glance at the screen I took my eyes off the road. It was C.J. still tryin' to change my mind. I wasn't. It was final. I'd already booked her on the one o'clock flight back to Miami, so I let it ring until it stopped.

Suddenly, it rang again. I frowned. I hated stalker broads. My eyes darted to the screen again. This time it showed unknown.

I answered anyway knowing I shouldn't have, but with major bass in my voice. "Hello," I said, turnin' onto a small side street.

The person on the other end thought shit was a game. They said nothin', and only light breathin' could be heard.

I hung up and kept driving to my destination. I was only five minutes away from an unexpected meetin' that already had me puzzled. But my jokester wouldn't give up. My cell rang again. After checking the call, it said unknown again. I pressed 'no' and turned onto the block at the far end of the street.

When I pulled up to Mrs. Lewis' house it seemed strange that her front door was open. It took a good five to ten minutes for me to even step from the car. I stayed put, monitorin' the cars passing by and the small amount of foot traffic breezin' past her front lawn.

Finally, I hopped out, zipped my waist length black, mink, and jetted up the stairs to the front door. The temperature hadn't reached forty for the day, but I'd worn my mink anyway because C.J. wanted us to match before we left the apartment. I could see Mrs. Lewis through the screen but called out to her anyway.

"It's me Mrs. Lewis. I'm here."

She stopped wipin' down the large brown chest on the living room floor, and looked my way. At least she gave up a half of a smile lettin' me know she was glad to see me.

"C'mon in," she said with her voice draggin'. "I was wonderin' when you would get here."

As soon as I walked inside the house she started hummin' one of the church songs played at the funeral. I couldn't recall the name of it, but she started back to cleanin' again like I wasn't there. It seemed odd hearin' her sing. She'd never done that before when I was around. Once again she turned her back to me, but I could still get a glimpse of her face from the side. Her face appeared flush and worn, almost as if she hadn't slept in days.

She started movin' around the livin' room slowly then made her way to the kitchen, still never givin' me eye contact. I followed as she told me, "Take that coat off. What is it, rabbit?"

"It's fur." I laughed lightly. "But I can't stay long," I said, leanin' on the wall just outside the kitchen area.

I couldn't wait for her to tell me what the problem was. She'd called me at 7:00 a.m. soundin' like she'd been cryin'. She said she couldn't sleep…hadn't slept in days. And that she had somethin' significant to tell me. She'd helped me out a few nights when I needed to talk to someone about my missin' child, or the child that I had no clue if she lived or not.

"So, what's the urgency? "I asked. "Is somethin' wrong?"

"Is it…" she began just as her phone rang.

I hadn't been in the house five minutes and had already become impatient. Truth was Mrs. Lewis wasn't my mother and wouldn't become my mother-in-law. So, showin' up was a common courtesy.

She answered, and immediately her mood changed for the better. By the way she talked, I knew I'd showed up at the wrong time. She stared at me as she talked as if the other person was talking about me.

"Yeah. He knows. He's right here," she said, then passed me the phone.

I knew it was Sed. *Fuck! Fuck Fuck!* I kept thinkin' to myself. I had given his mom the money needed to bail him out on Monday, and knew it was a matter of time before he caught up with me. He was still a liability, but one that had to be bailed out before he told every single detail about my operation. Unfortunately for me, he knew names, addresses, and shippin' sites of my German accomplice. I cleared my throat, placin' the receiver to my ear ready to fake.

"What's up my man? I see my money paid off."

"No doubt," he said in good spirits. "Dawg, why you did-

186

n't tell me you was gonna stop by mom's house?"

"Man, how was I supposed to call you? You did get rid of that phone like I told you, right?"

"No doubt. I'ma get a new one by tomorrow. Oh, and thanks for the money you left with my mother."

"No problem, Sed. You know you my man. You a'ight?"

"I'm straight," he answered, soundin' better than ever before. "I'll be better though when I get with this lawyer and he tells me how to keep my black ass from going back to jail," he laughed.

"It's gonna all work out. I just need a few days to get some business straight then we'll hook up. You feel me?"

"No doubt..."

He paused, lettin' me know he was about to say somethin' stupid.

"Man, shit is rough. I'm tryna pump myself up thinking all is good. But I got seven counts of car theft charges rangin' from fraud to transport charges. Make this shit go away man," he uttered usin' a different tone.

I stayed calm. "Sed, you got my word man. You got my word," I repeated. My eyes shifted to Mrs. Lewis again who looked like she'd heard enough about Sed. Her concerns remained elsewhere. "Lemme holla at your mother. Get back with me tomorrow, a'ight?"

It took me another three minutes to pry his talkin' ass off the phone. He was a problem for sure. I knew it. It was just another bullet on my list that needed to be handled. I hung up, turned to Mrs. Lewis and asked, "So, what did you want to talk to me about?"

"Rapheal, I'm gonna be honest with you..."

She paused, keepin' her head lowered then said, "It hurts me to even say it."

"Go ahead," I urged. "I'm listening."

"…There's no easy way to say it." Her voice kept trailing off as she spoke with a tremblin' sound. "I think Dominique had something to do with Monique's death."

A sudden coldness crept through my veins. And my mind didn't know how to process the news. Instantly I had flashbacks of Monique and Dominique's relationship. It was always messy. It was always a fuss or a fight. And the ultimate…Dominique really wanted me. I remained in deep thought, not saying a word, only digestin' what Mrs. Lewis had said.

"I know it's hard to believe," she continued, "but it's just that feeling that a mother has. An instinct. A mother's love."

She kept shakin' her head back and forth in a shameful kinda way.

"Now, I know I can't prove it, but I already got some people on it. I already told the police down there in the Bahamas. They don't have no jurisdiction here, but got some clues."

"Like what?"

She started shakin' her finger back and forth with speed.

"That DNA stuff is something serious. They said they can test Dominique's skin to see if it matches the skin that was beneath Monique's fingernails."

Her voice quieted, followed by a sudden melt-down. The first tear fell at a decent pace. After that it seemed like a stream flooded her saddened face.

"Aw, luv, it's gonna be okay," I said in an attempt to console her.

But she continued, "They said Monique fought off her assailant. And that's why she had skin underneath her fingernails."

"Nah.." I said, tryin' to make myself disbelieve what

she'd said. "You think she would really do somethin' like that? To her own sister," I added with a dumbfounded expression.

In my heart, I knew Dominique could. And would. And probably did. I had seen her devious ways and her demented thoughts when it came to getting what she wanted. As I thought more about her underhanded behavior Mrs. Lewis cried softly while tryin' to get her remainin' words out. When I saw her reach over to clutch at her stomach I reached out to her, but she bounced back like she was getting' herself together.

"Rapheal, if anybody can get her to confess, it's you," she sniffled. She paused, stood straight up then shot me a funny look. "I know she wants to be with you," she revealed. "She wanted to replace Monique."

I really didn't know what to think or how to respond. I wanted her to give me more since I was cautious about my words. "Ummmm…What do you mean?"

"The day I bailed her out of jail she refused to go home. She said her new home was with you. That's why I dropped her there. Did you make her leave?"

"Look, Mrs. Lewis. I don't know how to tell you this…but Dominique is mental. I mean she's really done some stuff to make me a believer."

Her doubtful expression told me she needed more to be convinced. She started cleaning up again and moved to her left to fold some unused tablecloths.

"She's been comin' on to me. Even before Monique's death," I snitched. "I thought I was helpin' by bailin' her out of jail. But that was it. I made her leave the very next mornin'."

I had both my hands in the air as I pleaded showin' my sign of surrender. I wanted her to stop with the household shit and be straight up with me. "I'm serious. That was it," I said again.

She stopped folding the table cloth. And with a gritty stance looked me directly in the eyes. "You messing with that girl."

"No Ma'am. You got my word. There's somethin' seriously wrong with her. I know that's your child but she doesn't take no for an answer. She's even been callin' my mother in Louisiana," I plead. "How she got the number, I'm not sure."

"Oh, you have no idea what she's capable of."

"And to top…"

I caught myself mid-sentence. I almost revealed what my mother actually said. Truth was-Dominique told my mother she was going to be a grandmother soon, and that she was pregnant with my child. Dominique was so full of shit I didn't know what to believe. I knew now I'd have to stop ignoring her calls. We needed to talk, for several reasons; one I needed to know if she really had anythin' to do with Monique's death. And two, if she did, what happened to my daughter? Lastly, the bitch needed to take a pregnancy test, and me-a paternity test.

"I'll talk to her Mrs. Lewis…see what I can find out."

"Oh, you don't know my daughter. She's sneaky and will catch on to you sooner than you think."

"I'll think of somethin'," I told Mrs. Lewis. "I know how to be slick too." I ended with a smile then moved toward the door.

She stopped me, movin' in front of my body with a tablecloth in her hand. "Have you called the police again lately to see if they have any leads on the baby?"

"No Ma'am," I said sadly. "I think I've sorta given up."

"Don't give up. You never know. Lemme make you

190

something to eat " she added out of the blue.

It was obvious she didn't want me to leave. She started movin' faster with her folding and talked a mile a minute. "You gotta find a way to get her to confess. I'd bc willing to bet my life she was in the Bahamas when Monique was murdered."

It was like the light-bulb effect had me by the balls. Maybe she had gone to the Bahamas? That shouldn't be too difficult to prove, I told myself. Even if the police had to get involved. I just smiled at Mrs. Lewis and rushed out of the door saying my goodbyes with my feet on the move.

"Call me as soon as you hear something, okay," she shouted behind me. "And I told Sed, to come home to stay. He's with some nappy head girl over by Stonecrest Mall already."

I listened but didn't respond as I walked backwards tryin' to make it to my car. C.J.'s plane would be leaving soon and I still had an important stop to make. So I hoped lunch time traffic would be mellow. I started the engine, thinking about Sed. At least he fell for my lies, I snickered pullin' from the curb.

My Blackberry was like crack. Addictive. I grabbed it as soon as I hopped back in the Camry to see if any text messages had come through. There was one from C.J. saying that she hadn't gotten back to the apartment yet, but was on the way. I knew she was tryna pull some shit, but she was leavin', whether she wanted to or not. It was my fault that my extra stop had taken so long.

I found myself ballin' out of the lot forgettin' that I wasn't in one of my high-powered vehicles. Luckily, there wasn't much traffic and I was only about ten minutes away from my spot. I turned the music up loud and ironically Donny Hathaway's, *For All We Know* came on. He was known for writing sad songs. Songs that made me think of death.

Listenin' to the lyrics made me think of my baby Monique; especially when he sang, "Tomorrow may never come."

"Damn, I really did love that girl," I mumbled to myself while pickin' up speed. She always had my back and I believe would've made a good wife.

I even thought about how when I initially met her, how she was gonna be a side-babe, one who would sign paperwork and be the front for my company, just as C.J. did in Miami, and Melissa in Vegas. That all changed when she warmed my heart with her laid back personality; and one who stayed out of my business.

Luckily, time passed quickly and some more upbeat music blared through the small system. I turned that shit up loud. It was Luda, my boy 'cause I'd found myself damn near in tears listenin' to Donny, somethin' I didn't do often. I slowed down when I noticed the cars in front of me inching toward my buildin'. It was hard for me to see since cars were backed up about a half mile back. When I stuck my head out the window, I saw lights flashing. Police lights. Damn, I breathed with nervous energy. Maybe it was a road block, since we were still at least inchin' along. Then my heart beat faster when the thought entered my mind that maybe five-o was lookin' for me.

Every second I came up with a new thought as I got closer to the action. Indeed the police were on the scene, and an ambulance too. As I pulled up to the officer who allowed the cars to pass by, he signaled for me to roll my window completely down. He was about my height with a monstrous belly, and a mean look on his grill. "You live around here?"

192

he asked me.

"Ah yeah," I answered, tryin' to dodge his movements. My goal was to get a good look at the action going on behind him. "What happened?"

At that moment my heart plummeted and my eyes zoomed in. Fear infiltrated my body. I spotted the rented Chevy Malibu over by the entrance to my garage. It was the Malibu I'd rented for C.J. while she was in town. Without warning, I put the car in drive and darted over to the scene as far as I could go. Three police cruisers blocked me from going any further. I could hear the officer who'd worked the checkpoint shoutin' and comin' behind me at top speed.

"Wait, wait! What the hell are you doing?"

I had my hands in the air when I jetted out the Camry shoutin', "I know her! I know her, man!"

My face was bawled up and full of emotion so they knew my sentiment was real. I broke into a slight trot getting closer to the Malibu second by second. I knew I wouldn't get too much closer 'cause about five plain clothes officers had made their bodies a barricade around the car. It didn't matter how big or small they were, my eyes had gotten the perfect view. That's when I saw it. I saw blood. Deep, red blood, gushin' from the side her head.

My knees buckled at the gruesome scene. And I just held my head between my hands and let out a loud moan. "Aw naw…Aw…naw!"

C.J.'s upper body was pressed against the steerin' wheel, and her eyes wide open showin' complete fear. She was dead. No doubt, but by who? Bullets had obviously shattered the broken glass on the driver's side window and she was hit just where they'd planned.

I started giving everyone around me cold stares; officer's, bystanders, and even workers from my building. Everyone seemed to be yellin' at me, wanting to know how I knew her. My feet had a mind of their own 'cause I could no longer think. I started walkin' backwards wonderin' who had shot C.J. in broad daylight tryin' to enter the garage. Somebody had targeted her. And I was sure... I was next.

Nineteen...

Dominique

If a White Chocolate Mocha with three shots of Expresso couldn't do the trick, nothing would. I sat in the back of the Starbucks at a table for two with my shades on pretending to feel good about myself. The three full length sheets of paper that had been delivered anonymously to my mailbox had my full attention. I always made it my business to stop by my place to check the mail, mostly collecting bills. But today somebody snuck me good. Somebody was fuckin' with me. Somebody was trying to be funny. Who? I didn't know. It was however, attention-grabbing even though it was an intentional attempt to call me out. It wasn't a death threat and thankfully no more court papers. It was a full listing of quotes having to do with jealously.

Some were funny. Some made me angry. And some the culprit had even circled in red.

Never waste jealously on a real man; it is the imaginary man that supplants us all in the long run.- George Bernard Shaw.

"Ha! That shit hit home," I told myself and slammed my double shot Expresso onto the table.

In jealously there is more self-love than anything.-Author Unknown

Jealously...a mental cancer. The envious die not once, but as oft as the envied win applause.- Author Anonymous

The jealous are troublesome to others but a torment to themselves.-William Penn

I found myself flinching at the table fighting off the madness. More than expected, the quotes touched me...had me a little fucked up. And they progressively got worse, targeting me personally.

Envy is the most stupid of voices, for there is no single advantage to be gained from it.-Honore de Balzac

Our envy will most likely destroy us and make the person we envy happy to see us suffering_ author unknown <u>unless you kill them, too</u>.-author unknown

The words *unless you kill them too-* covered the bottom of the page. It was an odd handwriting- one that couldn't be made out and written with a dark red pen. Out of the blue, I flipped into a tantrum. I started ripping the pages angrily into the smallest possible pieces wondering who would've sent me the bullshit. My eyes were blood shot red-partially from rage and partially from a lack of sleep. I stopped momentarily and pulled myself together when an older gentleman sat down to my left and whipped a laptop from his bag. I had become so paranoid lately, I scrutinized everyone with a watchful eye. I smiled, sipped my drink, then crossed my legs and played around with the tiny scraps of paper sprawled into the ashtray.

"Hello," I uttered in my sweet voice.

He looked to be in his early fifties so I expected at least a hello. But he gave up no vocals. Just a nod.

It seemed like I lived at Starbucks over the last week, trying to stay awake, attempting to keep myself calm from all the drama. Everybody had me pegged the wrong way, even Shawna. She'd been calling day in and day out, ringing my cell on some psycho shit like I was her man. That's why I finally agreed to meet her for a cup of coffee. After all she was my cousin, and if I could get anybody to believe me, it would be her.

I saw her enter the front door walking real fast and hood-like with a multi-colored scarf thrown across her neck. I attempted to wave her to the back but my cell sounded. It was Yuri again…and just like that, I hit no. I wished for a button on the phone that read; hell no!

"What's up bitch?" Shawna said loudly, coming toward me at full speed.

I got myself together real fast, seeing how she was asking me questions before she even got to the table.

"Bitch," sit down I instructed, swatting her like a fly. "You got everybody in our business." I kept looking around to see who was watching us. The man with the laptop was still typing and paying me no mind.

She sat across from me with tons of questions in her eyes and popping gum hard, and loud all in my face. "First things first. Why you neva told me you was in jail?" she fired, then purposefully leaned over to get a good look at my stomach.

My pillow was in place, but the size of my eyes still increased. Sensing that my explanation about the pregnancy would be complicated, I downplayed it. "Girl, that's next, let's start with the muthufucka who lied on me and had me locked down."

"Speak, hoe. I need to know now."

"Well," I began hesitantly then took a sip of my coffee. "You remember when we went to Magic City, right?"

"Ummm hmm."

"Well the guy I left with, Semo, must've been into

some cruddy shit. We got to the hotel on Peachtree and next thing I knew some big bouncer looking niggas burst in on us and shot his ass."

I expected more drama and animation from Shawna but got none. I wanted her to ask for details so I could lie. She sat there with a blank look on her face wondering where I was going with it all. I wanted her to be herself, loud and irritating; of course spreading everybody else's business in the street.

"So, how'd you end up getting locked up?" she asked with a doubtful expression.

"That's what the fuck I wanna know," I said convincingly. "The police said some guy saw me with him, so they had me participate in a line-up." I gave my shoulders a big shrug like it didn't really affect me. "I got a good lawyer though. So I'ma be straight. Trial starts in January," I added without looking her in the eye.

"You sound so sure," she said to me, still not acting like the Shawna I knew.

"Look, I'm out on bail, right? I got plenty of money, and…"

"…Pregnant," she said loudly, finishing my sentence. "You're fuckin pregnant and I wanna know by who?"

Her voice was firm and her eyes double dared me to lie even though I kept dodging her stare. It was insane how for once she held the upper hand. Her strong gaze on me made me feel like she wouldn't believe me either way. I was willing to bet someone had gotten into her head. I started to speak but the ringing of the phone saved me. I grabbed it and gave it one good look. It was Yuri again. "Hell no," I said out loud.

"So, that's your baby daddy calling," she asked, looking down at my phone.

"Funny." I shot her a sarcastic look.

"Girlll…all I gotta say is you got some shit with you. I

been callin' you since the funeral, only to be ignored," she smacked. "And now you pregnant and won't tell me who the baby's daddy is." Shawna ended with one big smacking sound of the lips and a flip of her weave.

"Look girl, I'ma go 'head and tell you the truth. You bound to find out." I breathed heavily giving her time to show how she was taking it thus far. She still wasn't feeling me. She was sitting straight up in her seat with perfect posture waiting for me to lie.

"It's Rapheal."

"What did you say?" She leaned in slowly, squinting her eyes at me. "Bitch, you said Rapheal? As in your sister's man?"

"Use to be my sister's man," I said in a lower, but dry tone.

Shawna hopped up, clutched her beat-up Gucci off the table and jetted toward the door. My first instinct was to run behind her, but the guy next to me was looking deep down my throat. Then to make matters worse, the phone rang. It was Yuri again. I didn't want to answer but knew I needed to. I sat down uneasily and said, "What's up, Yuri?" as I watched Shawna's backside disappear out into the street.

He yelled into the phone with all his might and caused me to yank it from my ear. I wasn't sure what he was saying at first until he calmed his tone a bit.

"Yuri, I got you. I told you I was on it."

"On what? On leisure time!" he shouted. "Have yuh been stakin' out Rapheal?"

"You damn right," I said, even though I hadn't.

I'd called him a few times but Rapheal wouldn't answer my calls. And I couldn't tell Yuri why. It was assumed that I could get next to Rapheal because he was my sister's man. We should've had some sort of connection at the moment, two grieving people left behind from an accidental death. But that was far from the case. Rapheal had stepped into new booty and I was a two-time murderer.

Shit was getting crazy. Yuri wanted him done by Thursday, Thanksgiving, the day we supposed to give damn thanks.

"I want his ass roasted, head on my table come Thursday!" he reminded me again.

"I got you," I said, blowing breath as if he bothered me.

"I'm sayin'…I'm tryna understand yuh. I had two jobs that paid good money. I told'cha to stay at home, chill, make Rapheal yuh priority. Are yuh doing that?" he asked me angrily.

"I am. You just don't see it," I said calmly.

"Yuh should be with him now! Maybe going over to the graveyard to lay flowers. I don't care what!" he said through clinched teeth. "Get over there!"

I held the phone to my ear even though Yuri hung up in my face. I was feeling antsy like a panic attack had crept through my body. I stood up but still didn't move. Things seemed fuzzy. How could all this have happened? Then it dawned on me-I brought it on myself, always going after what Monique had, always wanting the same benefits and privileges she had. Always wanting to be just like her.

I wondered if other siblings carried those same spiteful feelings; one for another. Or was it just me? Was I the lone idiot with a bad case of sibling rivalry? I was positive most sister's fought…maybe even a couple of jabs here and there. But murder… probably not too often. I knew family meltdowns went way back, but I'd pulled a Cain and Abel.

My mind started playing tricks on me. At that moment, I thought I saw Monique pass the front window of Starbucks. Her death had me stoked. It was almost as if the two killings were now taking a toll. I knew Monique really wasn't outside but I could've sworn the same Cherokee from the other day did pass by. My heart was beating fast, but I knew I had to make my important call.

I sat my purse on the table, opened wide and eyed my 9mm It was compliments of Yuri, supposedly for my protection. Yet it also had C.J.'s death written all over it. I hoped I wouldn't have to use it on the Allen Temple crew, but I was ready to at least smoke one of them.

Finally, I inhaled then took actual footsteps, leaving all my mess on the table. A dizzy feeling came over me as I walked. Some sort of mental melt-down. It was the type of anxiety that ran deep in my family; especially with everything piling against me at once. My mother had it out for me, Rapheal had dissed me for the moment, and Shawna showed she had some issues with me, too. But nothing compared to Yuri. He bothered me most. It wouldn't have surprised me if he'd followed me all along. He was probably sitting outside the Starbucks somewhere waiting for me to mess up.

As I made my way out the door and across the street to the payphone that sat on the corner, noticeably the older gentleman man who'd been working on his computer in Starbucks was now on the go, too. I saw him turn the corner at a rapid pace looking back over his shoulder the entire time. It was strange and seemed out of pocket for me. Or maybe it was just my suspicions, something else to get me off centered.

It took me a few seconds to locate my calling card. Then even more time figuring out what to do on the outdated pay phone. I'd called twice since back in the states, and each phone I used had different instructions. After I dialed what seemed like twenty digits, finally an international operator came on the line. I had to recite the same numbers I'd just dialed. It was a long wait, one that didn't seem like it would ever go through. Finally, an old, Bahamian accent sounded through the line.

"Yes…Yes…Yes..," she kept repeating.

"It's me," I said to her.

"Me who?"

Oh shit, I thought to myself. *This is more difficult than I thought.* "Your American friend," I said to her slowly. "Is everything good?"

Oh…oh…my dear, everyting is irie," she hesitated with a worn, sweet voice that reminded me of Glenda the good witch just at a much slower pace. I could hear the phone fumbling around like it had fallen from her ear. I said, "Hello," a few times, but there were still muffled sounds blaring into the phone.

Finally the subdued sounds calmed and she spoke directly into the phone again saying that she'd dropped the receiver. I could hear crying in the background which sounded like it came from two or three babies collectively.

"Hold'on a sec, sweetie, gotta help me young'on. She got her hand stuck in the door."

"Okay," I said, expressing my restlessness through my voice. I guess it shouldn't have been shocking that somebody's hand could've gotten stuck in the door. There were way too many children around there for her to keep an eye on. I remembered back to when I first rode up on the lady and her small-cottage like home. It was in one of the most desolate areas Nassau had to offer. It was the poorest area which was why I purposefully went there knowing money would talk. I'd passed many houses, and many ladies all of whom potentially could've worked. But there was something about Ms. Edna that I liked.

The children played wildly in the yard, all eight of them. So when I stopped to inquire about a local doctor, she informed me that most of the children were hers, and the other two, foster children. We talked for hours all about the motherhood thing. Of course she felt bad for me when I told her my husband beat me regularly.

Eventually it got late and she offered me a place to lay my head. I confessed early the next morning, about how I was on the run from my abusive husband. When I asked if she would watch my newborn, she hesitated, but agreed with a smile when I flashed the crisp hundreds before her face.

Her voice snapped me back quick. "You comin' to get your little one, this week, right?"

"Ummm. Not this week, Ms. Edna. Next week."

"Oh, baby, I thought it was this week. She does need her shots, yuh know."

"I promise next week, Ms. Edna. Everything else, okay? I mean, she has enough milk, right?"

"Chile we can feed all of Nassau and Freeport, too with the money you left. Of course she has enough milk."

I smiled.

"So, nobody's been around asking questions, right?"

"Like who," she asked, speaking even slower than normal.

"Anybody." I stopped and breathed into the phone roughly. "My husband got money. I'm sure he'll hire a private investigator soon. Maybe even contact the police."

"Chile, we ain't seen the police since 1988. Don't worry my dear." She laughed for several seconds while I tried to figure out if her comment was a joke.

I frowned. She kept laughing lightly; probably for the first time sinse the start of the conversation. She didn't find many things comical and neither did her children. They were all laid back, just glad to be alive. The noise level in her house roared again. There was screaming, running, laughter and then the crying. I wondered if one of the voices belonged to me.

"Well, I best be going now, dear. Time for me to prepare supper."

"No problem, Ms. Edna. Kiss my baby."

"I sure will," she said hanging up the phone.

A part of me got nervous. I wasn't sure if Ms. Edna would be able to handle any questions that came her way if the police did show up. She seemed uneducated, and unable to get hostile if needed. She simply wanted to shower her kids with love.

I knew if I showed up to claim my child and something really went down, I'd hire the best lawyer Nassau had to offer, and claim to be the next of kin. Shit, the baby thing wasn't really for me anyway, but if it was my ticket to getting Rapheal back, within a week I would be collecting our child.

Twenty...

Dominique

Three days passed and Thanksgiving had come and gone. It was the first time in life that I hadn't spent turkey day with my mother. She hated me. I was sure. More than she did before. When I called, her short-ass wouldn't answer, and even when I showed up at her home, Steve answered the door with an unwelcoming frown. His body language was clear, that I couldn't come in, and was evident by the way he stood stiff and close, guarding the front door.

I jetted from my bathroom after feeling ill for hours. It was the first time I'd been inside my place in months for more than a few minutes. It was dusty, had a faulty smell like the food in the refrigerator had been inside too long. Normally I would've only showed up to check the mail, and peep in on the spot, but today marked a day of real significance. For one, I had a reunion with my brother; and two we were getting together with our father. He wanted a face-to-face with us... so what better place for a little privacy than my place.

Sed was already out in the living room taking a nap while I took a cold shower. It was my hope the water would shake my nauseous feelings. Nothing would work. I tried crackers, bread, ginger ale, and even dry cereal. Nothing less should've been expected though… since I was finally pregnant *for real*. I'd gotten the doctor's results just yesterday and couldn't stop smiling. Six weeks was what he told me.

Shamefully, there was no one to share the good news with. Not even Shawna. I'd lied about being pregnant to everyone who knew me. So now that it was true, surely no one would listen. I had already convinced myself that it was Rapheal's and that we were going to be the perfect little family. Fuck the penthouse, fuck the fancy cars. I just wanted him and the little white house with the picket fence. I hoped for a boy, to go along with Ronnique once I got her back to the states.

As I stared in the mirror, pulling up my tight fitting Juicy Couture jeans and oversized knit sweater, I thought about Babyface. That nigga used to pump out them love songs. "Sing that song!" I shouted. "A girlllllll for you, and a boy for meeeee….."

Sed must've heard my voice cracking 'cause I heard him shout from the living room. "You callin' the dogs, baby. You callin' the dogs."

My singing sounded good to me and the storyline, too. I slipped on my favorite pink and purple knit socks and ran out to the living room running my fingers through my hair. I was scared to even comb it for fear of losing even one strand. I was letting it grow back because that's what I knew my honey loved. C.J. had long hair. And I'd heard Rapheal tell her the night of the storm that he loved her hair; especially the length. "God bless her soul." I had to laugh because now she was six feet under.

I killed the bitch with a gun shot to the head. As Yuri would say, "Yuh bumboclot me gunshot'cha." I laughed thinking about Yuri. He'd taught me well…both how to pull the trigger and how to do it discreetly. The entrance to the parking garage was perfect since it was a low-key area between the street and the inside of the garage. My mind raced back to how C.J. thought she was really doing something.

"Fuck that, tryna pull her car into my man's garage," I said loudly with a twist of the lips and a sharp roll of the neck. "That's some ole' housewife shit, and would be left for only me to handle."

"Who the fuck are you talkin' to?" Sed asked when I entered the living room.

Shit! I'd gotten so hyped I was fussing and expressing my feelings out loud. "Oh, to myself," I said with a huff. "Life has been crazy lately. Enough to make a bitch wanna take the easy way out and jump off a bridge."

I thought my comment was comical, but Sed didn't. He jumped up off the couch and walked over to the dining room table where I'd pulled out some old pictures from the big black photo album that I kept on the floor inside a magazine rack.

It was a picture from when we were all at summer camp in our early teens. Even then Monique had the face of a baby doll; being prissy and the leader of the pack. There were some of just me and Monique clutching one another by the shoulder smiling like real sisters do. I had the slightest idea why Sed wasn't in any of the photos. We kicked it a little more until Sed asked if I had anything to drink. I told him I hadn't been staying at the house and why. He got all googly-eyed like the Allen Temple boys had him scared, too. But, still he wanted something to drink. I got up to look for anything that had been left in the pantry. Sed's eyes lit up when I returned to the table with an old bottle of Grey Goose and one plastic, red, cup.

"One cup?" He frowned. "You not drinking?"

"Look fool. I told you my situation."

"You don't look pregnant to me."

"Well, I am," I shot back.

Without hesitation, he poured then took a long gulp which got him going real fast. He started making jokes and talking about people in the family; especially the ones I didn't like. I looked at Sed with a heartfelt feeling. He was always a handsome young man with his graham cracker complexion and light brown eyes. However, I had no clue as to where he got his big lips from. Soup coolers, didn't run in our family, so that characteristic was always questionable. It felt good having him around and having someone who was my sibling to hang out with. We even talked about Monique a bit. At times I had to bite my lip and turn my head, knowing that it was me who sent her to her death bed. I watched Sed closer and closer. Surely he was having a good time. He drank the Grey Goose like it was going out of style and never coming back. We got to fooling around and laughing about our childhood until all of a sudden Sed's demeanor changed. Something was troubling him. I could feel it.

"Look sis. ..I ain't gon' lie. I might roll over on Rapheal," he announced out of the blue.

Immediately, I put the photo album down and gazed into his eyes. I was pissed that he was talking about my man that way. "Why? I thought everything was going to work out?" My tone held a serious attitude.

"It might. You never know," he responded with a quick shrug of the shoulders. "I haven't been to court yet. Rapheal is slick you know. He knows how to paint a picture that says everything is okay."

"You been talking to Mama?" I asked anxiously. "She told you to do that. Didn't she?"

"Nah. I haven't seen her since the day I got out. She's been actin' all weird. You know I don't fuck with what's his name anyway?"

He started snapping his fingers like he was trying hard to remember our step-father's name. I was supposed to laugh along with him because I knew who he was referring to. I just couldn't find any humor in what I was hearing about Rapheal. When Sed said his next set of words it startled me.

"Besides, Ma has been traveling a lot."

A light bulb went off in my head. Where to? I wondered. "Look Sed, please don't do that," I begged. "Rapheal will make all this go away. Believe me," I pressed. "He got lawyers that can make shit disappear. You not behind bars are you?" I added as proof on behalf of Raphcal. "Bcsidcs, why mess up a good thing. I know he paying you major paper."

When I looked at Sedrick's dingy black t-shirt and baggy-ass Enyce jeans, I had to wonder what the hell he even spent his money on. He didn't dress anything like Rapheal.

Sed rubbed his newly bald held. "Money ain't everything Dominique. Shit…yeah, I'm out of jail, but one of the cops told me how Rapheal had sorta set me up to take the fall. It's not completely clear, but it's real. I'm just waitin' for my time to sing. You know what I mean?"

I nodded with an expression that told him I'd slipped into a demented state.

"Brotha, look-a-here," I began, trying to sound like Rapheal. "You've been outta pocket for a while. And….well, things have changed. I'm Rapheal's woman now," I announced proudly.

"Awwwww…sis. C'mon now. Not you?" he whined like I was being fooled. "He's a ladies' man."

"No! He's my fuckin' man!" I fired back.

With force, I kicked the chair opposite Sed down to the floor, and cursed all kinds of obscenities. It was wild how I could transform into an untamed beast when it came to Rapheal. He could do no wrong. Yes, I knew that Sed worked closely with him and probably knew a lot about him personally. But those other women meant nothing. They didn't have what I have, or the love he has for me.

"Dominique, hear me out, sis." He leaned over in his chair with his hands resting behind his head. He seemed to be extra emotional as he spoke at a snail's pace, making sure to pause between every word, "I- told- Monique-the-same-thing. She knew," he added, "even before she died."

I crossed my legs and bit my lip, then threw him a hard look into his eyes. "Are you a hater?"

"Oh my God! Are you that naïve," he hollered, allowing his hands to brush past his head from top to bottom. He was beyond frustrated and I was, too.

"Okay, I'm going to say this once and only once. He has women everywhere. International lover! Do you hear me?"

"Oh, I hear you," I said, calmly with my legs still crossed in a relaxed state.

"That's his M.O. He gets with these girls. Blow their mind…treat'em good and use them!" he shouted, making sure he emphasized the word used. "They open up businesses in their names for him. C'mon sis –don't fall for it. That nigga is real manipulative," he sighed. "There's this girl Melissa in Vegas, Brandy in D.C., C.J. in Miami."

"She's dead," I announced quickly and without a care.

His face lit up just as I pushed the photo album across the table with force, shoving the edge into his chest. I wanted my brother to know I meant business. Luckily for him, there was nothing sharp around because I was ready to show him a thing or two about loyalty.

Someone banged on the door as Sed simultaneously sat back in his seat. My guess was that he decided to take in all that I'd said. I saw him scrubbing his face with the palms of his hands as I moved anxiously toward the door. Even though I was still nervous about the Allen Temple boys, my heart told me it was who we'd invited.

After looking through the peep hole, it was confirmed. I opened widely, allowing our father to step inside. He looked sick in the face, his body frail, and weighing what I hoped was at least a buck forty.

Sed had gotten up and walked a few feet from the table toward the door. He was almost in awe after not seeing our dad for over eighteen years. Of course he thought he was dead just as I did until recently. Sed moved slightly behind me when the guest of honor stepped down into my sunken living room and looked around. It was almost as if he'd reverted back to being a child, hiding behind me or my mother because Daddy was coming home.

"Stop it, Sed," I said to him feeling a little nauseous again. "Dad, sit down here at the table. "We were just going through some old pictures."

I smiled, looking at him strangely. It was odd seeing some of my own features in him. We had matching complexions, and the same sized frame, with the exception of my womanly figure. His hair made me cringe. It was supposed to be a fade, but was unkempt along with his goatee that was badly in need of a shape up.

My father walked over to the dining room table and took the seat to the left of me. I took my same seat at the head of the table with Sed to my right. In the beginning, it was awkward because we all remained silent. My father sat straight up in his chair like he was ready for an interview while our looks asked the question, what should we say? What would we talk about first? I'd talked to him several times since the funeral but always just five minutes here-five minutes there. What did shock me was the heavy breathing coming from his side of the table. I'd never heard that over the phone. It was as if he'd developed a bad case of asthma. So I asked politely, "Can I get you some water?"

"No. I'm good," he said in his shrilly voice.

He kept his hands intertwined and stiffly on my glass table. He had his tweed coat buttoned all the way up to his neck like he had no intention on staying.

"Make yourself at home, Dad," I said in a sweet voice. It was a voice that no one had heard from me in years. Sed knew it because he watched me with his mouth open like he'd seen an alien.

All of a sudden my dad starting regurgitating which sent my face into a tight knot. It sounded nasty, coming from deep down inside his throat. To me, he needed to spit bad, and proved that he wasn't in the best of health. He'd obviously had a rough life, but it wasn't the right time to drill him on his nasty habit. After all, this was a family reunion.

"So Dad, you told me to invite Sed over because you had something to tell both of us. So what is it?"

He tried to answer, but once again started coughing up mucus. I'd never seen anybody regurgitate while sitting up, even though they'd had no food. The war had fucked him up bad because where I stood, if you still fighting some shit from thirty something years ago, that's a problem.

I offered him water like five times, only to get rejected over and over again. Finally I asked, "Dad, excuse my language, but what the hell is wrong with you?"

Sed just stared with big eyes and poured another cup of Goose.

With two sharp coughs blown into the center of his cupped hand, my father spoke hoarsely. "Heart condition, baby. Had it for over twenty years."

"Damn," was all I could say. He could tell I was concerned so he continued.

" ...Problems with my Aortic valve in my heart. When I got shot back in the army, the end result of removing the bullet during surgery caused my valve to become leaky. When the mitral valve becomes leaky, blood may back up into the lungs, causing shortness of breath and sometimes regurgitation."

"Oh shit. That sounds deep." Sed let out a worried sigh.

"You need surgery?" I asked

"Nah…it's all good," he said, sounding as if he'd loosened up a bit. "Don't ya'll worry. I had heart surgery years ago. I'm still kicking," he said jokingly, lightening the mood. "I mean the strength of my heart is declining, but it's beating."

He shot me a smile that warmed my heart instantly. It was a smile that I remembered from my elementary years. I smiled back, taking a real good liking to my father. I didn't remember much about him other than him paying close attention to me as a child. For some reason. I liked his personality…reminded me of my own.

"So, Dad, I gotta ask. How did all this come about with our mother saying you were dead?

"It's simple," he announced, stopping to take off his coat."

"Wow, this might be good," Sed uttered, showing us both that he was damn near fucked up.

"Go on. Go on. I need to hear this," I urged, leaning with both my elbows on the table.

"Somehow, I ended up in the psych ward at Walter Reed a hospital for Army vets and wounded soldiers. I had some mental issues for a while, both resulting from being shot at daily during the war. And also, because mental issues run deep in our family." He stopped and gave us both a funny look. "You know mental health issues are hereditary," he warned. "So, if you ever feel depressed or anything along those lines, get checked. There's medication for that."

"Neither Sed nor myself seemed interested in that. I just wanted the juice on my mother 'cause wasn't shit wrong with me.

"Well, she hung in there for a while. You and Monique were about eight at the time, and Sed about six. Your mother got pregnant…"

He stopped mid-sentence just as my tongue hung from my mouth. I was salivating like a dog hungry for the information. "What?" I begged. "What happened?"

Well I was laid up in the hospital, so the baby couldn't have been mine. We talked when I was sane and wasn't on my meds, but we sorta drifted apart. I started seeing her less and less until one day she showed up, with stomach out to here," he said, pointing about four inches from his stomach. He started shaking his head with embarrassment as he continued.

"I'm having the baby, Don." He shook his head again. "That's what your mother said to me. Next thing I knew, she had the baby by some man from the neighborhood, but gave the baby up for adoption because she met Steve just about the same time."

"See, that's why I can't stand his ass now," I uttered.

I'd been hanging onto my father's story step by step. It was intriguing to have your whole life story revealed within an hour and at a dining room table.

"So, where's the child now?" Sed asked.

My father shrugged his shoulders. "My guess is that she doesn't know either." She cheated on me for years, then I guess cheated on the other guy when she met Steve. Maybe she's calmed down since she's an older woman now."

"Oh, she's Miss Perfect now if you let her tell it."

"Hey baby girl, I've learned not to hold onto grudges. Your mother has been very dishonest, but she's still your mother. The only part still hurts is that I missed so much of your life," he told me sadly. "She moved y'all away while I was still in the hospital. She changed everything…addresses, phone numbers, schools-everything. But I'm just glad to have you back in my life now. I'm grateful that she even called and told me about Monique."

I looked into his eyes seeing that they were both welling up with tears. I didn't want anymore hurt to come to him so I told him not to worry and that we'd have a relationship from that moment on. He started telling me stories about how he loved his girls and Sed, too. He said he played with us daily before his extended hospital stay. When he told me that he and I were the tightest and that he took up extra time with me it warmed my heart.

"You know you were more outgoing than your sister." He laughed as if he remembered something in particular. "You followed me around," he sang, sounding extra cheerful. "But you and your mama, y'all didn't do too well together back then."

A tear slid down my cheek and into my mouth as I listened to the good times between us. I didn't think I had any. For a second it seemed like I did have a heart, despite what my mother had always told me. She was a deceitful and cunning lady as far as I was concerned. My father interrupted my bonding time when he broke the bad news.

"I do have some bad news," he announced.

"What's that?" I asked.

"Can't- be-be-be- too-too-too-bad," Sed stuttered with his head resting on the table.

"Sedrick you're not my son, although I did treat you as if you were."

My father's words ripped through my body like a massive tornado. Sed just sat with a blank look on his face. My thought was that he'd processed what was said but didn't know what kind of reaction to have. Well, I did. I was getting angrier by the minute, but didn't want my father to know. My mother had deprived me of having a father all those years.

Someone who really loved me. And for now, Sed didn't even have a father. I was gonna pay her ass a visit in the morning. And if Steve guarded the door and wouldn't let me in…I had something for them both.

Twenty-one...

Rapheal

I rushed toward the exit in the Lenox Square Mall carrying no bags, just a phone number. My strut was faster than usual, but of course I checked my surroundings to see if anybody had followed me out of the store. It had only been a week since C.J. had gotten her brains blown out in front of my building. Not to mention, it seemed like I was being followed every other day. Paranoid was what most people called it. But me, I wasn't a fool by a long shot. Something was about to go down.

I stopped, dug my hands into my jeans searching for a mint or piece of gum. My mouth was dry. Extra dry, probably from not eatin' all day. The churning of my stomach told me I needed to, but how could I? Shit was rough out on the streets and every second needed to be spent watchin' my back. The thought of sittin' down for a meal with so much drama going on seemed crazy. The beefs were strong and included everybody from me to Dominique, her mother, Sed, the Feds, and even Ansar.

I fired his ass and told him not to ever show his face again since he couldn't handle his business with the last few cars. I needed all the vehicles gone, like there'd been a magical disappearin' act. I even showed Ansar documentation of how he could get caught up and headed to jail just like Sed if he ever said a word. It's funny how he fell right into my plan. Even Sed fell for it all, too.

"The cards play funny for everybody," I said to myself.

Sed is slick, just not slick enough to come out on top, I thought as I stopped at a Coca Cola machine on the bottom floor of the mall.

Sed was done whether he realized it or not. The lawyer I hired for him told me when the trial came around he would convince Sed to take a plea bargain. All the evidence was stacked against him. And none against me. I grinned, slippin' the quarters into the machine. The best part about the Feds case was that everyone who would testify had been served and had only dealt with him. To date, my lawyer told me no subpoenas had been processed for me and Sed seemed to be takin' all the weight. I grinned inside. My lawyer was so damn connected it made me want to pay him extra.

Just as the soda came tumblin' down, a brown-skinned honey who worked in Abercrombie passed me and waved like a shy school girl. I smiled back but didn't bite. One prospective chick in one day was enough.

"Hey, what's up, sexy?"

"Why you ain't call me?" she asked flirtatiously.

"Oh, I will. Just give me a lil' time. I will."

I'd just come from meetin' up with Cynthia upstairs in the Express, somebody I'd met a few months ago. She was cool, definitely somebody I wanted to get with in the future. She had a good job as manager, so I knew her paper was right. I just needed to check her credit, I said making a mental note to myself. She had even come through for me on the hotel.

My new home for the past week was the Intercontinental in Buckhead, the best hotel Atlanta had to offer. Cynthia put the room in her name just in case the police or Dominique came after me. I thought about calling her back in the store just to say thank you one more time, but a silver Toyota Solara caught my eye when I pushed the door open to exit the mall. It was a face that I'd seen before, just couldn't remember where.

My mind raced as I walked as fast as I could to the Camry. I kept watching over my shoulder until I reached for the door handle and anxiously stuck the key in the lock.

The Solara was nowhere in sight, yet I jetted from the lot as if somebody was behind me. I couldn't shake my worried feelings. Just felt like somethin' would happen at any moment. I grabbed my cell from my pocket and dialed my mother's number. Ever since C.J died, I'd been callin' my mother every day to check on her. In my heart, I truly believed Dominique killed C.J. There was no way to prove it other than to get her to admit it. But in the meantime, I had to monitor anyone who meant somethin' to me. Dominique was fuckin' crazy to the third power and I knew it. My fear was that if she couldn't have me she would go after the only other woman she knew I loved. When my mother answered, she sang into the phone in her normal happy spirit.

"Yes… Coleman residence."

"It's just me, Ma. I'm just checkin' in."

She could tell I was worried about her.

"Boy, why you calling me every day. I told you I'm fine."

A sense of relief filled my senses. "Ma, did Dominique call you again?" I hoped the answer was no. Messin' with my mother would take shit to another level.

"No… haven't heard from her. You?"

"Nah…me either, but let me know if she calls." I paused. "And Ma..."

"Yeah."

" If she comes over , don't open the door," I ordered in a more serious tone. "I'm dead serious."

"I understand. I understand," she repeated. "Boy, I'll be glad when you get you one nice girl and settle down. That child, Melissa from Vegas been calling."

"Yeah. I know. I'll call her. And I'll call you later, too," I said, ending the call.

Before I knew it, I'd made it back to my hotel. The whole place was lit up lookin' lovely and here I was afraid to pull to the front. I didn't even valet park for fear that somebody would be in my back seat when I called for the car to be pulled back up. I was takin' all precautions. The sun had gone down, which had me more on edge so by the time I parked and got out, I started walkin' backwards searchin' for anybody who looked suspicious. I hadn't followed Dominique all day, and hadn't heard from my private investigator either.

As soon as I made it to the lobby, I whipped out my phone to call her. It was somethin' I should've done days ago. One, her mother was countin' on me to find out if she'd been to the Bahamas, and two, I needed her to confess to murderin' both C.J and Monique.

I found a small table in the back of the bar area waitin' for Dominique to answer. I'd been ignorin' her calls for over a week so maybe she would now turn the tables. I got antsy since it was on the fourth ring, but suddenly there was a voice. Her voice. I took a deep breath and put my game face on.

"What's up girl?"

"You?" she said like I was bothering her.

"You busy?"

"Not really. I'm surprised you called. I thought you'd have your nose somewhere stuck up C.J's ass."

"Nah…" I uttered calmly. She thought she was slick.

But I'd seen her kind before. She wanted to get a reaction out of me to see what I would say. I played it cool though.

"I haven't seen C.J.," I told her. "I've been out of town. "But enough about me," I said, quickly changing the subject. "I wanna see how you doing?"

"Is that a joke?" she asked me sarcastically.

"C'mon girl. Let's stop all the bullshit. I mean you pregnant with my baby and all. I think we need to change up how we been treatin' one another."

"You serious?" she asked with emotion in her voice. I could tell she was questionable at first, but the more I talked nicely she seemed happy and shocked all at the same time. "Where you at?" she asked, "I'm coming over."

"Hold fast. Let's take things slow. If we gon' do this I want it done right. I need to give you time to rid yourself of any niggas you messin' with and I'm a do the same."

"Shit, I can do that in thirty minutes," she blurted out.

"Nah...I'm for real. This way when we hook up, it's just me and you."

"Rapheal, I ain't gon' lie," she confessed with excitement in her voice. "I know you love me."

"I do Dominique. I really do. It just seems odd that this is happenin'. I can't shake the fact that I used to deal with your sister."

I bit down on my lip. I wanted to ask her right then and there if she killed C.J. My next step was to cover my mouth, in hopes of controllin' my anger. My thought was to meet up with Dominique and do to her what she'd done to both of my girls. But I stopped my thoughts immediately because a part of me wasn't sure about Monique. It could've been anybody, but Mrs. Lewis seemed so sure.

"Ummmmm Ummmmm...you hear me?" Dominique kept repeating loudly in the phone.

I had zoned out and forgotten that she was talkin' to

me. "Look, I want us to meet up as soon as I get back."

"When?" she asked extra fast.

"In three more days."

"No. I'll come to you. Where you at? What state?" she asked with persistence.

"Nah. Hold fast. Let me just handle this business, okay?"

She giggled sexily. I knew something crazy was comin' next.

"If you promise to give mama some of that good dick when you get here."

I closed my eyes. It was a struggle, but I said it. And I said it like I meant it. "You got it, luv."

"Three more days," she repeated just to make sure I was really coming.

"No doubt. I'll call you when I get in town so we can meet up to talk."

"Talk?" she snapped. "I thought we was gon' do the nasty and live happily ever after."

"Dominique, you are not movin' in just yet. I want us to take things slow. We need to talk first. And I want to spend some time gettin' to know the real you. Is that too much to ask."

"I guess not," she said showin' her disappointment.

"I wanna make sure we tell each other everythin'. No secrets," I said, givin' her a chance to come clean. "We can't be together unless the loyalty is there."

"Oh, well Rapheal there's something I gotta tell you."

"What's that?" I said, gettin' ready to hear a possible confession.

"Sed might be my brotha, but he ain't shit."

I swallowed hard. "Oh, yeah."

"Yeah. He said you was a womanizer. And I know about all your lil' girlfriends in every state. But that shit better end tonight. Call them all," she shouted. "Tell'em there's a new bitch in town. One that don't play. "Cause I'll whip ass if I have to."

"And what else," I pressed.

"Don't worry about what else," she said revertin' back to a sweeter voice. "I got it. You just watch Sed's ass. He said he might roll over on you if need be."

"Thanks for lookin' out." I shot her a loud kiss through the phone. "I'm not worried though…I haven't done any-thin'."

"Yeah…that's what the fuck O.J. said."

I said my goodbyes and finally convinced Dominique that I had to go. I hung up and breathed a heavy sigh. I felt that the call was a success; especially now that I knew she had turned on her brother for me.

Twenty-two...

Dominique

I sat quietly on the floor flipping through channels
with the remote. Yuri lay behind me on the couch, snoring his
ass off. It was a quarter to twelve and he was sleeping hard,
calling all the hogs in Atlanta. Little did that fool know he
sounded so unattractive, and so un-thuggish. The stench from
his hair even bothered me. I needed him to wash those mutha-
fuckin' dreads soon, and start smelling more like Rapheal.
Yuri showed up late last night, later than usual. And the couch
is where he ended up.

My days and nights had started to feel like prison.
Being cooped up in Yuri's spot had only one advantage- keeping me safe from the Allen Temple crew. Other than that, it
was a living hell. I had been back in his cramped up spot for
three days since I'd spent the evening with my brother and father. My heart warmed with even just a thought of Don, my
dad. When I left my apartment that night I told him that I
wanted him in my life, and wanted him to be a grandfather to
my child. Since then, we talked daily.

My thoughts came to a halt when something on
Channel 4, another one of our local news stations caught my

eye. Strangely, the scene touched me. And most things didn't. It was two small girls being pushed in a swing by their father. The story was about a single dad raising two nine year old girls. It seemed that nowadays anything relating to family moved me. At least now it was official…I had a father who was alive. Plus, my mind had been made up to change my last name back to Tucker the first chance I got. My mother changing our name to Lewis, Steve's surname was a violation. Don Tucker was my father's name, and would soon carry over to me-Dominique Tucker-Coleman. I grinned inside thinking about having a hyphen in my last name, and of course marrying and taking on Rapheal's last name. *This is truly some Jerry Springer type shit,* I told myself as I thought about me, Monique, and Sed.

Now, Sed was another story. He was all fucked up behind what was told to him about Don not being his father. I tried to convince him to go hard on my mother, confront her like a bitch in the streets, but he wouldn't. He said he didn't care about finding out about his biological father. The only thing he cared about was his upcoming trial. Unfortunately, he got some fucked up news the day before yesterday. His lawyer urged him to take a plea bargain.

He'd been staying at my spot even though I told him the chances of somebody breaking down the door and blowing his brains out were likely. Sed wanted me to stay with him, and couldn't understand why I was so fearful that I would opt to stay with Yuri. I wanted to tell him the truth about how I'd set Semo up, and maybe then he would understand why I knew retaliation was coming my way.

All of a sudden, Yuri yawned and his elbow jabbed me in the neck. I turned around ready to break, and noticed that his eyes were opened. He looked groggy, but irritated. "What's up with you?" I asked.

He switched positions from lying on his back to his

side. Nothing came from his mouth, but his eyes warned me that something was wrong. He had something on his mind.

"What?" I snapped while holding my left hand open. He still didn't say anything so I turned my focus back to the T.V., and rested my back against the couch.

Suddenly, he yanked my hair from behind. Nervousness took over while I wondered which one of my lies he'd found out about. With a slight turn, my eyes were able to catch a glimpse of his facial expression. He seemed tired and in deep thought.

"What do yuh really want from me?" he asked with squinted eyes.

I shrugged my shoulders. "I don't know. That depends on what you mean."

He scooted his body closer, up against my back, letting his dirty white T-shirt touch me. He was dressed in baggy jeans, a T-shirt that read GANGSTER, and dirty white gym socks.

"Damn, where you been at all night?" I asked, with a crazy look on my face.

"Takin' care of business. Yuh business," he added ruthlessly.

"Oh." I hit him with the shoulder move and flipped the channel again.

He started talking softly in my ear about how I was using him. Truth was...I felt the same way. So many times that nigga had ignored my calls, didn't come home at night, or showed me no affection other than in the bed. But now here he laid saying I was using him, too.

As he talked, my mind trailed to another world. The twelve o'clock news was on and Yuri's voice played like light background music. I started thinking about Rapheal again. In just a few days he would be back, ready to talk and make amends with our relationship. I just needed to stay with Yuri for a few more weeks until Rapheal agreed to let me move in with him.

Even though Rapheal wasn't a rough, gangster type dude, I figured I would be safe with him. I hoped he at least had a gun to protect me, his family. But if he didn't I did, and would use it again if necessary. No matter what Rapheal said, I had decided I was moving in anyway. This time, I wouldn't take no for an answer.

"Yuh hear me girl," Yuri said in a louder tone, and nudging me in the back."

"I hear you. I'm tryna watch T.V., though," I said dryly.

"So, yuh better start doing it," he announced.

I didn't have a clue as to what he was talking about. I just breathed heavily and nodded. Quickly, my mind switched back to my honey. I'd already programmed the number Rapheal called me from into my phone as HUSBAND. I used all capital letters to symbolize the strength of our relationship.

Suddenly, Yuri sat up on his elbows and stared into the television set that sat on a stand close to the floor. It wasn't a flat screen or even an updated model, but it was large enough for us to see the gruesome scene. My heart stopped when I heard the female newscaster say, "Allen Temple."

"Yuri, did you?" I asked wide eyed.

He was still behind me and my eyes were glued to the set so I couldn't see his expression.

"Shut yuh bumboclot mouth ans listen gurl."

Oh shit, whenever he changed up his words like that I knew trouble was near. "I just wanna know."

He smushed me in the head, snatched the remote, and turned up the sound. By now he'd gotten up, and was parked on the couch with his elbows on his knees and eyes glued to the news reporter.

The first flash showed the actual scene fenced in with yellow police tape, and two body bags on the ground, surrounded by uniformed officers. It must've been footage from the wee hours of the morning. Maybe a live broadcast, which explained the darkness and the bright, flashing police lights.

The cameras quickly flashed back to the day time. The reporter starting talking close up in the screen with a troubling look, and a high pitched tone. "Our city woke up to a horrifying site this morning. Atlanta police say this parking lot behind me, here in the Allen Temple neighborhood is the site of just one of two murder sites in the city last night."

She paused and the screen switched to some comments from the neighbors. Of course they found the people who couldn't use a verb and a noun in the same sentence. But most importantly they interviewed one man who talked about how the three men killed were the same boys who were responsible for tons of deaths in the city.

"They got what they deserved," he ended.

I looked over at Yuri and asked, "Were they some of the people following me?"

He swatted me with his hand. And the reporter continued.

"…Atlanta officers are seeking the public's assistance. If you have any information that will help with breaking this call our hotline….1-800-555-4222. I must note," she added as the cameraman closed in on her face. "The police are expecting more blood-shed. Tips have come in already noting retaliation."

Yuri clicked the television completely off, making it totally silent in the room. He was pissed, and I wanted to know why. Out of the blue a crazy thought whizzed through my mind. I thought about calling to snitch on Yuri's ass. *Killing is both a crime and a sin*, I told myself.

"It was supposed to be four murders!" Yuri yelled.

He got up, walked around throwing his hands in the air. His hand gestures were back and moving wildly above his head. "I took dem niggas out!" he bragged. "Boom boom boom, bumboclot!" he shrieked, showing the shooting action with an imaginary gun. "One by one, they dropped like flies."

He was heavily into the thrill...the work he'd done. Proud of himself... I guessed. I decided to seize the moment, and asked, "When you taking care of my witness?"

"What witness?" he shot back, followed by an evil stare.

"Semo's cousin?"

"First thing first," he told me.

I whined a bit when I spoke. "C'mon Yuri, if you do him I won't have any worries when I go to court. No witnesses, no worries." I smiled sweetly.

"I got yuh. But do yuh have me?" he grilled.

"What? Of course I got your back. Look, how many runs I been on with you?"

"That's not what I'm talkin' about. When we takin care of Rapheal?"

His words flowed like they came with ease. No emotion at all. No care about what we'd discussed before. For me, his words hurt. He wanted to take life away from me, personally. *Fuck that*! I told myself.

"So, when yuh gon' do it?"

I frowned. "Do what?"

"Meet up with the nigga. I told yuh to start callin' him more. Two to t'ree times a day at least."

"See, you talking shit like I'm not about my work." My head bobbed with attitude proving that I was for real. "I did call, so now what? And I have talked to him, twice," I added. "I'm trying to take it slow, Yuri. "We're meeting for lunch tomorrow."

"I'll be there, too. Where's lunch?"

I mentally scrambled for a good answer. I couldn't.

Finally, I named some off-brand restaurant in Dekalb County.

"Good. Yuh handle yuh business with Rapheal, and I'll handle the rest of the Allen Temple shit." He turned to walk away.

"Wait!" I shouted. "That's not over?"

"Yuh wanna know the truth?"

"Yep," I said strongly.

"It's not over 'til I take out all his soldiers, leavin' the weak ones to lie down."

When Yuri spoke those last words reminded me of the character, Screwface from the movie, *Marked for Death*. He bent down trying to balance himself while he put his boots on. As soon as he finished, he pulled a fat stack from his pocket and peeled off about ten soiled looking hundreds.

"This is for your pockets. I'm not sure when I'll be back."

I needed that loot badly. I hadn't been working with Yuri lately, so my money was getting low. Besides Christmas was coming soon, and Rapheal would need a special gift to celebrate our first Christmas together.

"Damn, aren't you gonna take a shower?" I asked, watching him gear up to leave.

"Warriors don't take showers during war," he said, grabbing a hooded sweatshirt from the edge of the couch.

He blew me a kiss as he walked to the front door, but I wasn't interested in blowing one back. I had gotten what I wanted-the Allen Temple boys off my back. Now it was a waiting game. Waiting for Rapheal to ride back into town and rescue me from Yuri's bullshit.

Twenty-three...

Dominique

Four days later, I got the call. The call which made
my heart sink. It fluttered and nearly skipped beats as I
thought of my man meeting up with me. It was a chilly December evening, perfect shopping time for buying Rapheal a
few Christmas gifts. Instead, I waited for him alone, and in
the dusk. I felt energized like I had been given a second
chance at life. I was hoping he'd surprise me with a brand
new watch, maybe a blinged out Cartier, or even a mink;
preferably like the one C.J. wore when she got smoked. I
smiled inwardly thinking, maybe I would be a happy housewife soon.

I walked casually through the open field near the
track, headed toward the bleachers where we agreed to meet.
The sun had gone down and darkness loomed over the track.
No one was out but me. Strangely, I had no fear. Yuri had
come through for me like the soldier he claimed to be. He'd
taken care of my problems in full. No more Allen Temple
boys to worry about and no more reasons to watch my back. I
even thought about dumping my gun buried in my satchel

bag, deep beneath my make-up and newspaper ads.

Life wasn't about killing anymore, it was about hopping on the sales I had peeped in the newspaper going on at the Baby Depot. The blueprint was ready. I would sweet talk Rapheal into letting me move in, and I would start buying baby shit for the new room immediately. Everything seemed to play out in my mind perfectly except how I would break the news to Yuri. Of course, I wouldn't tell him I was leaving him for Rapheal. Maybe I would say I just needed some time to do me. Or maybe I would play like I'd turned gay, hit him with some made up venereal disease, or tell him I had AIDS. Whatever lie I came up with would have to be worked carefully. Yuri was a like a disgruntled pit bull, who'd have to be let down easily.

As I finished up my last thought, I saw my knight in shining armor pull into the parking lot in a fuckin' old-ass Camry about ten yards away from me. He parked next to my car and got out looking smoother than ever. My neck jerked a bit when I spotted his coat. It was a short, black mink; the kind C.J. wore. Instantly, I got jealous. Here I stood, freezing my ass off in a short tan, Northface trying to keep warm. And he flossed hard in a mink. I started to lay down the law about how our relationship would flow, but caught myself. The goal was to show him I wasn't a time bomb waiting to explode. And that I could be a good wifey; one the world could be jealous of.

By the time Rapheal made it across the grass and over by the bleachers, I could tell the weather bothered him. "It's cold, isn't it?" I said sweetly, hoping to break the ice.

"It doesn't get cold here too often so it's cool."

He shrugged his shoulders then shot me a weird look. *He's worth it. He's worth it,* I kept telling myself. His attitude stunk so I needed some psychological motivation to help me stay the course. It was way too cold to be outside, but as my alter ego told me, *he's worth it*. Funny thing was-it seemed at times Monique was my alter ego. Maybe she wanted us to be together.

"Look Dominique, I gotta ask you something."

"What? Anything? Shoot!"

I was so damn excited he could've asked me to bark like a dog, or chew on his dick, whateva! I would do it!"

"Do you love me?"

"Why would you ask me something so damn stupid? Of course I do. I've loved you since the day I met you."

He smiled.

I smiled back.

I had no problems confessing my love for him. And even though there was no one around, I would've gladly hopped in my car, gone up to the next corner, and shouted, "I love this beautiful black man!"

"Ah, Dominque. did you hear me?" he asked, snapping from my thoughts.

"No. No, I didn't. But I think this is such a beautiful place to make our shit official. I mean, green grass, open field, nobody around. What else could we ask for?"

Rapheal didn't seem to be moved by my poetic words. He stood with his hands in his pockets, appearing to be frustrated. I watched him closely pull out his Blackberry, scroll down a few times then stick it back into his coat pocket. "Did you kill Monique?" he blurted out.

My eyes widened. I couldn't believe what he'd just said. "How could you ask me some shit like that?"

"I just need to know. You wouldn't lie to me, would you?" He gave me the puppy dog eyes. "I mean if it was an accident we can deal with that. I promise, we'll work it out."

"Rapheal, you don't understand, my feelings for you run deep," I admitted with my hands spread apart and open. "I would do anything for you," I wailed. "But lie and say that I killed Monique is not one of them."

"Your mother thinks you did," he confessed.

I knew I sounded like a sucka, but what did I have to lose. "My mother may have given me birth, but you've given me life again. As long as I have you who cares what the hell she thinks."

"What about C.J, did you…"

All of a sudden, the sound of Rapheal's voice trailed off. From the corner of my eye, I noticed a familiar figure ease from behind the bleachers. He came up behind Rapheal without him noticing a thing. His dreads dangled and frightened me on the spot. Tiny hairs stood up all over my skin.

How did he know where to find me? I questioned myself frightfully.

"Yuri, you following me?" I asked, looking like I'd been hit with a bolt of electricity.

"You and this pussy-ass nigga!" he roared, taking a few steps toward us both.

Rapheal looked surprised, but kept his hands in his pockets. He seemed to remain cool while I was in complete panic mode.

"Nigga, didn't I tell yuh not to bring no heat to me?"

Yuri was talking to Rapheal with his face screwed up into a tight knot. I took a step back from our lil' circle. We were all way too close.

"Whoa, whoa, whoa," Rapheal chanted with his hands in the air. "Yuri, let's talk about this. Man, how we get to this point?"

"When yuh sucka-ass sold me some shit yuh knew was foul!"

I knew things were going down-hill as I watched Yuri's hand gestures combined with his evil facials. Before I knew it, he'd whipped out a black pistol. It appeared to be a .45 Caliber, but from the way he had it gripped I couldn't be sure.

Immediately, I hopped into action.

"C'mon Yuri, rethink this," I begged, moving my body between him and Rapheal.

"Rethink what?" he snapped, then turned the gun my way.

My body jerked back quickly. But reflexes told me he didn't really want to take me out. It was Rapheal he wanted. And Rapheal I needed to save.

"Yuh think I'm stupid, don't yuh?"

"No, Yuri. I don't," I said, trying to pretend as if my heart hadn't fallen into my shoe. Yuri waved his gun around too casually as he fussed at me.

"Yuh got a thing for this nigga?" He paused, shot me a mean grimace then continued, "I know what the fuck I'm talking 'bout. Somet'ing's not right. Dominique, I told yuh he had to go weeks ago. But I gotta force yuh to set shit up!"

Instantly, Rapheal's head swiveled landing to his right, directly on me. His eyes surveyed me, wondering where the deceit had come in and why. For all he knew, we were meeting to discuss our relationship. That was my thought too, and I wanted to make that clear to Rapheal. He never said a word. He simply kept his hands in the air, near the width of his shoulders, waiting for us all to calm down.

My heart still thumped but I had to try something. "Look Yuri, let's talk about this. I know what we gotta do and I'ma do it."

I prayed Rapheal wouldn't try to read between the lines.

"I gotta better idea," he snapped, then leaped forward grabbing me by the arm.

Everything happened so fast I didn't know what he was doing. Yuri's tight grip on the upper part of my arm led me to believe he wasn't gonna shoot me. But the gun moving toward my face had me scared shitless. Suddenly, he yanked my arm toward my back, cracking every bone that could be cracked. I shouted, "Damn it, Yuri. That hurts. Lemme go! Pleaseeeee!"

Before I could even finish begging, he'd let go of his grip and was handing me the gun. We were all situated in a semi-circle with Rapheal directly across from me and Yuri to my right. Within a matter of seconds, my life had been saved and Rapheal's was in jeopardy.

"Shoot'em," he told me. "Now!"

The sound of Yuri's voice told me he meant business. I knew stalling wouldn't help, but I gave it a shot. I had been a plastic type chick all my life so now shouldn't have been any different. I started crying and begging like on the set of a movie, "Yuri, nooooo! I can't!" I cried out. "This is my niece's father!"

I even bent down clutching my knees waving the gun in the process. Rapheal dodged my moves hoping bullets wouldn't pop off, but Yuri took charge and stepped to me like I knew he would.

"Yuh bumboclot! Gettup, before me gunshot'cha!"

He was angry, and forceful as he straightened my posture and told me straight forward. "Yuh kill him now, or I'll kill you!"

Yuri took a few steps back off to the side and watched me like he was watching a Shakespeare play unfold. I had the gun pointing at Rapheal while both trembling and crying at the same time. I was caught up and my love triangle had me in a bind. I had been selfish all my life, never caring about anyone but myself. I wasn't capable of change. It was either me or Rapheal. One of us would die at the hands of Yuri if I didn't shoot.

"Shoot'em now!" he shouted.

I gripped the gun tighter as my adrenaline reached its max. All of a sudden, a spark burst through me reminding me what the future held for me. Without hesitation, I turned, fired, and realized Yuri had been knocked to the ground. The deafening sound of my gun told me to worry. I remained in place shaking, unable to contemplate my next move. Tears streamed from my eyes. It wasn't the fact that I'd taken a life. It was the fact that it was Yuri's. He wasn't the love of my life, or my future husband. *The worthless nigga couldn't even make me cum*, I told myself. But he did have my back and I had shot him straight in the temple, killing him dead. I glanced down at his lifeless body wondering what had I done.

Rapheal had started taking baby steps toward me. His face showed fear wondering if I would do him, too. "Dominique, put the gun down, luv. Put it down," he repeated.

My eyes remained glassy as I glared at him coming my way. I couldn't let go of the gun even though I wanted to.

"He can't hurt us anymore," he preached. "We will be together."

Rapheal lunged forward landing on my side, and removing the gun slowly from my hand. Still in a state of shock, my body shook for several more minutes while Rapheal caressed my back with his warm hands. His attempt to calm me and my heavy breathing wasn't working. I needed more. I needed a hug. Hell, I needed tongue.

I turned to him, stuck my tongue in his mouth hoping he'd tongue me back. The temperature seemed to drop even more, but with the warmth of his body I was right where I wanted to be. Finally, he kissed me back, resting his hand on my lower back, and calming my nerves. It wasn't the kiss I was expecting where sparks flew and fireworks sounded, but under the circumstances it was enough.

"Let's go," he instructed. "We need to get outta here."

"What about him?" I pointed to Yuri on the ground.

"We can either call the police and claim self defense, or we can just leave…your call. I'll back you no matter what."

"Leave him," I said taking off, rushing toward my car. I've got important matters to worry about this week." As soon as I was able to get my final sniffles out, I told Rapheal, "No matter what…I do need you to go with me to the doctor's this week. I'm having your baby, you know. So, I want you there."

"I'm as good as there," he told me in a caring tone. "You got my word."

"You sure?"

He nodded as we rushed from the field. I didn't want to break the news about Ronnique just yet, but it was just a matter of time.

Twenty-four...

When all the deceit ended...

The perfect Christmas Eve....what can I say? My senses filled with both joy and excitement as I rushed out to the U-haul to meet my father. I had just gotten myself some crackers to help my morning sickness go away. For days I'd gotten up feeling nauseous, and flopped right back into bed. But today nothing could keep me down. It was moving day. The day I made an official leap to live with my man.

I bounced happily toward the mailbox like a child with a new toy. I'd just completed forwarding my address at the post office, but needed to check my box one last time. As soon as it opened, a frown formed on my face. There was only one piece of mail which showcased the same unknown handwriting on the envelope that had been mailed before.

I snatched the letter as I heard my dad laying down on the horn. It was loud and probably annoyed everyone in the neighborhood. We needed to turn the truck back in by two o'clock since we'd had it for two days loading up all my shit. This time, I didn't label any boxes, nor did I try to pack neatly. The excitement of my new home had me unable to do anything in a normal way.

241

This time the headline read; Murder and Betrayal

I got angry and instantly started ripping the two pages to shreds. I didn't want any more negativity in my life. And wanted the culprit to stop before I had to flip back to the person I really was. As I jetted toward the truck I let the pieces fall to the ground as a sign that I'd forgotten about the bullshit already. Through more talks with my father, he shared with me his mental history. He was bi-polar and bet his next check that I was, too. He offered to get me checked, but I declined. As long as people didn't fuck with me…I wouldn't attack them. I smiled, bouncing back within seconds.

When I hopped in the truck, my father could tell something still worried me. Yet, he pulled off choosing to release his words carefully.

"Whatever the problem, let it go, baby." he preached. "You're on your way to a new life, bigger things," he added, while glancing at my stomach.

"I know. I know," I said while snatching my phone from my purse. "I just gotta get this out," I announced while dialing.

When Shawna answered, I blasted her, "Look chick! Now I been real fuckin'patient. I've been calling you. You won't return my calls. I've been trying to talk to you, but you don't seem to want to be bothered. It's cool though. But don't keep bringing these stupid, fuckin' letters to my house!"

Shawna hung up. It was nothing new. Both she and Jennifer had been doing that over the last month, along with any other female friends that I used to fool with, every now and then. *Fuck'em all*, I told myself with a wide smile. I had my two men in my life who loved me for me.

My father preached a little more, trying to instill life lessons in me on our short drive. I sat back and listened, also thinking about my mistakes in life. Some I regretted, others were just stepping stones. What did stand out was when he told me he'd never abandon me again. My heart melted, and I finally thought I could change for the better.

Before long, my father pulled up to the curb at my penthouse. I hopped out with major swagger like I owned the place, and reached into my purse for my sunglasses; the new sunglasses that had just come from Saks Fifth Avenue and were now labeled my new, favorite pair. The sun shone and was unseasonably warm for December. I just figured it was a sign about how my love life was starting to shine. Terrace waltzed out and greeted me with a smile, while hitting me with the male version of a curtsy.

"How can I help you?"

"Oh, I'm just moving in," I responded cheerfully.

I thought he was going to give me flack, but he didn't. He showed me to the service elevator, and told me he would check on me when he got back from lunch.

"Thanks for everything, Terrance," I said to him, looking forward to a friendlier relationship.

"No problem. I'll see you around," he said as he left the building.

I convinced my father to leave the truck out front so that we could both go up and tell Rapheal to come down. It didn't take long for him to agree and follow me inside. It seemed I had him wrapped around my finger like most men I encountered in life. He held the elevator door like the perfect gentleman and treated me like his little princess.

As soon as we got off the elevator, I stopped abruptly. With only two yards away from the door's entrance, something came over me letting me know there was a problem. The front door was half-way open, not a move that Rapheal would pull. I knew he was excited about me coming, but with Yuri dead and C.J. dying out on the street he wouldn't be that careless. My mind started wondering as I inched slowly toward the door. What if someone had retaliated for Yuri? What

243

if Rapheal was inside hurt or dead? With that thought, I picked up the pace with my father's lil' frail-ass right behind me.

With a few light pushes on the door it opened wide, allowing me to step inside with caution. Once inside the apartment it became obvious to me I'd been had. I stood in the middle of the floor lost as my mind juggled all kinds of thoughts. No matter how much I tried to fool myself, reality set in. The apartment was completely empty. Bare. Vacant. There was no furniture at all, just boxes of unwanted items and trash, cables cords, and all the shit most people left behind when they left a place in a hurry.

All of a sudden I covered my mouth when it all sank in. My father took two steps forward and just gently placed his hands on my shoulder for support. I was full of emotion and tried my best not to cry. I wasn't the crying type. I closed my eyes to the count of four trying to pull myself together.

A glimpse of a piece of white paper over on the kitchen counter caught my eye. Before I could even make it to the sheet, my heart weakened letting me know I couldn't handle much more. It was a letter. A letter from Rapheal. I got angry instantly. Letters were beginning to annoy me.

Dominique,

I'll make this short and brief. You came into my life in a way I never expected. I know I was wrong for leading you on, but I just can't do it anymore. The last few weeks that I spent with you, I feel I got to know the real you. The plastic you. It's not the right time in my life to settle down and not with someone who would murder their own sister.

Now that we've taken the paternity test, just know that I will take care of my responsibilities. Hit me up on the Blackberry— I'll be in touch.

I became ill instantly. And just as bile rose up in my

stomach, I had to remind myself this wasn't a nightmare… this wouldn't go away. Rapheal had really dumped me. I raised my chin and looked off into the thin air. I guess my father could tell I was still in a daze.

He started to speak, "Dominique, what….," but was interrupted by the loud noise coming toward us.

I heard the rattling, the chatter, and the rapid footsteps, but I remained glassy-eyed near the kitchen. My father jumped into action assuming something was wrong. He rushed toward me, grabbed my arm and pulled me toward the front of the apartment.

Before we could make it even to the living room area, which was several feet from the front door, three uniformed officers appeared along with two plain clothes officers. It wasn't Carter or Barnes, so I wondered what they wanted. Of course my mind flipped to Yuri's death. But then I wondered how could they have anything on me. Suddenly, it clicked. Rapheal had done me dirty.

"How could he?" I asked myself covering my face.

I felt so betrayed it took everything in me not to faint. I could feel the water welling up in my eyes, but kept it together.

All at once the officer's came rushing toward me, with one heavy-set policeman moving my father back away from me. He was the only thing holding me together so as soon as I felt the release of his grip, my first tear fell.

The tallest officer who appeared to be in his early fifties stepped forward and read me my rights, "Dominique Lewis, you have the right…"

The sound of his voice trailed off as another officer pulled my arms gently behind my back and cuffed me. At that point it clicked. I heard the officer say for the death of Monique Lewis. He'd also said that I would be extradited back to the Bahamas to stand trial. A gust of guilt shot through my veins as they talked, but I still managed to keep a straight face. I didn't deny it and I didn't admit to anything.

My stomach filled with terror, and anxiety took over my entire nervous system. I was pregnant. I couldn't go to jail. What the fuck was going on! How did they know?

Out of the blue, one of the officer's shifted his weight, and a vision of my mother coming through the front door startled me. Her eyes met mine and we stared at each other for what seemed like minutes. I was still in the same position as the officer's talked and my mother began to encircle us.

From the corner of my eye, I saw Steve walk through the front door, too. He was carrying something in his arms that I couldn't make out, but since he wasn't a threat my focus adjusted quickly back to Ruby. She seemed to be the one mugging me with her face in a tight knot.

It was more like a prance, than a walk. It was a strut of victory. All of a sudden she pulled my old sunglasses from her bag, dangling them near my face.

"Remember these," she taunted.

I had to think quick. "Those aren't mine!" I fired, talking for the first time.

"Oh, yes they are. Your favorite pair of shades…found in the Bahamas."

Her smirk confirmed that she thought she had me. I hoped that my silence told them all her alleged accusations wouldn't be entertained. Of course my shades had been missing since the Bahamas, and yes they were mine, but those words would never come from my mouth.

It would take a whole lot more than some shades to convict me. And as soon as I got my one phone call, I would call Rapheal and he would get me out. That I was sure of.

Finally, Ruby stopped walking in circles and stared at me deeply. "I hope what you read in those letters will someohow help you."

"You're the one who needs help," I told her. "Keeping me from my father all these years. Having children out of wedlock."

She simply shook her head and didn't respond to anything I said. The scene painted the perfect picture. My mother on one side, my father on the other, and the police moving me toward the door. My mother trailed along like a stalker trying to keep up with us as she talked.

"Dominique...do you know what you are?" she asked me.

I said nothing. But asked the question, what? with my eyes.

"You're nothing but a Carbon Copy. Always has been, always will be."

Luckily, my escorts had a firm hold on me, and my mother was now behind me. My stepfather, Steve was now in perfect view. I knew he wouldn't say anything, but his face troubled me, along with the package in his hand. Suddenly, I heard a baby cry. The baby who was swaddled in a white blanket. I stopped in my tracks trying to get a good look, but Steve wouldn't allow it. Unexpectedly, my mother darted over next to him trampling over any officers in her way. She rubbed up against Steve, all along making goo goo sounds and coos toward the baby girl.

I couldn't believe she'd found Ronnique. My baby. My rightful daughter. I just broke out into this crazy laugh. "Ruby, take care of my girl until I get out. I'll be out soon," I said heartily. "Or I'll send Rapheal by to get her. And oh yeah...he *will* get me out!" I shouted with confidence.

"You'll never see this child again!" she shouted from behind me.

I couldn't see her face as the police led me down the hall toward the elevator. Both my mother and Steve stayed behind but my father was still by my side. He walked alongside the police quietly with a look that confirmed he would never abandon me again. It was crazy how he was the person who walked into my life when everyone else walked out.

ALSO BY AZAREL

A Life To Remember
Bruised

BRUISED 2   **DADDY'S HOUSE**

Meet Azarel, author and CEO of Life Changing Books. Azarel comes to the publishing world as a former teacher and native of North Carolina. She received her BS degree from University of Maryland Eastern Shore, and earned a Masters of Arts in Teaching degree from Bowie State University in 1999. Her love for writing sparked a career change in 2002. She resigned from her teaching tenure in the Prince George's County public school system to fulfill her dream of becoming an author. After writing her first novel, 'A Life to Remember," written in an attempt to help change lives of young men, Azarel launched her own publishing company, Life Changing Books (LCB).

Now with over thirty-one titles published to date, LCB is one of the most well known and successful African-American owned publishing companies in the publishing industry. Many titles produced by Azarel have continuously topped the charts on the national Essence Best sellers list and many national book store chains, including her own titles Bruised 1 and 2, and Daddy's House..

Although Azarel publishes a wide variety of adult fiction, her title roster includes "Teenage Bluez" an urban series of books for teens. Teenage Bluez is designed to capture the hearts of teens across America by providing them with entertaining stories in a positive manner.

As a wife and mother of two, Azarel enjoys spending time with family and friends and lending support to those in need. By mentoring teens and speaking at shelters for abused women she continues to achieve that goal.

Azarel currently completed her latest baby, Carbon Copy which goes on sale July 18th, 2009.

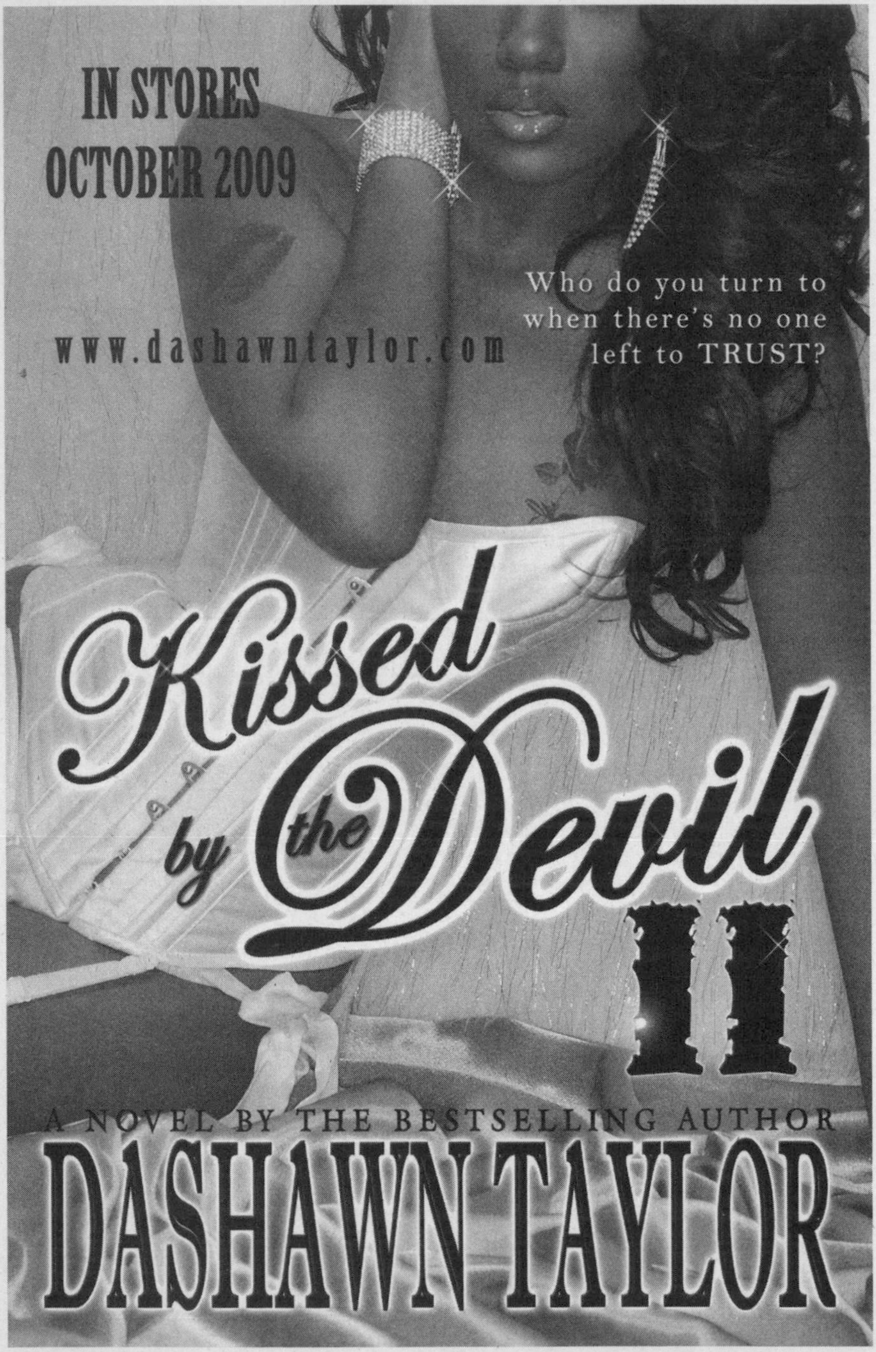
IN STORES
OCTOBER 2009
Who do you turn to
when there's no one
left to TRUST?
www.dashawntaylor.com
Kissed by the Devil
II
A NOVEL BY THE BESTSELLING AUTHOR
DASHAWN TAYLOR

MAIL TO:
PO Box 423
Brandywine, MD 20613
301-362-6508

FAX TO:
301-856-4116

ORDER FORM

Ship to:

Address:

Date:	Phone:
Email:	

City & State:　　　　　　Zip:

Make all money orders and cashiers checks payable to: **Life Changing Books**

Qty.	ISBN	Title	Release Date	Price
	0-9741394-5-9	Nothin Personal by Tyrone Wallace	Jul-06	$ 15.00
	0-9741394-2-4	Bruised by Azarel	Jul-05	$ 15.00
	0-9741394-7-5	Bruised 2: The Ultimate Revenge by Azarel	Oct-06	$ 15.00
	0-9741394-3-2	Secrets of a Housewife by J. Tremble	Feb-06	$ 15.00
	0-9724003-5-4	I Shoulda Seen It Comin by Danette Majette	Jan-06	$ 15.00
	0-9741394-4-0	The Take Over by Tonya Ridley	Apr-06	$ 15.00
	0-9741394-6-7	The Millionaire Mistress by Tiphani	Nov-06	$ 15.00
	1-934230-99-5	More Secrets More Lies by J. Tremble	Feb-07	$ 15.00
	1-934230-98-7	Young Assassin by Mike G.	Mar-07	$ 15.00
	1-934230-95-2	A Private Affair by Mike Warren	May-07	$ 15.00
	1-934230-94-4	All That Glitters by Ericka M. Williams	Jul-07	$ 15.00
	1-934230-93-6	Deep by Danette Majette	Jul-07	$ 15.00
	1-934230-96-0	Flexin & Sexin by K'wan, Anna J. & Others	Jun-07	$ 15.00
	1-934230-92-8	Talk of the Town by Tonya Ridley	Jul-07	$ 15.00
	1-934230-89-8	Still a Mistress by Tiphani	Nov-07	$ 15.00
	1-934230-91-X	Daddy's House by Azarel	Nov-07	$ 15.00
	1-934230-87-1-	Reign of a Hustler by Nissa A. Showell	Jan-08	$ 15.00
	1-934230-86-3	Something He Can Feel by Marissa Montelih	Feb-08	$ 15.00
	1-934230-88-X	Naughty Little Angel by J. Tremble	Feb-08	$ 15.00
	1-934230847	In Those Jeans by Chantel Jolie	Jun-08	$ 15.00
	1-934230855	Marked by Capone	Jul-08	$ 15.00
	1-934230820	Rich Girls by Kendall Banks	Oct-08	$ 15.00
	1-934230839	Expensive Taste by Tiphani	Nov-08	$ 15.00
	1-934230782	Brooklyn Brothel by C. Stecko	Jan-09	$ 15.00
	1-934230669	Good Girl Gone bad by Danette Majette	Mar-09	$ 15.00
	1-934230804	From Hood to Hollywood by Sasha Raye	Mar-09	$ 15.00
	1-934230707	Sweet Swagger by Mike Warren	Jun-09	$ 15.00
			Total for Books	$

* Prison Orders- Please allow up to three (3) weeks for delivery.

Shipping Charges (add $4.25 for 1-4 books*) $

Total Enclosed (add lines) $

For credit card orders and orders over 30 books, please
contact us at orders@lifechaningbooks.net
(Cheaper rates for COD orders)

*Shipping and Handling of 5-10 books is $6.25, please
contact us if your order is more than 10 books.
(301)362-6508